Away

MARILYN CAMPBELL
"Fantastic Fantasy." —*Rendezvous* for *Topaz Dreams*
When Leanne Shepard hires the elderly handyman, she
doesn't realize he's actually one hunk of a fugitive in
disguise. Soon she finds herself falling for
"A Most Wanted Man."

THEA DEVINE
"The Queen of erotic romance . . ."
—*Romantic Times* for *Sinful Secrets*
Determined to teach dashing, successful Hunter Devlin a
lesson, Leslie Gordon wins a date with him at auction. But
the handsome investor has lessons of his own in mind—
which he'll teach her in
"Love Sessions."

CONNIE MASON
Romantic Times Storyteller of the Year and Career
Achievement Award-Winner!
Stranded by her fiancé on what was supposed to be their
wedding cruise, Cara Brooks finds respite in the arms of
sexy Dom Domani. His bronzed, muscular body is the
answer to her every fantasy, and his searing kiss
makes her cry,
"Promise Me Pleasure."

Other, *Leisure* and *Love Spell* anthologies:

Swept Away

MARILYN CAMPBELL, THEA DEVINE, CONNIE MASON

LEISURE BOOKS NEW YORK CITY

A LEISURE BOOK®

August 1998

Published by

Dorchester Publishing Co., Inc.
276 Fifth Avenue
New York, NY 10001

ISBN 0-8439-4415-3

The name "Leisure Books" and the stylized "L" with design are trademarks of Dorchester Publishing Co., Inc.

Printed in the United States of America.

Swept Away

A Most Wanted Man

MARILYN CAMPBELL

For Judy DeWitt and Susan Koski of the Bookworm—
Thank you for your constant, unconditional support.

Chapter One

Full-time handyman needed to renovate old house. Room, meals, allowance included. Retired gentleman only.

He was absolutely perfect.

The moment Zachariah Gibbons entered her office, Leanne Shepard knew he was the man she had wished for when she'd placed the ad. In fact, after two weeks of interviewing unsuitable prospects, he was almost too good to be true.

Frazzled, shoulder-length gray hair stuck out from beneath a battered, wide-brimmed straw hat. A bushy gray beard covered the lower half of his face, and dark sunglasses shielded his eyes, leaving exposed only a very tan nose and two slashes of cheekbone. A wooden toothpick jutted out from the beard, about where his mouth would be.

He wore a loose, long-sleeved shirt patterned with parrots and jungle flowers that were faded from too many washings, and his threadbare jeans looked a size too large. Old, leather sandals completed the Ernest Hemingway image.

"Mr. Gibbons?" she asked, just to confirm that he was the one who had called earlier that morning.

"Yup."

She held out her hand to him, but withdrew it when he made no move to take it. Perhaps he was one of those old-fashioned men who did not approve of shaking hands with women. "I'm Leanne Shepard. As you can see, I'm not quite settled in yet," she explained, with a wave of her hand at the stacks of storage boxes crammed inside the small office. "Please have a seat." She motioned toward the metal folding chair she had brought in from home, then perched herself on the corner of the desk.

As Mr. Gibbons stepped closer, it occurred to her that he had probably been quite tall in his youth. Even with his back hunched from age, he was still a head taller than her own five feet, five inches.

He shuffled forward slowly and, with a muffled groan, settled his large frame on the small chair. "Might's well get one thing straight right off. No one calls me Mr. Gibbons. Zachariah'll do just fine." His speech was grated out through jaws clenched around the toothpick.

She couldn't help but wonder if he was as unfriendly as he seemed. For what she had in mind, that could pose a problem. "Excuse me, Mr.—er, Zachariah, but would you please take your sunglasses off? It's difficult to judge someone when you can't see his face."

The toothpick bobbed up and down rapidly within its coarse, gray nest. "Rather not. They're prescription. I'm a mite nearsighted, an' I lost my reg'lar pair."

"Just for a moment then. And I'll come closer if it really makes you uncomfortable." He still didn't comply. She was about to force the issue when she came to her senses. It wouldn't do to antagonize the only decent applicant she had had. "Never mind. It's not that important. Where are you from, Zachariah?"

"Born in Tennessee. Lived there all my life, 'cept when Uncle Sam needed me, o' course. But the last few winters have been mighty hard in them mountains. Got me hankering fer some warmer weather."

Leanne smiled. "Well, there aren't many places warmer than the Florida Keys in August. I've got to tell you, you remind me a lot of my Grandpa. He was a conch . . . lived all of his life right here in Key West. He passed away two months ago and

13

left me his house." She let out a soft sigh as a loving memory came to mind.

"You can't imagine how many people advised me to sell it. Oh, I know that would be the logical thing to do, but I decided against it. Not only because he loved that house, but after what I've been through the last—" She stopped before the bad memories had a chance to resurface. "At any rate, are you . . . in good health, Zachariah?"

"Fit as a fiddle. Not quite as fast as I used to be, an' I don't last quite as long, an' like I said, the eyes aren't so good, but everythin' else still works well enough."

Had he been a younger man, she might have assumed his comment was suggestive, but there was nothing about his tone of voice to make her suspicious. "That's good to hear. I'm afraid the house is in pretty bad shape, and it does have two stories, three if you count the attic. When you called this morning, you mentioned that you did construction work before you retired. How are you with plumbing? Out of three bathrooms, not one is fully functional."

"No problem."

She let out the breath she'd been holding. "Electrical wiring? I can't tell you what's wrong, but most of the outlets are dead."

He nodded and gave her a thumbs up sign.

"Wonderful. Once those two necessities are taken care of, there are a lot of less urgent things like replacing rotting wood, refinishing cabinets, sanding floors, and cleaning up the yard. You know, general renovation work. Will that be all right?"

"Yup."

"Great. As I mentioned in my ad, you would live in the house. The job pays a small allowance besides room and board. Do you have any questions?"

"Yup. Where would I git hold o' you if I needed to?"

"Oh, I'll be living in the house also."

His nose twitched as though he smelled something foul. "Don't sound like that house is fit fer a little slip o' gal like yerself."

"I have no choice," she said with a slight shrug. "My . . . financial situation is a bit . . . let's just say I have to keep my expenses down at the moment."

"Gotta have my privacy. Don't cotton to somebody lookin' over my shoulder when I work."

"It's a very big house, and I assure you that I will respect your privacy. Anyway, during the day, I'll be busy getting this office set up."

"Hmmph. Just so's yore not tryin' to adopt a granddaddy like some do-gooder."

Although that thought had crossed her mind, she smiled and shook her head no.

"An' one other thing," he continued without waiting for a verbal response. "I ain't 'bout to do none o' yore cookin' or cleanin' or washin' yore unmentionables, like one o' them newfangled houseboys. I lived this long without ever waitin' on some filly. Ain't gonna start now."

Leanne stifled the giggle that threatened to burst forth. He was going so far out of his way to prove what a gruff old grizzly he was, she would bet he was probably the exact opposite—a cuddly teddy bear, just like Grandpa had been.

"Don't worry about that, Zachariah. I'll tend to the cooking and laundry for the both of us. As for cleaning, well, when you see the house, you'll understand why housekeeping is the least of my concerns. I assure you, I need a husband . . . not a wife."

The toothpick flew out of his mouth on a puff of breath and landed in her lap. "*Husband*? Yore ad didn' say nothin' 'bout gettin' hitched!"

"Oh dear, no," she said quickly, suppressing another giggle as she brushed the toothpick off her skirt. "I only meant that I need someone to do the chores that an old-fashioned husband would have done. Okay?"

He dug a fresh toothpick out of his shirt pocket and stuck it in his mouth. "Okay. When can I start?"

"Would this afternoon be too soon?"

"Nope. Got everythin' I need in my pickup outside. Jus' gimme the address, an' I'll find it."

As she wrote out the directions for him, she said, "I'm determined to make some progress here today, but I should be home by five. Can I expect you for dinner?"

Zachariah nodded once, then uttered a groan as he slowly rose from the flimsy chair. At the door, he stopped and took another look around the room, which was filled with boxes. "What is it yore gonna be doin' here?"

She stood and straightened her shoulders proudly. "I'm an investment counselor." She heard a sharp intake of breath, and his body seemed to go rigid for a moment. "Zachariah? Are you all right?" She reached out to touch his forearm, but he jerked it away.

"Fine. See ya at five."

Ellwood Zachariah Gibbon Rush—better known as Zach to his immediate family and E.Z. to everyone else—forced himself to continue the old man charade as he headed for his truck.

Of all the damn luck! When he saw the ad in the newspaper, it had seemed like the perfect solution to his most urgent need: a safe place to hide for a while that wouldn't cost him anything. Having to disguise his appearance to get the live-in job made it even more desirable. Even if his employer/landlady was shown a photo of E. Z. Rush, she would honestly deny knowing him.

He should have realized that it was too good to be true. Nothing in his life had gone right lately. Why would this?

The first hitch was the fact that his new employer would be living under the same roof with him. Her friendly personality pretty much guaranteed that he would have a hard time avoiding her completely, which meant he would have to maintain the uncomfortable disguise most of the time.

It was already quite clear that he would never be able to tolerate the tropical heat with the extra padding he had donned to conceal his well-toned physique. He hoped she hadn't paid much attention to his body shape in the short time they had spoken.

He congratulated himself for coming up with a reasonable excuse for wearing sunglasses indoors, but how could he explain the hat? Since the beard was only held on by stretchy strings around his ears and the gray hair was attached to the hat, he would have to keep it on whenever she was home. What he needed was a good quality gray wig, but he didn't have that much money. When no sensible explanation came to mind, he pushed that detail aside for the moment.

His flimsy disguise was only one reason to keep his distance from her, however. There was no denying the physical response his body had had to watching her breasts stretch the fabric of her tee shirt with every breath she took. Why couldn't she have turned out to be an old hag, or, at the very least, plain?

Whenever the question of his bachelorhood arose, Zach always gave the same answer. He was still unmarried at the age of thirty-three because his perfect woman had yet to appear. When prodded, he would run down the list of her perfect attributes.

Of course, she should have a professional career compatible with his own, be intelligent and independent, but also soft-spoken, compassionate, and considerate of others. Physically, she would be completely feminine, right down to a voluptuous figure. She would be of medium height, and around his age.

Her hair would be shoulder-length and the color of wheat. Her eyes would be bluish-green, framed with long lashes. Her lips would be full and—

Zach shook his head to banish the erotic image. In all the years since he'd first noticed that girls were different from boys, he had never found anyone who had come close to being his perfect woman . . . until thirty minutes ago. Leanne Shepard could have been engineered out of his imagination. Only her eye color was wrong. No, not wrong, just different. Now that he had seen his fantasy with brown eyes, he decided to change that item on his list.

How could he possibly sleep under the same roof, night after night, with the woman of his dreams, and never touch her? He shoved that question aside even quicker than the first. There were more serious problems to consider, the lesser of which was the gross exaggeration about his construction skills.

When he moved into his last apartment, he had smeared a white substance into the small holes in the walls left by nails and touched up the paint. He also had experience spraying a lubricant onto door hinges to stop them from squeaking. Once, during his college years, he sort of replaced a broken doorknob. His roommate had actually performed the task while he read aloud the instructions on the package.

That summed up his experience as a handyman.

If something went wrong with plumbing or electrical fixtures in his apartment, he called the building superintendent, and it got taken care of while he was at work. It had never been important to him to know how such things operated. And yet, he had implied that renovating an old house would be "no problem."

He reminded himself that he was a fast learner. Hadn't he mastered the complexities of both the commodities and stock markets before graduating from high school? Surely there was a book that could teach him whatever he needed to know to master something as simple as household repairs. All he had to do was stick to patching holes or oiling hinges while he learned the other skills required.

Key West being a rather small island, it didn't take him long to find a bookstore, but its inventory was mainly geared to tourists and beach reading. The clerk suggested he try the hardware store on Duval Street.

Entering BC Hardware was a bit like stepping into the twilight zone for Zach. To his knowledge, this sort of small, poorly lit store, with its narrow aisles and floor-to-ceiling shelves crammed with stock, had been replaced by corporate mega-stores. A sole proprietorship simply couldn't compete with such efficiency. He doubted that this store's owner even had a computer.

"Can I help you?"

Zach turned toward the friendly male voice. Two elderly men sat behind the cluttered counter, apparently in the middle of a game of checkers. They fit in the setting as perfectly as a Norman Rockwell painting.

The man with the deeper tan and least white hair grinned and spoke again. "Was there something you were looking for?"

Since Zach was not inclined to spend more than a few minutes inhaling the accumulated dust and mildew that was already tickling his sinuses, he replied, "D'ya have a book on home repairs?"

"Not much call for them, but I have a few." He leaned down behind the counter and brought up a large hardcover book and four paperbacks. With a quick puff, he blew the dust off the top book, then spread them out. "There's your basic how-to, and separate guides to carpentry, electrical, plumbing, and building gazebos. Somebody ordered that one a few years ago, but never came back to pick it up. Probably changed his mind and put in a pool."

Zach sneezed three times before he could speak. His allergies demanded that he get out of this store as soon as possible. "How much fer all o' them?"

The man's eyebrows raised slightly. "Well, seeing's how I've had these awhile . . . twenty dollars."

That was more than half of all the money Zach had left, but he decided it was a necessary investment in his new career.

As the man took Zach's money, he asked, "What sort of project are you planning?"

Zach sneezed again and picked up the books. "Just some repairs . . . on an old house." He started for the door but the man stopped him with another question.

"On the island?"

Zach was about to lie, but he realized that the repairs might require his returning to the store for supplies. "Yup." Another triple sneeze kept him from having to say more.

"Two thousand milligrams of vitamin C and zinc lozenges. That'll stop that cold in its tracks."

Zach waved at him and hurried out the door before the man could make another attempt to involve him in a conversation. Besides helping him acquire the books he needed, the encounter made him think that Key West might actually be like a small town where every resident knows every other resident's business. If so, he had one more thing to worry about.

By late afternoon, Zach had familiarized himself with the entire island—its limited network of streets and avenues and its miles of sandy beaches. Using a map he bought at one of the multitude of souvenir stands, he found the sign that marked the southernmost tip of the United States as well as the homes of both Ernest "Papa" Hemingway and John James Audubon. Perhaps, if he stayed long enough, he might be able to check out some of the bars that all claimed to be Papa's favorite hangout.

He also observed a number of *unusual* people—unusual by Boston standards, that is.

The whole time, he tried to avoid thinking about the primary reason he should forget this whole crazy idea, and why he couldn't.

After a month on the run, keeping one jump ahead of his pursuer down the whole eastern seaboard, he had apparently landed right in a spider's web. If Leanne Shepard were a doctor or a beautician, the name E. Z. Rush would probably have no meaning to her. But as an investment counselor, she had probably read every news article covering his downfall and subsequent disappearance. She must have seen photos of him. She would have already found him guilty.

And yet there didn't seem to be any alternatives left. Besides being exhausted and out of money, he needed to stay in one place long enough to set up a safe system of communication with Dolores back in Boston. Despite all the risks, hiding in a stranger's house, disguised as an old man, looked like his best option for the moment.

He had always had considerable talent when it came to dealing with the opposite sex. Surely he could deceive one woman for a few weeks.

Chapter Two

At precisely five o'clock, Zach pulled into the pot-
holed driveway of the address Leanne had given
him. He had located the street earlier, just to make
sure he could find it, but he hadn't actually *looked*
at the house. For several minutes, he simply stared
in amazement at the monstrosity before him. The
outside appearance of the property was gruesome
enough to give children nightmares.

The yard was overgrown with weeds and lit-
tered with dried brown palm fronds. Ancient or-
ange and Key lime trees drooped from the weight
of unpicked fruit and broken, moss-covered limbs.

Only one guide wire, used to anchor the house
during a violent storm, remained attached to both
the roof and the ground, while another swung

freely in the breeze. Zach doubted the house would survive a heavy rain shower, let alone a hurricane in its current condition.

Wooden slats were warped and curling away from the main structure, shutters hung by splinters, several posts of the wooden railing around the front porch were missing, and one complete length of that railing lay in the yard. The second-floor balcony and the widow's walk on the rooftop appeared to be in the same precarious state. Noting that pieces of wood covered the dormer windows in the attic, he easily imagined bats taking up residence in there.

In total contrast, a large, intricately designed stained-glass window had survived unscathed above the front door. Zach couldn't help but notice its beauty. A hundred years ago, this was undoubtedly a very impressive house. Now, it would probably take an army of workers and a vault full of money to restore it to a livable condition.

And he had told her it would be "no problem" to fix it up himself. If only he could access just one of his money market accounts— No, he couldn't allow himself to brood over his financial problems at the moment.

Like a condemned man on his way to the gas chamber, Zach slowly approached the house. He was wondering whether a hard knock would cause the door to cave in, when it swung open. His breath caught in his throat. It hadn't been his imagination. She was his dream woman, all wrapped up in one package.

"Hi!" Leanne smiled brightly and waved him into the foyer. "Welcome to the Shepard mausoleum. Come in, please. I wish I could say it's not as bad as it looks, but I don't lie well."

"Have ya thought of levelin' it an' startin' over?"

"Them's fightin' words, mister," she said in a deep voice, then laughed. "I love this house, and I want to bring back its dignity."

Zach had heard that love could blur one's vision, but this was ridiculous. His gaze traveled over the yellowed wallpaper and cracked paint on the antique-foyer table and coatrack. Leanne, in her thoroughly modern jeans and snug tee shirt, did not fit in this picture.

She belonged in a sleek, contemporary environment . . . like the bedroom of his penthouse apartment in Boston. He gave himself a mental kick. That was exactly the kind of thought he had to abort before it took hold and he found himself instinctively acting on it.

"What about one o' them historical groups?" Zach asked, mainly to clear the other thought out of his head. "I seen some old houses today with signs in the yards. They was fixed up real nice."

Leanne smiled. "I know. But this house doesn't qualify. First of all, it's several decades younger than Key West's oldest houses. Second, no one famous ever resided within these walls—not even for an overnight stay. Finally, it's had so many alterations and additions put on that it's too much of a mutant for the Historical Society to be interested in preserving it. Why don't you leave your bag and hat here while I give you the fifty-cent tour?"

Zach set down the bag and said the only thing that came to mind. "Umm, I never take my hat off. It's . . . it's my . . . lucky charm."

Leanne gave him a look of disbelief, but didn't argue. "Okay. I'll start with the positive side. The foundation and main structure are solid, and the roof was replaced four years ago, so any water stains you see are either old or from the leaky pipes.

"Plus, most of the doors and windows open and close and there are screens, which is very important since the air conditioning isn't working—something connected with the electrical problems I think. Luckily, the stove runs on propane gas and the refrigerator is hooked directly to a generator so they both work fine."

Zach followed her lead, nodding when it seemed appropriate, as she pointed out what was wrong in each room, which ceiling fans were safe to turn on, which outlets had power, and which plumbing fixtures functioned.

The house was much larger inside than it had appeared on the outside. From the foyer, a stairway led upstairs to several bedrooms, including the master suite where Leanne slept. Nothing in either bathroom upstairs worked adequately.

"You know, these are all hardwood floors," Leanne told him proudly. "I'd like all these musty old carpets hauled away and the floors buffed to their original condition. And one day soon I intend to sort through the mish-mosh of furniture and get rid of all the clutter."

Grimacing, she picked up a starched doily and a dusty little vase. "I never understood why Grandma felt it was necessary to have so many *things*."

"Growing up in poverty," Zach murmured absently as he fingered the silky tassels on a lampshade. "Living through the depression affected an entire generation."

Leanne stopped in her tracks and stared at him. "Would you mind repeating that?"

The bewildered expression on her face clued Zach into the fact that he'd accidentally slipped into his real speech pattern. He let out what he hoped was a hearty laugh. "Ya liked that, huh? Heard it on one o' them talk shows an' thought it sounded so smart, I kinda memoried it the way the feller said it." She seemed to accept that, but the close call reminded him of his decision to spend as little time with her as possible . . . no matter how strongly his body kept trying to get closer to hers.

He was in complete accord with her directive to dispose of the musty carpets and dust collectors. The allergy pill he had taken after leaving the hardware store was still working, but he knew he'd have to take another before going to bed. At this rate, though, he was going to have to find a way to refill his prescription.

To the right of the foyer downstairs was an archway into a large living room. The hallway straight ahead led to the bedroom Zach would be staying in and the only bathroom with a working shower. Unfortunately, the flushing mechanism inside the toilet tank was broken, so it was necessary to use the commode in the utility room.

To the left of the foyer, another archway framed the entrance to a formal dining room, with the kitchen, utility room—originally called the mud room—and a garage aligned beyond that. To Zach's surprise, the garage was crammed with lumber, hardware, and tools.

"Grandpa was always buying supplies to renovate the house, but he lost interest in keeping the place up after Grandma passed away two years ago. I think he had gotten into such a habit of taking care of things only after she complained about it, that without her, he didn't know what to do first. So, about a year ago, he decided to take a trip around the world and forget all about the house."

She took a deep breath that made Zach more uncomfortable than he already was. He tried to put more space between them but only succeeded in knocking over a pile of lumber. At least restacking it gave him something acceptable to do with his hands.

"Anyway," she continued, "he played tourist for

about ten months, and had a fatal heart attack three days after he was back. I was planning to drive down to visit him the next weekend."

She sounded so close to tears, Zach wanted to take her in his arms and hold her until the grief flowed away. Instead, he said, "Mebbe his travelin' was just his way o' runnin' from the loneliness in this house without yore grandma. Mebbe he loved her so dang much, he just wanted to go an' be with her agin."

She blinked the dampness from her eyes. "Why, Zachariah, that is exactly what I needed to hear. But it sounded like you were speaking from personal experience. Are you running from loneliness as well?"

Zach had a split-second of weakness during which he wanted to tell her exactly what he was running from, to bear his soul to her and discover what it would be like to be comforted by her, but he came to his senses. "Nope. Never married. Never missed it. Only thing I run from was another freezin' winter."

His response seemed to give her an idea. "First thing tomorrow morning I'll take you to meet Billy Chesterfield. He was Grandpa's best friend, and he was never married either. You might enjoy visiting with him when you need a break. He has a boat, by the way, in case you like to fish."

Zach shrugged indifferently, but inside he felt a stab of panic. It was one thing to deceive her, but he wasn't sure he could fool one of her grandfather's cronies. "If that's it for now, I'd kinda like to git settled in and mebbe take a shower before dinner."

Leanne flushed slightly. "Of course. I should have realized— I only meant to give you a quick tour, and I got all carried away. You go on. I'll have dinner ready in about an hour. I hope you like spaghetti and meatballs."

"Anything you fix'll do fine," he said, and shuffled away.

Leanne had considered barbecuing a steak, but she wasn't sure if Zachariah had any teeth. Though their relationship had progressed since their initial meeting, she didn't think they were up to discussing something as personal as his ability to chew meat.

She knew salad was in the iffy category, but figured if she cut everything into small pieces, he might manage it. On her way home, she had picked up a loaf of Italian bread and a bottle of Chianti. Altogether, she felt she had planned a fine first meal for her new housemate.

As she prepared the food and set the table, she tried to review what she had told him so far to see if there was anything she had forgotten. Instead, it was the little odd things that kept popping up in her mind.

His insistence on wearing his hat and sunglasses indoors was peculiar, but she supposed she could get used to such an inoffensive idiosyncracy. At least he had shed some of the gruffness he had displayed in her office earlier.

It must have been her imagination, but he also seemed to have shed weight. For some reason, she thought he had a stockier build when she first saw him.

What kept replaying in her head the loudest, however, were the two phrases he had uttered about poverty and the depression. She had definitely *not* imagined the change in his voice. He had explained that he was simply imitating someone he'd heard on television, but it still seemed rather odd.

On the other hand, both her intuition and her intellect told her she had nothing to worry about. If either of those reliable senses had sent up a red flag, she would never have hired him to work on her home, let alone live in it. There wasn't a doubt in her mind: Zachariah Gibbons was her reward for surviving the last two impossibly difficult months.

Grandpa's death had been totally unexpected, but the fact that she hadn't seen him in almost a year made the grief nearly unbearable. It was no surprise, though, that she had inherited the spacious old home in Key West. After spending so many happy childhood summers there, she was the only one in the family who felt the same way as Grandpa did about it. She would never sell it out of the family.

She had imagined herself using it as a weekend

retreat, and perhaps retiring there one day with her husband—a pleasant dream that had disintegrated within weeks of the funeral.

Because she had been taken in by a well-polished—and completely fraudulent—investment prospectus, a number of important clients had lost a great deal of money. The firm's partners didn't blame her; they simply asked for her resignation, immediately.

All because of a sleazy con-artist named E. Z. Rush, she'd lost her position at the stock brokerage firm in Palm Beach where she had worked for six years. If only she could get her hands on that man for five minutes, she'd . . . well, she had never actually decided what she would do to him, except that it would be drastic.

Two of those clients were her fiancé, Eric Lazarus, and his father. The senior Lazarus had threatened to sue her personally. Eric had declared that her reputation was ruined in his "circle" and bluntly requested the return of his engagement ring.

She was actually quite proud of how she'd handled that selfish request. She hadn't cried or begged for understanding. She had simply taken the three-carat diamond solitaire out to the stable and planted it in a pile of manure freshly provided by his favorite polo pony.

It didn't seem to matter to any of them that she had also invested and lost a portion of her own savings in the phony company.

In the depths of despair, Leanne had made a sweeping decision. Her career goal had always been to set up her own brokerage firm, but Palm Beach was no longer a viable location. Key West, another magnet for both old and new money, would do just as well. She had put her townhouse up for sale, packed her clothes, and headed south. The realtor had warned her that the townhouse might not sell until the winter season, but Leanne figured she had enough money to get by until then.

The first problem with her plan for a new life was the disastrous condition of the house. It seemed hard to believe that it could have deteriorated so badly since she had last seen it, but, as Grandpa's friend Billy quickly reminded her, it takes constant attention to maintain a house in the tropics, and no one had paid attention to this house in quite some time.

Within a few days she'd discovered firsthand how limited Key West's labor force was. The few local contractors who showed up to inspect the property had demanded outrageous prices for their services. When she heard that some developers imported their labor from Miami, she tried doing the same, but no one was willing to travel so far for such a small job.

Billy had offered to help, but he had his own business to attend to, and she only wanted to impose on his kindness as a last resort. When she had told him about her idea to hire a retired gentleman like Grandpa, it had been his suggestion that one might be willing to work for less pay in exchange for room and board. Of course, he also suggested he interview the man before she made any final decision.

On the positive side, a surprising number of men had answered her ad. The downside was that every applicant had made a red flag of warning pop up. Some were objectionable because of their youth or bad habits, others just gave her a negative feeling, but her inner feelings about people were usually accurate, so she followed them.

If only she could have met that wretched excuse for a man, E. Z. Rush, in person, instead of on paper, she probably would have saved herself a lot of misery. She had no doubt that her intuition would have picked up on his dishonest nature.

Although she had promised Billy not to hire anyone until he gave his approval, Zachariah was just too perfect to take the chance of losing him. Besides, he reminded her so much of Grandpa, she was certain Billy would like him, too.

To Leanne's disappointment, Zachariah reverted to one-word responses over dinner. No matter what subject she introduced she could not engage him in conversation. She suspected that part of the problem was the difficulty he was having with the spaghetti. With each mouthful, he seemed to take in a few hairs of his beard while most of the sauce stayed outside.

As soon as he cleaned his plate, he excused himself and left the house to take a walk.

* * *

Zach sat on the beach, watching the ocean ebb and flow until the sun slipped completely below the horizon. When the stars began to show and he was sure he was alone, he stripped down to his boxer shorts and ran into the warm water. Having noted the abundance of jagged coral rock formations that were known to shelter a variety of fish, including barracuda, he didn't venture far from the shore.

That was okay. All that mattered was that, for the moment, he was free of the irritating disguise, free to stretch, free to be himself.

Free. He would never again take freedom lightly. Gazing up at the clear night sky and feeling the waves gently lap against his body, he decided that, if his fate was to get caught and put in prison, at least his last days of freedom would be in paradise. The only thing that could improve his circumstances would be if Leanne was willing to share this time with him . . . the *real* him, that is.

His imagination immediately ran with that thought, conjuring her up in the water with him. She was wearing a modest, one-piece bathing suit— He hit his mental delete button. If he was going to have a fantasy, he could do better than that.

Like a mermaid, she emerged from the water a few feet in front of him, wet and sleek and incredibly beautiful. She wore a string bikini, with a thong bot-

tom, that barely covered her nipples and the triangle between her legs.

She smiled seductively. "I hope I didn't keep you waiting too long."

Her perfection rendered him speechless. He shook his head.

"I saw you staring at my chest before." She ran her hands up her thighs, over her stomach, and cupped her full breasts. "Is this what you were imagining?"

"Not quite," he answered hoarsely, and drifted toward her. Taking her hands, he repositioned them behind her back. She kept them there as he untied the two strings that held the top scraps of material in place. "This is what I was imagining." He peeled away the skimpy top and let it float away. The sight of her puckered nipples took his breath away, but it didn't stop him from accepting what she was offering so willingly. His hands moved to—

Something alive nibbled at his calf, startling him enough to shatter the vision in his mind. It was just as well. Playing with that sort of fantasy was only going to make it harder to fall asleep tonight.

When he thought it was late enough for her to have gone to bed, he got back into disguise and headed back to his new home.

His timing was slightly off.

He was seconds away from slipping unnoticed into his bedroom when Leanne stepped out of the bathroom carrying a battery-operated lantern.

The fragrance of freshly bathed woman assailed his senses. Her wet hair was slicked back from a face devoid of make-up. Although the rest of her body was completely covered by a long blue velour robe, his water fantasy was still playing with his head.

He saw her untying the belt and slipping the robe off of her shoulders. She was by far the most erotic creature he'd ever laid eyes on.

The vision affected him so strongly, it took him a moment to realize she was also staring at him with a look of amazement.

She forced a smile. "I, uh, I was afraid you got lost . . . or something." She blinked several times and cleared her throat. "I'm, uh, all finished in the bathroom . . . if you . . . whatever." She lowered her head and hurried past him. "Good night, Zachariah."

" 'Night," he responded, and ducked into his room before he could give in to the urge to follow Leanne to hers.

Gathering his wits, he remembered that the small lamp on the dresser was the "safe" one to turn on. The first thing he noticed was that his bed had been turned down as though he were a guest in an upscale hotel. The pillow was fluffy enough to be new, and the sheets looked crisp and inviting. He only hoped the water stain on the ceiling above them was one of the old ones Leanne had spoken of.

His gaze continued to scan the room until it

came to an abrupt halt at the dresser mirror. Looking back at him was the old man he had created, but one important piece of the disguise was missing—his sunglasses! They were still in his shirt pocket where he'd stuck them when he went swimming.

Damn! Now he knew exactly why Leanne was staring the way she had. With the lantern light glowing right in his face, she couldn't help but see one of the tell-tale features he had tried to conceal.

Those eyes! Leanne could not remember ever seeing a mature man's eyes like Zachariah's, and she knew a considerable number of elderly men. Their eyelids tended to droop, the lashes were sparse to non-existent, and the iris color usually had a washed-out look.

In fact, even among much younger men, those eyes would never be considered average.

Unless her mind and the lantern light had conspired to play a huge joke on her, Zachariah's eyes were a vivid blue, clear and bright, and framed with thick lashes. No drooping eyelids above or sagging flesh beneath. Just a few lines. In a word, Zachariah's eyes were . . . *beautiful*.

And his head-to-toe appraisal of her with those eyes had made her feel as though she were standing there naked.

No. She had to be wrong. It must have been the light. And her worrying that some mishap had befallen him. And too much stress over the last two months.

But just in case her intuition had failed her about Zachariah, she locked her bedroom door. She was able to fall asleep by reassuring herself that Billy would pass judgment on her new housemate tomorrow. If there was anything seriously wrong with Zachariah, Billy would figure it out.

Chapter Three

Zach was enormously relieved the next morning when Leanne did not try to initiate a conversation, or worse, ask him to take off his sunglasses for another look at his eyes. He hoped it meant she hadn't noticed anything strange last night after all.

"Are you ready to go?" she asked as soon as he finished his breakfast.

"Go?" Was she throwing him out without a discussion?

"To meet Grandpa's friend, Billy Chesterfield, remember? I decided it would be best to get that introduction out of the way before you got started on anything here. Besides, he probably knows as much about this house and what's stored out in the garage as Grandpa did. Of course, if there's anything else you need, Billy can get it for you and charge it to my account."

Zach followed her through the utility room and out the door that led to the back porch. The word "account" raised his curiosity. "What does Billy do?"

She frowned slightly. "I thought I told you. He owns the hardware store."

It took supreme effort for Zach to get into the passenger seat of her car. Concern that his disguise might not pass the scrutiny of an older man was now superseded by an added complication. Assuming that Billy Chesterfield owned BC Hardware, that meant they'd already met, and because of his purchase at that store, Billy must have deduced that he was a novice at home repairs.

Despite his need to figure out a way to get through the upcoming introduction without being exposed, he was distracted by how withdrawn Leanne was. Though he'd only met her yesterday, he already knew her well enough to sense that something was definitely wrong. As Zach, he could probably get her to tell him the problem with a little probing, but Zachariah would never do such a thing. He had no choice but to mind his own business.

By the time she pulled into a parking space in front of the hardware store, Zach had a partial plan of action formed. He would simply have to improvise the rest as he went along. "I stopped in here yesterday," he said, as though he didn't realize this was the store she had referred to.

"Really? You must have met Billy then. He's always here."

He shrugged. "Didn't meet nobody by name. Wasn't here that long."

The instant they entered the store, Zach knew Billy recognized him, remembered his buying the how-to books, and was suspicious of why he was there with Leanne.

"Good morning, Billy," she said, giving him an affectionate hug and peck on the cheek.

"Good morning, punkin'. What brings you by today?"

"I thought I'd bring my new handyman in to meet you, but he just told me he was in here yesterday. I gather you didn't exchange introductions though. So-o-o, Billy Chesterfield, meet Zachariah Gibbons. He answered my ad yesterday, and I hired him on the spot."

Billy held out his hand in greeting, but his eyes narrowed as he shook Zach's hand. "How's the cold?"

"Took your advice," Zach told him. "Woke up feelin' fit as a fiddle agin, thanks to you."

The verbal pat on the back worked. Billy grinned. "Do you play checkers?"

"Used to. A lot. But then this feller I knew back home passed on . . ." Zach purposely left his sentence hanging.

Billy nodded with understanding. "Leanne, honey, why don't you go on to that new office of yours and leave Zachariah with me. I'll see to it he gets home."

Leanne smiled happily and gave Billy another hug. "That would be great. I'll see you both later then."

Billy shook his head as she walked out of the store. "You'd never know it by looking at her, but that girl has seen more bad luck in the past few months than some people do in a lifetime."

Zach wanted details, but Billy changed the subject before he could figure out how to ask.

"Ever been married, Zach? Okay if I call you Zach?"

"Yup, and nope, ain't never took a wife. Thought women was too dang much trouble when I was young, and when I got old, seems like I was the one who was too much trouble for them."

Billy snickered. "I know just what you mean. Never married myself. Tom and I—Tom was Leanne's granddad—we had hoped she would be settled with a husband and a couple kids by now. Instead, she's setting up house with an old geezer like us."

Zach leaped at the opening. "Why ain't she married? Somethin' wrong with her?"

"Hell, no!" he retorted, clearly taking the question as a personal offense. "God never made a prettier, sweeter, more thoughtful girl. She just seemed to be more interested in her career than any man she met. As a matter of fact, she *was* engaged to some high-society guy, but after what happened . . . Well, I wouldn't be surprised if she never trusted a man her age again."

Zach's curiosity overpowered his restraint. Anyway, it sounded like Billy was enjoying the chance to gossip. "She done picked herself a bad apple, huh?"

"Hmmph. The fiancé was just an ass. The real bad guy was the one that started all the trouble. He even had a con-man's name: *Easy* something or other."

Zach's heart nearly stopped. Billy hadn't grasped all the specifics, but he related enough for Zach to draw a fuzzy picture. The bottom line was that he was somehow responsible for all the misfortune in Leanne's life.

Abruptly changing the subject, Billy said, "Leanne was supposed to let me check out anyone she wanted to hire, but it looks like she jumped the gun with you. You might as well know, I'm pretty protective of Tom's little girl. Tell you what, let's set up the old board and get to know each other a bit."

For the first half hour, Billy asked the same sort of questions Leanne had and interjected anecdotes of his own experiences. Luckily, he didn't seem to think Zach's idiosyncracies about his glasses or hat were that unreasonable, since he had a few quirks of his own.

Prior to this visit, Zach's old-man charade had been based on a character he remembered from a movie. As he closely observed Billy, he noted a few little details that could make his act even more realistic.

Billy won the first game of checkers before Zach even remembered the basic rules. Just when he began to feel confident that he was being accepted for what he appeared to be, Billy asked the one question he'd been dreading.

"So, why did you buy those books yesterday?"

Zach chewed on his toothpick a bit and purposely moved a checker into a vulnerable position before answering. "I don't like havin' ta admit it, but there's times when my memry ain't as good as it used ta be. It's been a few years since I done some o' the kinda work she hired me for. If it were my house, I wouldn't care none if I made a mistake or two, but it ain't mine, an' I don't rightly figger that house could stand fer no mistakes."

Billy laughed out loud and jumped Zach's checker. "King me. You're probably right about that house. It sure is going to take a lot of work, and Leanne's just stubborn enough to see it get done."

He paused and his expression grew serious. "I'm not one to beat around the bush, Zach. I think you and I could get along fine. And believe me, I wouldn't mind a new face around here now that Tom's gone. But I can't let you get away with lying to Leanne."

Zach swallowed hard and waited for the axe to fall.

"A handshake tells a lot about a man. For instance, yours was firm and quick, which means you're strong, but you don't feel a need to prove it. That's good. Your palms were a little damp, so I'd guess you were a bit nervous about meeting me. That's good, too.

"But I also know that whatever you did for a living most of your life didn't put enough callouses on your hands for it to have been hard labor. What's your story, mister?"

Zach could only hope that the one he'd come up with on the way here would gain Billy's sympathy. He took a few seconds, as a proud man probably would. "I ain't a liar. I just pushed the truth a bit. Things ain't gone so good fer me the last few years." He sighed and hung his head.

"Yore right. I ain't done much hard labor. Just one construction job before the war. I been a cook mostly. A dang good one, too. But haven't been able ta get work fer a while 'cause o' my age, an' social security sure ain't near enough to live on. Lost a couple friends last winter. Nothin' left ta keep me in them hills."

He paused and sighed again before continuing. "Spent some time in Key West when I served in the Navy an' decided that was where I wanted ta finish what was left o' my time. Saw Leanne's ad the day I got here an' figgered it was a kinda sign from God."

Zach gave Billy a moment to consider that much before pushing for a commitment. "I'll understand if ya feel the need ta tell her that I ain't 'xactly what

I said, but if ya could see yore way clear ta keep it ta yoreself, I swear I'll do a good job fer her." Billy took so long to answer, Zach was sure he'd failed to convince him.

Finally, he huffed and shook his head. "It's a damn shame. That's what it is. A man works hard all his life, even risks that life serving his country, but let his hair turn gray, and suddenly no one has any use for him." He ran his hand over his nearly bald head. "If it weren't for my owning this store, I'd probably be in the same shape as you."

Zach could hardly believe his ears. He had somehow managed to tell all the right lies.

"Okay," Billy said. "I won't tell Leanne that she hired herself a cook to rebuild her house. On one condition."

"Anything," Zach said too quickly.

"I'm going to help you fix up the old place."

Zach faked a sneezing spell to give himself a few seconds to think. On one hand, he welcomed the offer of help from someone who knew the difference between pliers and a wrench. On the other hand, he didn't relish spending so much time with Billy. He was far too observant. Sooner or later he was bound to catch on to the really big lie.

"That's mighty kind," Zach finally told him. "But I don't wanna be the cause o' yore losin' business here."

Billy laughed. "That's no problem. Phil comes in every afternoon whether I pay him or not. He won't mind covering for me for a while. Hell, the truth is, I miss putzing around that dinosaur of a house. It would be like old times for me . . . except Tom had an inkling of what he was doing." He laughed again. "I do have one very important question though."

Zach cocked his head. He was still reeling from the double-edged sword he'd just been handed.

"Who's your favorite singer?"

The name, Mariah Carey, almost slipped out before Zach caught it. "Hmmm. Let's see. My favorite, huh?" He racked his brain for a name that his father might have mentioned and recalled something about George Clooney's aunt once being a popular singer, but he didn't know her first name. It was all he had. "Clooney."

Billy grinned. "As Bogie once said, I think this is the start of a beautiful friendship."

Rather than wait for Phil to show up, Billy called him. In no time, they were on their way to the Shepard house.

They started with an inspection of the supplies in the garage. All that seemed required of Zach was to trail behind and nod or chuckle at various times during Billy's numerous stories. Zach sincerely hoped he had thousands of them stored away. Any subject was fine, just so he didn't have to deal with any more pop quizzes about "the good ole days." He doubted that he could pull another magical "Clooney" out of his straw hat.

"Where do you think we should start?" Billy

asked after he had mentally inventoried every inch of the garage.

The image of Leanne coming out of the downstairs bathroom flashed before his eyes. As much as he would love sharing a shower with her, he needed to prevent the temptation. "Her bathroom upstairs. She says nothin' works. An' it ain't fittin' us sharin' facilities."

Billy agreed and immediately headed up there to check it out.

To Zach's delight, Billy really did enjoy "putzing" around, and he seemed to enjoy teaching even more. To Zach's surprise, however, he was enjoying being the student.

At midday, Zach repaid him by making lunch. That was the one thing he hadn't lied about—he *was* a good cook.

It was after four o'clock when Billy called it a day. "I'd rather be gone when Leanne gets home. You can tell her I hung around awhile, but don't let her know I was working here all day. She has the foolish notion that she doesn't want to *impose* on me. Can you believe that? She gets that from Tom. He could be a stubborn cuss at times."

Zach saw Billy out, then went upstairs to put Leanne's bathroom back in order. Even though he couldn't honestly claim credit, he was quite pleased with what he'd helped accomplish. Drains had been snaked, and a broken pipe, toilet tank innards, and gaskets had all been replaced. Even a new massaging showerhead had been installed.

Billy had noted that Leanne would probably want to put in all new fixtures and tile eventually, but for now at least, everything functioned the way it should. All that was left for him to do was put the tools away and give everything a hard scrubbing with the chemicals and cleansers Billy had pointed out.

Leanne breathed a sigh of relief after her chat with Billy. It was so typical of him to stop by her office before he went home, just to put her mind at ease. As she had hoped, he not only approved of her choice, he *liked* Zachariah, and was looking forward to having a new companion. It was good to know that her intuition was still on target.

On her way home, she picked up some Chinese food and rented a movie from the video store. If Zachariah chose to go out again after dinner, at least she would have something to keep her mind occupied.

She wasn't thinking of anything in particular as she opened the back door and entered the utility room, but her mind went completely blank when she saw Zachariah. In his left hand was a bucket filled with cleaning supplies. In the right was his shirt, dripping water on the floor.

In between was a very bare, very *masculine* chest and a flat, tightly muscled stomach.

"I brought dinner," she said to the indented navel showing just above his low slung, baggy jeans.

"Yore bathroom's fixed," he muttered, quickly

setting down the bucket and tossing his wet shirt over the washbasin.

Before Leanne could respond to his announcement, he was gone. She supposed he must have been embarrassed by her blatant stare, but who could blame her? She knew thirty-year-old men who would kill for a body in that condition.

It was really quite remarkable. First his eyes, now this. She wondered what he would look like with his hair and beard neatly trimmed. Just because he was well past retirement age didn't mean he couldn't be an attractive man. She thought of Sean Connery and Gregory Peck and Cary Grant. Their maturity certainly didn't prevent them from being called handsome or sexy.

Suddenly she saw herself pulling Zachariah out of his self-imposed coccoon and turning him into a butterfly. There were probably a number of mature, single women on the island who would be interested in making his acquaintance.

That thought led to another that made her giggle. After getting a glimpse of his hidden attributes, she'd bet there were a number of *immature* females who would be interested as well.

Putting the Pygmalion fantasy aside for the moment, she left the Chinese food on the kitchen table and went upstairs to see what Zachariah meant about her bathroom.

For several seconds, she simply appreciated how clean it was. She didn't know what he had done, but even the rusty stains on the porcelain had been whitened.

"Everythin' works now," Zach said from behind her.

She glanced over her shoulder. He had put on another large, flowered shirt. *"Everything?"* He nodded, but she had to see it for herself. First she turned on the water in the sink, then she flushed the toilet, and as a grand finale, she turned on the shower full blast.

She was so ecstatic, tears filled her eyes. "I can't believe it! You're a miracle worker!" Without hesitation, she launched herself at him, gave him a firm hug, and kissed his hairy cheek.

As she stepped back, she was laughing and crying at the same time. "I brought home Chinese food, but after this surprise, I should take you out to dinner to celebrate."

"Chinese'll do fine," he mumbled and strode away.

His abruptness instantly dulled her pleasure. Why was he like that with her? According to Billy, Zachariah was friendly and had a good sense of humor. He said they enjoyed their visit together.

Suddenly the answer hit her. Zachariah had never married. He had almost feminine eyes. He chose to retire in Key West, a place with a reputation for its acceptance of alternate lifestyles. Obviously, Zachariah preferred the company of other men.

With that in mind, she advised herself not to

hug him again until he realized the gesture held no sexual implications for her.

Before joining Leanne for dinner, Zach took a brief, but very cold shower.

Chapter Four

She was so happy. Everything was perfect. Hugging him close, feeling his strength, she could have stayed in his arms forever. But she wanted much more than a hug.

She stepped back and slipped her fingers around the top button of his flowered shirt. It came undone easily, as did all the rest. He stood still as she pushed the shirt off his shoulders. It wasn't enough to see his nipples peak in anticipation, she had to touch . . . and taste. And he let her take as long as she needed.

"It's your turn," he whispered, and suddenly she was standing naked before him.

He lifted her into the bathtub, but as they lay down, it turned into her bed.

She didn't want to go slowly any more. She parted her legs and lifted her hips, knowing this would be perfect as well. Gazing up into his beautiful blue eyes, she—

Leanne's nose twitched. Something was trying to wake her, but she ordered it away. She wanted to finish the sensuous dream.

In a lightning flash of double awareness, she realized she'd been having an unacceptable dream about Zachariah, and that smoke was the cause of her twitching nose. In the next second, she bolted from her bed and dashed downstairs. A crashing sound directed her to the kitchen.

A thick cloud of smoke billowed out, momentarily blinding her. Waving her arms in front of her, she could make out Zachariah frantically whipping a throw rug against the wall, knocking over everything in his way. Fiery sparks burst into flames along an exposed wire faster than he could smother them.

Squinting her eyes and holding her breath, Leanne scrambled for the fire extinguisher she'd stored beneath the sink. Without wasting another moment, she released the safety lock and sprayed the white foam at the burning wall and everything around it. By the time the canister was empty, specks of white floated through the heavy smoke, making the whole room appear to be a victim of a snowy blizzard.

Leanne's eyes burned, and she began coughing uncontrollably. She had to get the doors and windows open before they were asphyxiated. As she stepped cautiously across the foam-splattered tile, her foot nudged an obstacle in her path. Squinting through the smoke, she realized why Zachariah wasn't choking like her. He was unconscious on the floor!

Beginning to feel faint herself, she stumbled to the utility room and shoved the outside door open. She took a deep breath of fresh air, then hurried back into the kitchen.

"Zachariah!" she cried and shook his shoulders. No response. A little of the smoke was dissipating, but she was certain he would be better off outside. She positioned herself at his head and worked her hands under his arms. To her dismay, she couldn't get her footing in the slippery residue bent over like that, and his upper body seemed to weigh a ton.

Laying his head back down, she moved to his feet. Clamping each of his ankles beneath her armpits, she was able to drag him backwards to the open door. She was so intent on what was behind her as she inched her way outside, she misjudged the length of her burden.

Thunk! His head slid over the door ledge and down the short drop to the porch. Leanne abruptly dropped his feet and hurried to check on what additional injury she had caused.

In desperation, she sifted through her memory to recall the first-aid course she had taken eons ago. She remembered a little about treating someone for drowning, but what was the treatment for smoke inhalation? One thing was certain. He probably shouldn't be moved again; she might have hurt his back or even broken his neck.

Oh my God, she thought. *What if I've killed him?*

She knelt down and held her palm near his nose, but she couldn't feel any breath. Frantic, she unbuttoned his shirt and pressed her ear to his heart. Either it wasn't beating or the pounding in her head was too loud for her to hear. Her fingers searched beneath his beard for the carotid artery. His skin felt cool and clammy, but she found a pulse—a frighteningly weak beat that nonetheless gave her an ounce of hope.

Mouth-to-mouth resuscitation. That's what she was supposed to do. Unfortunately, she only had a vague recollection of the proper steps.

Tip the victim's head back and pinch closed his nose. She prayed she hadn't already broken his neck.

To make her efforts easier, she removed his glasses and tried to clear the beard hair away from his mouth. Like a splash of icy water in her face, her mind registered what she was seeing. Zachariah's hat had come off when she dragged him onto the porch . . . and his scraggly gray hair had stayed with the hat.

No longer blinded by smoke or panic, she could see that his real hair, although matted down, was thick, wavy, and dark brown. She could also see that the beard had strings on each side that wound around his ears.

Bewildered, she yanked off the phony beard. This was no elderly man! Zachariah was a fraud! She wanted to scream at him, beat him to a pulp, then turn him over to the police.

But first she had to make sure he didn't die on her porch.

No longer concerned about being gentle, she tipped back his chin, closed his nostrils, and opened his mouth. She inhaled deeply, formed a seal over his mouth with her own, then blew the air from her lungs into his.

Head up. Count to five. Do it again. The procedure seemed right, but it took nearly a dozen more breath exchanges before he responded.

His chest finally rose with a jerk, and he began to gasp for air. When his gasping graduated to violent coughing, she helped raise him to a sitting position and pounded his back.

"*Enough!*" he pleaded in a hoarse whisper.

For a moment, Leanne was again distracted by the beautiful eyes trying to focus on her. But the anger returned as she watched him draw a handkerchief out of his pocket, wipe his teary eyes and blow his nose. His expression revealed the exact moment when he realized his disguise was missing.

"I can explain," he began, but no explanation followed.

Leanne sprang to her feet. "Don't bother! You're

a fraud! What sort of sick game are you playing? What could you possibly hope to accomplish with this ridiculous farce? Never mind. I don't care. Just pack your things and get out of my house."

He tried to rise, but didn't make it. Squinting painfully, he pressed his fingertips to his temple and took a raspy breath. She felt only slightly guilty about being the cause of his headache.

"I wasn't playing any game," he whispered. "I just ran out of options."

She was still furious with him, but the look in his eyes was so pitiful, she decided to let him try to explain. "What do you mean?"

"When you've got money and a regular job, everybody's your friend. When you don't, nobody's willing to give you a break. I was hungry and tired of sleeping in my truck. I just wanted a fresh start." He dragged in another breath and coughed out a bit more smoke.

Leanne stared at the man slumped at her feet. Even covered in soot, he looked too good to be true. There was no way he could be a homeless person. He simply didn't match the picture that the word homeless conjured up for her. "I find it very hard to believe that you couldn't get a job."

"Would you have hired me if you knew I had a prison record?"

Her mouth dropped open and she stepped back a foot.

He shook his head. "See? It wouldn't have mattered if I explained that it was a non-violent crime, or that I was very neatly framed."

"No, it wouldn't have mattered to me, because I was determined to have a retired gentleman, not a . . . a man, who . . ."

"Who would rape you in your sleep?" he finished. "I've never committed a violent act in my life, but I guess I can understand your position. I don't suppose you could give me a chance to prove myself, say, for a week? Long enough to clean up the mess I made in the kitchen and maybe get your electrical problems worked out."

Her better judgment warned her not to listen. This man was a liar and a damned good actor. Maybe he was lying now. How had her intuition messed up so badly? How had he fooled Billy?

Arms crossed defensively, she paced back and forth across the porch. Was there any possibility that both her and Billy's instincts *were* correct? That Zachariah *was* a good man forced to act out a charade for the purposes of survival?

"I could put the disguise back on. You seemed comfortable enough with Zachariah. He kept his distance from you, didn't he?"

He *had* done his best to avoid spending time with her. And he hadn't moved a muscle when she'd thrown herself at him last night. Lord knows, if his ulterior motive was to get his hands on her, it would have been easy enough.

Her thoughts skipped to the miracle he had worked in her bathroom. How was she going to get the rest of the house in shape if she threw him out?

"I swear, if I do one thing that makes you nervous, you can tell me to leave, and I will without another word. Please, just give me a chance."

Her mouth pursed and her eyes narrowed as she weighed the risks of letting him stay against getting the electricity flowing. Considering the possibility of having air conditioning again made her ask, "Exactly what crime did you commit?"

"I didn't commit any crime," he retorted without hesitation. "I was framed." He coughed again, though his lungs were obviously clearing up. "For . . . stealing the petty cash from the construction company I was working for."

Leanne looked dubious. "You went to jail for petty cash?"

He shrugged. "They used it for bribes, to inspectors and such. It was over three thousand dollars. But I didn't take it. I think I know who did, but I couldn't prove it."

"What's your real name?"

"Zach."

"Hmmph. I don't suppose you needed to lie about that. I'll tell you what. I'll give you three days, but if you give me one reason—"

"I won't."

She crossed the porch one more time. Now that the crisis was over, the memory of the erotic dream came back to her. Apparently, her libido had seen through his disguise with no problem.

She told herself that the dream meant nothing except that she was feeling a little lonely. Zach was completely undesirable to her—an unemployed ex-convict. Regardless of how lonely she was or that he had dreamy eyes or an enticing body, his status would be enough to hold her hormones in check.

"All right. As of this minute, you're on probation, but I would prefer that you continue to wear your disguise outside the house. I don't want the neighbors talking any more than they already are. Also, I would rather Billy not learn of your deception. He would definitely not approve of your staying here with me no matter what your story is. Now, if you'll excuse me, I'm going to get cleaned up and go out to breakfast."

Zach sat where she left him for a few more minutes. He had never told as many lies in his entire life as he had in the last forty-eight hours. Actually, it surprised him how good he was at it for having had so little practice. Nevertheless, he would give almost anything to be able to come clean with Leanne.

The word *clean* made him laugh as he noted how filthy he was and thought about the mess that awaited him in the kitchen. It took some effort, but when he rose this time, he managed to stay upright. Feeling a more localized pain in the back of his head, he located a tender bump and guessed that he'd hit it when he fell—

He hadn't thought to ask what had happened or how he'd gotten out onto the porch, but it wasn't too hard to figure out. Through a series of assumptions, he got to the point where Leanne must have given him mouth-to-mouth resuscitation.

It wasn't just a dream or a hallucination. Her mouth *had* been on his. And her breasts *had* been pressed against him when he came to . . . just like they were last night in her bathroom, only this time there was nothing but her thin cotton nightshirt between them.

The fact that he had been able to keep his gaze off her nipples—which were impossible not to notice, the way the shirt was clinging to her—and improvise a credible explaination was a fair testimony to just how desperate he was.

Zach still felt a little dizzy as he went back into the kitchen. The damage he encountered there didn't help.

One entire wall was burned black, the cabinets and appliances were coated with soot, and the black-and-white linoleum was a sea of foam, water, coffee grounds, and various items that had once been on the counter.

All because he'd wanted to have a pot of coffee ready for Leanne when she came downstairs.

He blamed the disaster on his feeling a bit cocky from yesterday's success. When he had plugged in the coffee pot and nothing happened, he had removed the outlet cover. He remembered how well cleaning worked for pipes and figured it would do the same for dusty old wires.

When he tried to wipe the sticky wiring with a dishtowel, there was a loud pop. The next instant, the towel and the wallpaper were on fire and sparks were shooting out of the wall faster than he could react. The last thing he could remember was getting sprayed with foam.

Then he woke up with her mouth on his.

Zach knew he couldn't waste any more time thinking about the opportunity he'd missed. If he didn't impress the hell out of Leanne in the next three days, he'd have to hit the road again. That possibility eliminated the one item on his to-do list today. He couldn't very well send a cryptic message to Dolores if he wasn't sure where he would be when she got it.

They had agreed that he wouldn't call her on the phone or use E-mail in case her calls were being monitored. The last thing he wanted to do was implicate her in his mess more than she already was.

The next item on his list could not be put off. He absolutely had to get a refill on his allergy medicine if he was going to function at all in this house. If only the air conditioning were working . . . But it wasn't, and there wasn't any use fantasizing about such a luxury. Hopefully, his Boston pharmacist could fax a copy of the prescription to the drugstore he'd seen near Billy's.

The one positive note was that Leanne had requested that he maintain his disguise outside of the house. That was more than okay with him. Keeping his real identity concealed was still a priority for him. When he saw himself in his bathroom mirror, he knew there had been little chance of her recognizing him even if she had had a photo of E. Z. Rush in her hand. Whether she would recognize him when he was cleaned up was yet to be discovered, though he intended to put off that moment as long as possible.

An hour later, *Zachariah* had his refilled prescription in hand and was on his way to beg Billy's help.

By midafternoon, Leanne could not ignore her guilty conscience another minute. There was nothing in her new office that couldn't wait another day, but her home wasn't in the same condition. Yes, she was angry about Zachariah's—or rather, Zach's—deception, but she really should have stayed to help him clean up. After all, it wasn't his fault that the electrical wiring was faulty.

That thought led to his asphyxiation and the injury she'd caused him in trying to help. She probably should have taken him to a doctor to be checked out. What if he had a relapse or a concussion? For all she knew he was unconscious now, lying in a heap on his bathroom floor.

In record time, she locked up her office and sped home. To her surprise, Billy's truck was in her driveway. Good heavens! What if Zach had answered the door without his disguise? What would he have told him? Billy was so protective of her, how could she explain that she had such a big soft spot for people in trouble that she had decided to go completely against her better judgment? With no idea of what might be awaiting her, she went inside.

To her great relief, Zach was scrubbing a cabinet in the kitchen, fully conscious, and in full disguise.

"You're early," he said in a tone of voice that let her know he was not pleased about it.

"I felt guilty about not helping you with the mess." She glanced around the kitchen in amazement. There was obvious evidence of the fire, but the room wasn't in bad shape otherwise. "I can see you did fine without me, though. I saw Billy's truck outside." It was more of a question than a statement.

"Um, yeah, he, uh—"

"Hey there, punkin'," Billy said, coming into the kitchen from the utility room. "You're home early." He held up two very dirty hands to discourage her from giving him a hug. "I'll take a rain check. You know, it was the funniest thing. Something told me to drop by and see if Zach wanted to join me for breakfast. Of course, once I saw what happened, I couldn't walk away."

Leanne clucked her tongue. "Billy, what did I tell you about—"

"You just hush now. You're not imposing on me

because you didn't ask. And neither did Zach. I'm helping out because I had nothing better to do today. You'll be happy to know that I—*we* got to the bottom of your electrical problem. The main connection from outside into the fuse box was bad. And as long as we were working on that, we installed a whole new box. Tom had bought one, but never got around to replacing it.

"There's still a good deal of rewiring that should be done inside, but it'll go faster with two of us working on it. I should warn you though, it may require knocking some holes in walls."

She started to object, but he cut her off again. "We're talking about your safety here. So I'm going to help with this, no matter what you say. Tom would probably start haunting me if I didn't. And as far as the store goes, Phil's been fighting with his wife again, so he'll welcome the opportunity to put in the extra time."

Knowing she couldn't really win an argument with him, Leanne just smiled and shook her head. "Then I guess there's only one thing for me to do: change my clothes and take over the rest of the clean-up in here so that Zach can get back to doing something more *constructive*."

The rest of the afternoon passed quickly and productively. As the daylight waned, however, they had no choice but to put work on hold. Since Leanne insisted Billy stay for dinner, it was well into the evening before she and Zach were alone, and then Zach immediately went to take a shower.

Leanne was finished cleaning up from dinner and on her way upstairs for her own bath when he emerged from his room. "Are you going out?" she asked.

"No. There's something I'd like to see on television . . . if you don't mind."

"Of course not. I was only wondering why you were still incognito."

"I, uh, thought you would be, you know, more at ease with Zachariah."

She smiled. "I don't think it makes any difference how you look. I'm not going to forget that it's a costume. In fact, knowing that makes it a little silly when it's just the two of us. Please. Take it off. Get comfortable. I'll be okay. Really." She climbed a few steps then said, "You got a lot done today. Thank you."

He nodded and headed slowly back to his room. It was rather strange, actually. She thought he'd be relieved to take the disguise off. Instead, he acted as though it was the last thing on earth he wanted to do.

After her bath, it took much longer than usual to decide what to put on. She would be most comfy, and most covered, in her velour robe, but she was afraid that it hinted at an intimacy they didn't share. Finally, she donned jeans and a plain cotton shirt that didn't seem to hint at anything.

"What are you watching?" she asked as she came into the living room and saw him focused on the television set.

He shot a glance at her, then quickly looked back at the movie in progress. "*Three Days of the Condor*. It's old, but I never saw it, and I heard it was very good."

She sat down in the nearest chair. She had to. The sight of Zach, au naturel, turned her legs to rubber. He didn't just have great eyes. The whole Zach package was devastatingly handsome.

She did her best to get interested in the movie, but she couldn't stop herself from sneaking peeks in his direction. A few damp curls of dark brown hair fell over his forehead and the tops of his ears. The shadow of a beard, just beginning to grow in, gave him a rugged, manly look that balanced out his almost feminine eyes and lashes.

His jeans and short-sleeved pullover shirt were fitted well enough to confirm that the glimpse of well-toned body hadn't been her imagination.

Zachariah Gibbons was a hunk, with a capital H!

He's completely undesirable, she reminded herself.

He's down on his luck, her soft spot countered.

He's a convicted felon.

He said he was framed and I think I believe him.

Hah! He lied to you about his age. He could be lying about his crime.

That was a white lie, told only to get the job, and a place to live, and he is doing an excellent job, by the way.

He's—

Billy likes him and that's enough for me.
Okay, but don't say I didn't warn you.

"Are you sure this is okay?" Zach asked without looking directly at her. "You seem . . . tense."

"Tense? Don't be silly. I'm fine with . . . *this*. It's just been a tense day, I guess." She shifted into a more relaxed pose in the chair and stared intently at the movie.

Zach knew she was lying. His first thought was that she recognized him, but his male instincts were telling him otherwise. He could feel her visual exploration and, from the flush on her cheeks, she was more than a little intrigued by what she saw.

Having a woman be attracted to him wasn't that rare. Getting dates was never a problem for him. But there were three big differences with Leanne. First, his attraction to her was unlike anything he could remember experiencing before. After all, she was his fantasy woman in the flesh. The second difference was that he was not free to do anything about the mutual attraction. One aggressive move on his part could get him thrown out regardless of how intrigued she was by his looks.

It was the third difference, however, that made the situation unresolvable. It was one thing to stretch the truth about small details that didn't hurt anyone, but his conscience would not allow him to take advantage of the physical attraction without telling her who he really was. And she despised that man.

If only he could be sure that love really was blind. Considering the electricity that seemed to be flowing between them, it probably wouldn't be that hard to develop the physical attraction into emotional love. Then when he told her the whole truth, she would believe him without hesitation. *If* love was truly blind.

But since he had never been in love, he couldn't be positive it would work out that way.

The instant the credits began to roll at the end of the movie, they headed for their separate bedrooms, despite the fact that neither expected sleep to come easily.

Panic catapulted her body into action. If she didn't hurry, he could die, and it would be all her fault. As though she were moving through quicksand, she dragged his heavy body outside. Trembling fingers tore open the buttons on his shirt, revealing a muscled chest. Her hands glided over the smooth flesh, and she felt her body begin to get aroused.

But first she had to help him breathe. She bent her head, then pressed her lips to his, and the magic of her kiss gave him life. In the next instant, his mouth took control, sucking her breath into his lungs, sweeping her mouth with his tongue.

Without breaking their kiss, she stretched out on top of him, and his palms covered her bare bottom. She didn't know where her nightshirt had gone and didn't care. The important thing was that he was finally pressing his hardness against the soft core of her need.

But he was still wearing his jeans, and she wanted to feel his hot flesh against hers. She wanted him all the way inside her body.

Her fingers groped for the opening in his jeans, but there wasn't one. She tugged on the denim, trying to pull it down over his hips, but it wouldn't budge.

She searched his beautiful eyes for the answer.

He shook his head sadly and whispered, "I'm so sorry, but you can't have me until you figure it out for yourself."

Leanne let out a frustrated groan that woke her out of the dream. What the hell was that supposed to mean?

Chapter Five

The dream was still bothering Leanne so much the next morning that she made breakfast for Zach, then left without sitting down and sharing it with him. She told him she had a lot of important work to do today, which was true. This was the day she had planned to begin calling all her former clients to let them know she had opened her own brokerage.

By late afternoon, she had put a small dent in her mailing list . . . and a large one in her optimism. Only one client was willing to transfer the handling of their portfolio to her new office. The rest were either unavailable for her call, vaguely promised to think about it and let her know, or turned her down flat. She heard a number of excuses, but she knew it was her credibility and judgment that were the real problems.

After yesterday's destruction of the kitchen, she thought she had seen the worst it could get. Boy, was she wrong. Most of the downstairs appeared to have been attacked by a team of demolition experts. Billy had said they might need to make some holes in the walls to get to the wiring. It had never occurred to her that some of those holes could be several inches wide and run from one side of a room to another or from floor to ceiling.

"Hello," she called out. "Were there any survivors?"

"We're back here," Billy shouted from Zach's room.

Leanne found the two men, happily destroying another wall. "Please tell me again how this is a good thing you're doing."

Billy laughed. "If you weren't Tom's granddaughter, I'd think you didn't trust me. Believe me, we made some real headway today. You wouldn't believe how much energy this old geezer has. He opened up ten feet of wall for every one I did!"

"That's absolutely amazing, Zach," she said, arching a brow at him. "Why, I know men half your age who couldn't keep up with Billy." She paused for a beat, then let Zach off the invisible hook. "I'm in the mood for grilled hamburgers and home fries tonight. How's that sound, guys?"

They both grunted their approval and she

warned them to be ready to eat in an hour. After changing into a much cooler outfit—shorts and a sleeveless tee shirt—she started dinner. As she got out all the ingredients, she eyed the bottle of Chianti she had bought for Zach's first dinner, but had never opened. She didn't know whether either of the men would be up for a glass, but after last night's dream and the day she'd had, she certainly was ready for one.

By the time they sat down to eat, she was on her third, and when neither of her guests opted to partake, she finished the bottle.

"I don't seem to remember you enjoying wine quite so much, punkin'," Billy said with a frown. "Have your tastes changed or is there something you'd like to talk about?"

She frowned back at him. "You look much too serious. You should have some wine. It doesn't fix anything, but it makes it nearly impossible to worry about it . . .'cause your head is all fuzzy . . . like Zachariah's beard." She thought that was very funny, but neither man was laughing, so she got serious also. "I'm fine. I just had a lousy day. I'm sorry." She rose unsteadily and started to pick up their dishes, but Zach took them out of her hands.

"Billy, why don't you make sure she gets up to her room an' I'll take care o' the kitchen fer one night."

As soon as Billy left, Zach practically ran to his room to peel off the hot disguise and scrub off the layer of sweat and dust that had resulted from the day's hard, dirty work.

Once he felt thoroughly clean, he slipped on a pair of comfortable shorts. With Leanne passed out upstairs, he didn't think he needed more clothing than that.

From what Billy had said, he gathered that Leanne was not in the habit of drinking, so he couldn't help but wonder what had happened that she wanted to avoid thinking about. Was it something that had happened regarding her business? Was it the mess the house was in?

Was it him?

On impulse, he tiptoed upstairs, just to make sure she was sleeping peacefully and hadn't fallen off the bed or anything. His first surprise was that her bedroom door was open. He would have thought that Billy would have closed it. His second surprise was that Leanne was not on her bed, or anywhere else upstairs.

Apparently she had left the house while he was in the shower. Good God, he thought with a spear of panic, what if she decided to drive somewhere? She could barely walk when Billy led her out of the kitchen. He descended the stairs two at a time in his rush to check on her car.

To his great relief, both her car and his truck were exactly where they should be. That meant she was on foot. He imagined her staggering down the sidewalk, falling, and— Worse, she could try to cross the street and get hit by a car. Or even worse, some lecherous man could see her, force her into his car, strip off her clothes—

He grabbed his truck keys and raced out the door to find her before it was too late. Luckily, his first thought was the right one. He found her sitting on a blanket on the same stretch of beach he had walked a few nights before. He told himself to leave her alone and go home. If she had gotten here, she'd find her way back without his help. His feet didn't listen.

"Zach!" she scolded when she realized who had walked up on her. "You scared me."

"Which is a good reason why you shouldn't be out here alone in your condition."

She giggled. "My condition? I'm perfilly fine. In fact, I was jus' thinking that I obviously had not imbibed quite enough."

He knelt down beside her on the blanket. "I don't have any more wine, but I have two good ears if you'd like to talk."

She looked up at him with a half-smile, but as her gaze traveled from his eyes down to his bare chest, she groaned and lowered her head to her bent knees.

Quickly grasping her shoulders, he asked, "Are you going to be sick?"

"Yes," she whined, "But not the way you mean."

He released her and sat back. "I don't understand."

She looked out at the softly swelling ocean and took a deep breath. "Neither do I. In fact, I don't seem to understand anything in the whole world anymore. I don't understand why Grandpa had to die before I got to say good-bye to him. I don't understand why his house has to be torn apart to make it livable again."

"You know—"

"I don't understand how a person can be called a genius one day and stupid the next. An' I don't understand how a man can give you a ring and say he wants to be with you forever and then ask for it back just because some bastard made a fool of me." She sniffled and a tear leaked out of the corner of one eye, and suddenly there was no holding back the grief.

Zach hesitated for a full second before wrapping his arms around her. Her head on his chest, he gently rocked her until the sobbing was reduced to an occasional sniff. Without moving out of his arms, she used her tee shirt to wipe the tears from her face and his chest.

"First things first," Zach said in a hushed voice. "I've heard enough of Billy's stories to know that your Grandpa knew very well how much you loved him. I also know that even if his heart gave out, there's a little bit of him in every room in that house, out here on the beach, in the ocean, and looking down on you from those stars up there. If you feel the need to say good-bye, say it. He'll hear you."

She sniffled again and the movement of her

head on his chest let him know she understood and appreciated what he'd said.

"I believe the next thing was the problem of the house, but we both know the mess is only temporary and when it's all done, it will be even nicer than when Grandpa lived in it. Moving on. Anyone who would think you're stupid is too stupid for their opinion to matter to you, and you're better off without them. If you're referring to the people you used to work for, you should be grateful to them. After all, because of their stupidity, you now own your own brokerage, which is much better than being an employee."

She tilted her head up at him. "How did you know about that?"

"Billy told me." He had no intention of commenting on the bastard she'd referred to, but he certainly had a few words about the bastard who'd thrown her away. "As to the idiot who broke your heart, no matter what his reason was, I would be most happy to confront him and challenge him to a duel."

She laughed. "That is very gallant of you, sir, but hardly necessary." She straightened up, and he reluctantly let his arms fall away. "Eric broke the engagement and I felt betrayed, but he didn't actually break my heart. After it was all over, I realized everyone else had always been more excited about our relationship than I was. The truth is, I accepted his proposal because everyone kept telling me I'd be crazy not to, and I wasn't getting any younger, and no one else had ever come along who . . ." Her shoulders slumped.

He waited, but she didn't finish. "Who . . . what?"

She glanced at him, smiled, then looked back at the ocean. "Nah. You wouldn't understand. It's a girl thing."

"C'mon, try me. I've been told I can be very understanding."

She sighed. "I guess I read too many fairy tales and romance novels, but I always thought that one day, my prince would show up on a white horse. Our eyes would meet, and I'd hear music or bells or something."

He grinned. "What about when he kissed you?"

"Hmmm," she murmured dreamily. "When we kissed, the whole world would disappear, and time would stop."

"Sounds great. What about . . . when you made love?"

She closed her eyes and took a slow, chest-rising breath. "It would be a journey to heaven."

Zach never wanted anything in his life as badly as he wanted to accompany her on that journey. "I gather that Eric didn't quite . . . take you to heaven."

"Hmmph. Eric barely got me off the ground."

In his mind, Zach jumped up, whooped, hollered, and did a victory dance around the blanket. "That proves that you're lucky to be rid of him. He wasn't the one."

82

"The *one*? I've pretty much given up on the *one* miraculously showing up in my life. Enough about me. What about you? Has Zachariah Gibbons ever met his *one*?"

He waited for her to look directly into his eyes, then he held her gaze until he was absolutely certain about the attraction being mutual. "I'm almost positive that I've met her. But I can't do anything about it. You see, I made her a promise that if I did anything to make her nervous, she could send me away, which is the last thing I would want to happen."

Leanne licked her lips. "What if . . ." She took another of those breaths that nearly unmanned him. "What if you had already made her *very* nervous, and the last thing it made her want to do was send you away?"

He raised his hand to stroke her cheek, but drew it back again. "If that was the case, she'd have to let me know exactly what she would allow. For instance, if it was all right for me to touch her face or hand, she would have to look me in the eyes and smile."

Ever so slowly, her mouth curved into a soft, inviting smile.

Just as slowly, he reached out and touched her nose with his fingertip, then traced the line of her jaw with his thumb. Being allowed that much gave him the courage to move that hand to her shoulder and lightly trail his fingers all the way down her arm. The gooseflesh he felt let him know that

83

an attempt to enclose her hand in his would not be rebuffed.

"Do you hear harp music?" he asked boldly.

She smiled again. "I think one of the neighbors must have their stereo turned up too loud."

He gave her hand a small squeeze, and she returned it in kind. "That's certainly encouraging, but I wouldn't want to jump to any conclusions because of a little music. For example, let's say my special lady wanted to find out whether my kiss would make the world go away. She'd have to give me more than a smile. I think she'd have to lean toward me, close her eyes, and say, 'May I have a taste?'" For a moment, he thought he'd gone too far, but then she leaned forward, tilted her head back, and closed her eyes.

"Please, sir may I have a taste?"

For the first time in his life, he was nervous about a kiss. If he didn't get it just right— He hushed the unfamiliar voice in his head and touched his lips to hers. A hint of a spark convinced him it was going to be fine. Although a part of him wanted to dive into the kiss with his whole body, a greater part demanded that he give her only what they had negotiated for, *a taste*.

He lightly brushed his lips over hers, gave a peck, then moved his mouth to her cheek and down her neck, before returning to her mouth. He continued to tease her with baby kisses and warm breaths until he felt her growing anxious. Only then did he outline her mouth with his tongue, and when she parted her lips for him, he gave her the taste she had requested.

A second after their tongues touched, he drew back from her and waited.

She blinked at him in confusion.

"Where are you?" he asked.

"I have no idea," she whispered back honestly. "Please, sir, may I have some more?"

That request was the reward for his patience, as well as the confirmation that patience was no longer necessary. When he joined their mouths this time, there was no restraint. This kiss demanded that every part of their bodies be passionately involved in the act.

He wanted her to know how badly he had wanted to do this since he first saw her. He wanted her to feel the passion she aroused in him. He desperately wanted to ignite a fire in her like no other man had ever done. In the next instant he had everything he wanted.

She became the aggressor, claiming his mouth and tongue with a devouring kiss that left him breathless and craving more. Her hands moved over his bare chest, arms, and back as though they were feeding on him as well. Her desire made him feel weak and empowered all at once. And he was more than willing to let her use him until she had her fill.

But when her fingers touched his sex, he knew, if he didn't slow her down, it would be all over before he'd had a chance to satisfy a hunger of his own. "Not yet," he murmured, and moved her hand. "I want to see how close my imagination got to the real thing."

She didn't understand, and he didn't explain. He simply grasped the hem of her tee shirt and raised it over her head. The lacy bra came off seconds later, and he filled his hands with the most beautiful breasts he had ever seen. "You're incredible."

She smiled shyly, and he lowered his head to the valley between her breasts. He covered every inch of that beautiful female flesh with caresses before allowing himself the pleasure of capturing a peak. He took his time suckling and teasing one hardened nipple with his teeth before moving to the other, and he could have happily gone back to the first for a second helping had she not interrupted his feast.

"Zach, *please.*" Unable to say what she wanted, she took his hand and slid it down between her thighs. Pressing his fingers hard against herself, she repeated, *"Please."*

He needed no further urging. Returning his mouth to hers, he gave her his tongue to suck while he undid her shorts and found his way to the pulsing bundle of nerves that were begging to be relieved. She was so wet and wanting, he only needed to stroke her, and she cried out her climax.

That sort of quick release was hardly the journey to paradise he had intended to take her on. However, the blissful expression on her face told him that she had no idea it could get better. He was so very glad her fiancé had been an idiot.

Tamping down his own need, he removed her shorts and panties.

Leanne sighed with contentment as Zach positioned himself between her legs and went back to kissing her breasts again. The alcohol-induced haze had pretty much worn off, but Zach had her floating in a far more delightful way. It didn't matter that they hadn't known each other long. It didn't matter that he was an unemployed exconvict. She knew without a single doubt that he was the prince she had dreamed would miraculously appear someday. She knew this because:

She had had two erotic dreams about him—one even before she knew what he really looked like.

She had heroically rescued him from the jaws of death.

Their eyes had met, and there was music.

They had kissed, and the rest of the world had disappeared.

He had touched her, and the burst of pleasure throughout her body was the most exciting thing she had ever experienced.

Until he licked his way down her stomach and used his mouth to take her back up to the top of pleasure mountain. Her second climax was so powerful, she thought she had gone to heaven.

"Oh, Zach," she said once she could speak again. "That was . . . I don't know what it was. I can't think straight." He stretched out beside her and nibbled on her ear and neck as he lovingly kneaded her breast. "Mmmm. I could get very self-ish about this. But it is very definitely your turn to have some fun."

He laughed. "I thought I was having fun."

She kissed him and eased her hand between their bodies. She was pleased to find him just as hard as he was when they began, but the fact that he was still wearing his shorts after everything he'd given her made her chuckle. "Here, let me get these off of you." She unbuttoned the waist and pulled down the zipper, but he stopped her from taking the shorts off.

"Wait. I can't do this."

Chapter Six

Leanne assumed he was kidding and gave his erection a squeeze. "I think you'll manage just fine, but I promise to give you all the help you need." To her bewilderment, he stopped her efforts again, more firmly this time.

"I'm serious." He sat up, and it was his turn to stare at the waves breaking on the sand.

She suddenly felt very naked and very vulnerable. She reached for her clothes. "Thank you, Zach. You have just managed to ruin the most beautiful experience I have ever had."

"It was wrong of me to start this, knowing you had too much to drink. I can't take more advantage than I already have."

"I may have been a little tipsy after dinner, but

I'm sober enough to know that you didn't take advantage of me. Try again." She pulled on her panties and shorts.

"We don't have any protection."

"That's true, but you didn't need protection for what I was going to do for you. Unless . . . do you have . . . a contagious disease?"

"No."

"So protection is not the real problem either."

"If I tell you the real problem, I'm afraid you'll hate me."

"If you don't tell me, I'll hate you for sure. You certainly can't think we could live in the same house together after what just happened and not explain. So you have nothing to lose. You may as well talk. And this time, I want the whole truth. Who knows, you may luck out, and I'll believe you . . . *again.*"

"Will you promise to hear me out completely?"

She finished dressing, then exhaled heavily. "Sure. Why not."

"I was down on my luck, and needed a place to stay, like I said, but not for the reasons I gave you. Also, I was accused of a crime I didn't commit, but I don't have a prison record."

"Why would you lie about— Were you cleared?"

"No. I ran before I was arrested. I'm still a wanted man."

"Oh, swell. I'm harboring an escaped criminal."

"I'm *not* a criminal. I was framed."

She made a bored face. "Oh, yes. You said that

before. But if you were so innocent, why did you run?"

"Because I overheard the real perpetrators discussing the hit man they had already hired to kill me and make it look like suicide. They had no intention of letting me tell my side of the story. If people thought I'd killed myself, everyone would believe I had committed the crime, and the real bad guys would get off free."

She let that much sink in. "Are you telling me that you intend to hide out for the rest of your life? If you're really innocent, you could go to the authorities and demand protection."

"I could, if I had one piece of solid evidence, but all I have is my word against theirs. And if I turn myself in, and they put me in jail until a hearing is set, there's a good chance the killer could get to me there. I have a friend, my secretary actually, who promised to search for something I could use to prove my innocence."

"And has she?"

"I don't know. I haven't been able to contact her for a couple of weeks. I was hoping I could do that while I was here."

Leanne massaged her temples. "Wait a minute. You called her your secretary. Since when do construction workers have clerical help?"

"I, uh, wasn't truthful about my former career."

"What a surprise! Well, don't stop now. I can't wait to hear the rest of this soap opera."

His mouth twisted from side to side. "I, uh, I was a stockbroker."

"What?"

"And I was very professionally tricked into promoting a stock offering for a new company. They had all the right backers, at least they had good forgeries of signatures of impressive names, which were conveniently confirmed by middlemen. They had all the right forms and the numbers were just below the too-good-to-be-true point.

"All they needed was a highly successful broker from a major firm to add his endorsement and push it to everyone in the business. Since I had a reputation for picking winners right out of the gate, a lot of investors jumped on the offering without checking it out themselves."

"This is beginning to sound way too familiar," she said, feeling sick to her stomach.

"Let me finish. Within weeks, hundreds of millions of dollars had poured in. Needless to say, I had made a fair amount in commissions. Then the inevitable happened. One of those impressive names came forward and denied knowledge of the enterprise. As the fraud was uncovered, my name kept coming up as being the brain behind the scam. There was even a record of a large deposit into a Bahamian bank account in my name. My frame-up was as brilliantly arranged as the fraudulent company."

Leanne could hardly breathe. She already knew

the story he was relating, but that would make him— No. That was not possible. God wouldn't do this to her. Yet she had to know for sure. "What is your name?"

"I didn't do it, Leanne, I swear."

"Your name, dammit!"

"Ellwood Zachariah Gibbon." He paused then said the name that was as fatal as sticking a knife in her heart. "Rush. My family calls me Zach, but most people know me as E.Z."

She felt the rage build until she could no longer contain it. *"O-o-o-oh!"* she roared and punched him in the chest. In an instant, she was on her feet. "You pig! Wasn't it enough that you destroyed my life? You had to move into my home? You . . . you had to make me want you? How dare you put your hands on me?"

She grabbed the edge of the blanket and yanked with all her fury. She was only slightly satisfied to see him fall over into the sand. "I'm going home to burn this and scrub myself with lye soap! You may pick up your things tomorrow while I'm at my office."

Leanne walked an extra few blocks in an attempt to burn off her anger.

You were warned, her little voice reminded her.

Shut up.

What good is having intuition if you're not going to pay attention to it?

Excuse me? It was my wonderful intuition that told me to hire him and give him a chance after I discovered his first lie. It was my intution that told me he was the prince I'd been waiting for. Paying attention to my intution is what got me into this predicament.

My point exactly.

Leanne questioned the illogic of her own thought process, but the little voice had stopped talking.

By the time she walked home and went to bed, the red anger that had muddied her thinking was muted to blue self-pity. After several hours of wallowing, her little voice decided to start nagging again.

Have you figured it out yet?

Why are you reminding me of that dream?

Why do you think he wouldn't let you please him? If he was really such a bad guy, wouldn't he have taken advantage while he could?

Don't confuse me. I hate him.

The important question is, do you believe him?

Leanne instantly tried to form a negative answer, but couldn't manage it.

Just for a moment, try to let go of the hurt and anger. Pretend you have no personal stake in the answer. What does your intuition tell you about his story?

I no longer trust my intuition. For some reason, it is completely unreliable where he is concerned.

Then try putting yourself in his position. You know that what he described could happen.

It would be extremely difficult to pull off.

*Didn't he say "hundreds of millions of dollars"
were involved? Some people would take up the challenge for that kind of money.*

She didn't want to believe his story. It was easier
to stay angry and keep blaming him for everything
bad that had happened in her life recently.

The memory of Zach comforting her as she
cried in his arms drifted through her mind. What
he had said about saying good-bye to Grandpa
was unbelievably sweet. And she certainly
couldn't logically blame him for the condition of
Grandpa's house.

His opinion that she was lucky to be away from
the narrow-minded people and in business for
herself also had a strong dose of truth in it. And
he had proven in a most dramatic way that Eric
was not the best man for her.

The biggest argument on his behalf, however,
was the fact that he had made love to her, but
couldn't let her do the same for him as long as a
lie stood between them.

There was no use fighting it. She believed him.

Following her intuition once again, she decided
to go back to the beach to see if he was still there.
As it turned out, she didn't have to go that far. His
truck was parked in the driveway outside, and he
was asleep in the cab.

She reached inside the open window and
touched his shoulder. He was immediately alert
. . . and leery. "Come inside, Zach. We aren't fin-

ished talking." Rather than wait for him, she turned and went inside alone.

He joined her in the living room seconds later. "I never meant to hurt you. You've got to believe that."

"I do," she responded simply.

He was so ready for another rejection, it took him a moment to absorb her words. "You do?"

"Yes. And I might be totally out of my mind, but I also believe you're innocent of any crime." His face broke into a broad smile and he stepped toward her, but she held up a hand to keep him from getting closer. "There's something I want you to do, though, to prove that I'm not just reacting to . . . you know, what you did for me."

"Anything. Name it and it's done."

"I want you to get on a plane with me and go visit an old fishing buddy of Grandpa's. He's with the Securities and Exchange Commission, and if anybody could help you, he could."

Zach looked doubtful. "There's a difference between 'could' and 'will.' "

"He'll help if I ask him to. Of course, I may have to invite him here to stay for a few weeks so that he can have another try at hooking a marlin."

"When do we leave?"

That question, and the excited look in his eyes, was all the confirmation she needed. She might be a fool, but her heart felt a hundred pounds lighter. "I'll have to check the airline schedules, but I think we can put that off for a few more hours. There's one more test you have to pass first."

His frown returned. "Okay."

"Do you think I'm at all inebriated at the moment?"

"You don't look it," he said, cocking his head. "Are you?"

She clucked her tongue at him. "Of course not. I just wanted to make sure you were clear on that point. Next, are there any more lies you have to straighten out, or truths you've kept hidden?"

He gave that a few seconds of deliberation. "There are a few thousand details about my life I haven't told you, but I don't suppose that's the sort of thing you mean. As far as anything that would make you want to punch me again . . . I guess I should admit that I don't know the first thing about home repairs."

"Then how—" She figured it out on her own. "Billy, right?"

He lowered his head with guilt. "Yup. I'm afraid I told him a few lies also, and he took pity on me. In my defense though, he did say that he had wanted to get back to 'putzing' around this house, but you wouldn't let him. And I did help, by the way."

"Hmmm. Okay. Anything else?"

"I don't think so. Oh, yeah, there is one other thing—it's more of a confession actually—but this probably isn't the best time—"

"Spill," she commanded in a threatening tone.

97

"I'm warning you—"

"Now!"

"From the first time I saw you, I had . . . impure thoughts about you."

She bit her cheek to keep from laughing. *"Impure thoughts?"*

He acted as though he were very embarrassed, looking sheepish while shifting from one foot to the other. "Fantasies, actually."

Recalling the erotic dreams and rather wicked thoughts she had been having about him, she asked, "What sort of fantasies?"

His gaze slid down her body and back up to stare intently into her eyes. "Very, *very* sexy ones. They usually involved getting you naked. And you wanting me to touch you, kiss you, lick you. All over. From head . . . to toe." His gaze lingered on certain sensitive areas in between.

Her tongue moistened her dry lips. "And, uh, where would these fantasies take place?"

"Anywhere. Everywhere. In the ocean. In my truck. In the shower. On the back porch. I'd be happy to show you."

She could see him holding his breath for her response, but she had no intention of letting him off the hook that easily, not after everything he'd put her through. "Follow me," she ordered and strode to the stairs.

Once inside her bedroom, she made him wait a bit more while she unearthed a box from the closet and found what she was looking for. Keeping as straight a face as she could, she tossed two foil-wrapped condoms on her bed. "Do you know what those are?"

His curious frown turned into a lascivious grin. "Protection?"

"Exactly. I am not drunk, there are no lies between us, and you have your protection. I believe that takes care of all your objections against letting me make love to you, unless you have some new ones."

His grin broadened, and he shook his head. Glancing at the condoms, he asked, "Two?"

"Too many?" she teased.

"Too few," he countered.

"Touché," she said with a nod of approval. "Then what are you waiting for? Take your pants off. I'm not removing one stitch until you're more naked than I am." When he laughed and dropped his shorts, she quit fighting her own smile. "Well," she said admiring his semi-erection. "I'm relieved to see that your hesitation about removing your pants was not due to any . . . shortcoming."

In a flash, he closed the distance between them and lifted her into his arms. "If I remember correctly, you've already had a *short* coming, and a medium one, too. Do you think you could wait for a long one this time?" He set her down on the bed and took off her nightshirt. When he realized she was completely nude beneath, his sex came to full attention.

Wrapping her fingers around the length of him,

she whispered, "I'll bet I can hold out longer than you can." As she took him deeply into her mouth, his groan of pleasure confirmed that he had already lost. Leaning back again, she said, "Now, I'd like to hear some details about one of those fantasies you've been having. If you make it interesting enough, maybe I'll be willing to act one out with you."

As she circled the tip of him with her tongue, he inhaled sharply through gritted teeth then assured her, "You already are, believe me."

She smiled seductively. "Too easy. The test is that you have to tell me one of your stories while I try to distract you." Her fingers moved to softer flesh and played with her new toys. "If you don't start, I'll stop." She withdrew her hand and sat back.

He chuckled and shook his head. "All right, but you should know, I have very strong powers of concentration."

"Hmmph. We'll see."

"You remember when you gave me mouth-to-mouth out on the back porch?"

"Mm-hmmm." Her fingertips tickled his bottom.

"Uh, I, uh, ahem. I imagined that it didn't work, and you—" He had to stop for a moment when she nibbled her way down his shaft. "And you opened my shirt and licked my nipples." Another pause to appreciate her efforts. "And when that didn't work, you took off my pants and—" On the verge of losing control, he rushed through the story's climax in one held breath. "And you did what you're doing now and that's how you brought me back to life. Dear, God, Leanne. I don't think I can—"

The only concession she allowed him was to lie down on the bed before he fell down.

He tried to hold out, but she had her mind fixed on evening the score between them. Besides, she was looking forward to that "long one" he'd mentioned and wanted him to be able to stay with her for the whole journey.

As had happened with her, all that the first release accomplished was to take the sharp edge off. Zach's energy level—and his erection—was back up in a few minutes, and he reclaimed the lead. With his mouth and hands, he seduced her back to that delicious place she thought of as pleasure mountain. But this time, he stopped midway so that they could climb to the summit together.

Leanne had never known such a vivid sense of arousal as when he joined their bodies. She felt him deep inside her, on top of her, all around her. It was as though they were no longer two separate beings, but one, moving in time with the rhythm of their united heartbeat.

And when she was certain they could go no higher, he proved her wrong. Her entire body was suddenly flooded with exquisite happiness, and together they soared far above the top of the mountain, directly into heaven.

She didn't remember falling asleep, but the sun

was beating through the bedroom window when her eyes opened again.

"Good morning, beautiful," Zach murmured in her ear. "You were smiling in your sleep."

"Mmmm. I was having a yummy dream about Ernest Hemingway," she teased, and he pretended to be hurt. She kissed him quickly. "But then it turned out to be a very sexy, much younger man, in disguise."

"Were you angry at him for deceiving you?" He kissed his way from her neck down to her navel.

"Yes," she told him, then drew his head to her breast. "But he was so good at pleasing me, I decided to forgive him."

He caressed one nipple, then the other, before asking, "About everything?"

She gave him a long, deep kiss. "Yes. About everything. I can't explain why, because it certainly isn't logical."

"I think I know why," he said quietly and snuggled her into his embrace. "It was fate. Pure and simple. Just look at the timing of everything that has happened to each of us to bring us together in this house. If you ask me, I think Grandpa may have had a hand in this."

She chuckled. "I think that might be stretching a bit too far for an explanation."

"Maybe," he continued seriously. "But you have to admit, it's all been rather extraordinary. Most of my life I've known what my fantasy woman would be like, but I never met anyone who even came close. Then I walked into your office, and I knew that instant. It was almost as though I didn't need to get to know you, because I already did. You're the one I was looking for."

When Leanne remained quiet, he leaned back to see her expression. Her eyes were damp. "I wasn't going for tears with that speech—"

"They're happy tears," she assured him with a smile. "That was by far the most romantic speech I have ever heard."

"Good. Then I feel secure enough to finish it. I . . . Leanne Shepard, I think I love you."

Her cheeks flushed. "I think I love you, too, Ellwood Zachariah Gibbon Rush."

Their mouths came together slowly and the kiss was more reverent than passionate.

"I have an important question," Zach said after a quiet moment. "Since neither one of us has ever been in love, how will we know when we go from *thinking* we're in love to definitely *being* in love?"

"Good question. We should probably make up a test of some sort."

He grinned. "I usually do pretty well on tests. What do you have in mind?"

She sat up and propped her chin on her fist. When Zach tried to say something, she hushed him so that she could think. Finally, she snapped her fingers. "I've got it. If you're right about our meeting being fated and so on, then this is a classic fairy-tale romance. And everyone knows that sort of story always ends happily ever after."

Zach was intrigued, but could not tell where she was headed. "So, what's our test?"

"Don't you see? It's the ending that makes it true romance. If we can exact a happy ending—one where your name is cleared, and we are free to live together happily ever after—then it must be true love."

Worry clouded his eyes. "But what if—"

She pressed her fingers to his lips. "Uh-uh. No doubts. Only happy thoughts. Anyway, if you're right about Grandpa engineering this match, I'm sure he'll continue to stick his nose in it to the very end. Are we in agreement on this?"

"Happy ending equals true love," he said, though he clearly had some unspoken reservations. "I suppose that's as good a test as any."

"Good, because there's the matter of some unfinished business between us." She let him wonder what it could be for a moment, then showed him the condom they had yet to use. "I believe you were the one who said two would be too few."

Much later, she was making lunch while Zach took a shower. When she heard a knock at the door, she assumed it was Billy, coming to do some more work, and automatically opened the door.

Instead of Billy, however, there was a stern looking gray-haired man in a short-sleeved white shirt and loosened tie. He flashed some sort of identification in front of her and said, "I'm Detective Andrew Wyckoff. Have you seen this man?" He showed her a good photograph of Zach. "His real name is E. Z. Rush, but he could be going by anything."

Leanne swallowed hard and ordered herself to remain calm. What was she to do? The legally correct thing would be to turn Zach over to this man, but that would risk his life. On the other hand, if she didn't admit to knowing him, she could be convicted of aiding and abetting a criminal. Her heart made the decision. "Sorry. He doesn't look familiar."

Wyckoff arched an eyebrow at her. "No? That's odd. Because someone claiming to be E. Z. Rush picked up a prescription refill at the local drug store, and the pharmacist said that man gave this address as his current residence. Another odd thing is that the truck in your driveway matches the description of the last vehicle E. Z. Rush was seen driving."

"Is that Billy?" Zach called as he came down the hallway toward the foyer.

Chapter Seven

Leanne's heart nearly leapt out of her chest, but one glance over her shoulder assured her that Zach was in full disguise, right down to the toothpick in his mouth. "Uh, no . . . *Tom*. This is Detective Wyckoff. He's looking for someone named—I'm sorry, what was that name again?"

"E. Z. Rush. I didn't catch your name."

Leanne made herself smile. "I'm Leanne Shepard. And this is Tom . . . my . . . grandfather. That's his truck out front."

The detective looked at the truck, then at each of them. He didn't appear to be completely convinced. "Would you have any objection to my taking a look around?"

Leanne straightened her spine. "As a matter of

fact—" Zach cut her off by squeezing her elbow.

"Ain't no reason ta object, lessen yore some kinda criminal plannin' ta rob us. Ya got any ID I kin take a look at?"

"Of course." The detective handed him the case he had flashed at Leanne.

Zach studied it for a second. "This here says yore one o' them private eyes, not a real police detective like they have on that cop show. So who you workin' for?"

"I'm sorry. That's confidential."

"Then we're mighty sorry, too. Our home is one great big confidential matter, an' 'less you have a piece o' paper that gives you the right ta trespass, yore business is finished here." Zach closed the door on him and turned the deadbolt.

"Dolores Yankowicz," Wyckoff called from outside. "I was hired by—"

Zach reopened the door.

"—Dolores Yankowicz to find her boss, E. Z. Rush. She has been trying to get some very important information to him that he would definitely want to hear . . . if I could track him down."

Zach hesitated another few seconds, then said, "*If* we knew how to find this Rush guy, I'm sure he'd wanna have some proof about who done hired you an' what for, before he'd be willin' ta talk ta ya."

Wyckoff took out a wrinkled handkerchief and wiped the beads of sweat from his forehead and upper lip. "It sure is hot out here in the sun. I'd really appreciate an invitation inside and a cold drink."

Leanne glanced up at Zach and he gave her a nod. "Would a glass of sweet iced tea be all right?"

"Perfect," he replied, looking very relieved when Zach led him toward the living room.

Leanne joined them with three glasses of tea before the two men were finished discussing how well the ceiling fans worked to keep the house cool.

Wyckoff drank half the glass then got back to the subject at hand. "Dolores thought her boss might be leery of anyone coming after him, so they had decided on a code phrase that no one else could know. But I was only to say it to Mr. Rush. If I tell it to you on the off-chance that you might run into him, then I've failed to keep it a secret, haven't I?"

Leanne looked from one man to the other. It was like a Mexican standoff.

"I don't suppose there's anythin' we can help ya with then," Zach said. "If yore finished with yore tea, I'll see ya ta the door."

Wyckoff walked out, but paused before leaving the front porch. "This heat is really something. Don't think I could stand living here myself. It's enough to turn my brown eyes blue." He stepped off the porch and waved a hand. "See you around."

"Wait!" Zach exclaimed. Wyckoff had just said Dolores's key phrase: *It's enough to turn my brown eyes blue.* "Do you have a match?"

"Sure do," he said and walked back to Zach. He took a matchbook out of his pocket and handed it to him.

Zach could hardly believe it. As they had agreed, Dolores had given her messenger a souvenir matchbook from her daughter's wedding. Quickly, he took off his straw hat, sunglasses and beard. "I'm E. Z. Rush. Please come back inside."

As they returned to the living room, Wyckoff said, "You've certainly given me one hell of a chase, Mr. Rush, and since I'm one of the best trackers in the business, that's really saying something."

"Why would you say that? How long have you been looking for me?"

"From the day you left Boston."

The sound of the men's voices drew Leanne back into the room. Seeing Zach without his headgear confused her, but he didn't look upset, so she tried not to be. "What's going on?"

Zach smiled. "He really is a messenger from Dolores. She's the secretary I mentioned to you." To Wyckoff, he asked, "Did you say, from Boston?"

"Yes, but I wasn't officially working for Dolores until three weeks ago. Before that I was working for Rupert and Finney, the two men who set you up."

Zach slammed his hand on a table. "I knew it was them. But how did you— I mean, do you have proof—"

"Hold on. It all gets a bit complicated, so I'll just

give you the big picture for now. Rupert and Finney hired me to keep an eye on you, because they said they were trying to find out what you were up to. Later I realized they planned on using me to show how they were suspicious of you all along.

"The night before you disappeared, they took me out to a fancy dinner and made me an offer they thought I couldn't refuse: a half-million dollars to bump you off and make it look like suicide. Don't worry. I don't do that sort of thing, but apparently, they didn't know the difference between a tracker and a hit man. Too many bad movies, I guess.

"Anyway, I told them I'd think about it, while I did a little checking on them. Then you took off right before the doo-doo hit the fan, so I figured I needed a scorecard to figure out who was what. That's where Dolores came in. She's a real looker, you know? Smart, too. When I get back—"

"Mr. Wyckoff, *please* go on," Leanne interrupted.

"So we put our talents together. I kept Rupert and Finney on the string by tracking you and sending them reports, and an occasional photo, while she stayed on the inside, taping conversations, searching for evidence, accessing hidden computer files, that sort of thing. She found the numbers of two Swiss bank accounts where they've been transferring funds."

Zach shook his head. "This is unbelievable. Are you telling me that you're the one I've been running from for the past month? And if I had let you catch up to me, *nothing* would have happened?"

Wyckoff shrugged. "Since you hadn't spoken to Dolores, there was no way for you to know that she and I were in cahoots. At any rate, you never really lost me until you hit Florida, and then it was like you dropped off the Earth.

"It was the prescription refill that gave you away. Dolores knew you couldn't go too long on the supply you had left, so she had made discreet arrangements with your regular pharmacist to let her know if anything came in with your name on it."

"So what's the bottom line?" Zach asked. "Is it safe to go home, or not?"

"Yes, but you'll want to keep your return under wraps for a bit longer. Dolores and I have come up with the perfect sting to pay those two guys back and see to it that they go to jail for a long time. We need your help to pull off the final act though."

"That's fine with me. Anything's better than hiding."

"I can fill you in on the flight back. How soon can you be ready to go?"

"Ten minutes. Just let me—" He stopped when he saw the worried expression on Leanne's face. "—pack a few things. We'll be right back." He grasped her hand and led her to his room.

As soon as they were inside with the door closed, he kissed her with all the excitement he was feeling, but her response was lukewarm. "I'll be back," he promised. "I'd take you with me, but if this is some kind of elaborate trap, I don't want you implicated in any way."

Her frown deepened. "You think it might be a trap?"

"No, of course not. I just don't want to take any chances with you. I'll call as soon as I can, I promise."

Two days later, in Boston, Wyckoff met with Rupert and Finney. Unbeknownst to them, he was wearing a wire and had the FBI standing by. He showed them a photo of Zach, looking quite dead, hanging from a chandelier hook by a noose. He also let them examine a photocopy of Zach's handwritten confession/suicide note that was left at the scene.

But he withheld the location of the decaying body until they paid him his half-million dollars in bearer bonds and had a friendly chat about the enormous scam they had gotten away with.

When they grew tired of boasting about their success, they demanded the location of Zach's body, and he handed them a sealed envelope. It contained a piece of paper showing the address of the building they were sitting in.

Before they had a chance to figure it out, Zach and a squad of agents dropped in for a surprise visit.

*   *   *

A week later, Leanne gave up waiting for Zach to call. Apparently, it wasn't true love after all.

The sting Wyckoff had referred to made all the news, and his and Zach's faces were on every channel and in every paper. She was happy for him. Really she was.

Each day she spent a little longer at the office, not wanting to go home to the big empty house before she absolutely had to. At least she could be pleased that she was starting to make some progress with her client list. Not everyone blamed her for their losses, especially after watching the latest development on the news.

Telling herself for the hundredth time that her heart would feel better tomorrow, she locked up the office and headed for her car.

But her car wasn't in the space where she had parked it that morning.

Instead of her car, there was a very large, very white horse. And sitting astride that horse was a very handsome Ellwood Zachariah Gibbon Rush . . . dressed up as medieval royalty, from crown to stockings.

He leaned over and offered his arm. "You might want to use the stool," he suggested, pointing at the short stepladder next to the parking meter.

She was sitting sidesaddle in front of him atop the great horse before she found her voice. "You're crazy, you know that? What did you do with my car? Why didn't you call me? I thought . . . I didn't know . . ."

113

Marilyn Campbell

He tilted her head and kissed her questions away. "Your car is at home. I used your extra set of keys. With regard to my not calling you, I almost did a thousand times. But once I got this idea into my head . . . You see, there are no telephones in any of the fairy tales I ever read, and I didn't want there to be any question left in your mind as to whether or not I was the prince you'd been waiting for."

"Hmmm. You certainly look the part. And your kiss certainly made me forget about everything else. But I wouldn't want to get involved with a prince that was just passing through my village."

"I have given that matter considerable thought and decided that I definitely prefer a tropical island to Boston. Do you think you could help me find an empty office where I could ply my trade and a castle to sleep in?"

She laughed. "A castle might be a little hard to come by, but I think I can arrange something." She lowered his head for another long kiss. "I love you."

"I love you, too."

"Are you absolutely certain? You don't just *think* you love me?"

He kissed her again. "You're the one who said the test for true love was a happy ending."

She stopped him from giving her another kiss. "Take me home, Prince Zachariah, and I'll give you a happier ending than all your fantasies combined."

And they lived happily ever after. . . .

Love
Sessions

THEA
DEVINE

Always, always, always for my guys:
John, Michael and Tom

And, my gratitude to Alicia Condon

Chapter One

"Hunter Devlin did *what?*"

Leslie Gordon wheeled around from her computer to see her editor lounging in the doorway.

"You heard me," Natalie Balter said. "I'm shocked you didn't see it."

"Tell me again," Leslie invited, folding her hands in her lap. Clenching her hands. *Hunter again. Hunter forever. Hunter everywhere. You couldn't get rid of Hunter, who sought the spotlight like a flower sought the sun.*

"He bungeed onto the set of the *Today* show right into Katie Couric's lap."

"Omigod," Leslie murmured, shaking her head. "And to think I missed it. What that man won't do."

"A stunt like that," Natalie said, "definitely warrants a Leslie Gordon commentary, don't you think?"

"As cheap as it gets," Leslie said, her eyes gleaming at the possibilities. "What's his deal this time?"

"*Fashion Forward* magazine named him clothes hunk of the year."

Leslie groaned. "Give me a break. Everything that man touches turns to gold. And now he's the best-dressed icon too. It absolutely escapes me how he does it."

"Well," Natalie said, drawing the word out. "Maybe you have an opportunity to find out."

Leslie shook her head. "I already know more about Hunter Devlin than I want or need to know."

"Yeah, I know—same old, same old. Same best private schools; same super-intellectual college. He dropped out, you didn't. He made money, you made Phi Beta K."

"That's the sum and substance of it," Leslie agreed. But it wasn't nearly the whole story. It really went more like: he'd been rich, popular, confident, magnetic. And she'd been the sad little rich girl: overweight, undervalued, unwanted, with an unregenerate intelligence that she'd made sure was deliberately off-putting. All she'd cared about was covering her behind.

She shuddered to remember those days. She'd been an overbearing, dictatorial prig until that glorious moment when Hunter "got" her. And all it had taken was one wicked, skewering editorial in the Dumbrille School newspaper early in their junior year.

It had only changed her life.

She'd known him forever. Or so it seemed. Yes they had attended the same private boarding schools, which he had relished and she'd hated, having been shunted there by her widowed army-general father who'd had no time for her. Hunter, on the other hand, had made his own decision to come after a globe-trotting childhood with doting parents that had provided lots of love and adventure, but little stability.

They'd had mutual friends, disparate interests. Until the Commentary.

The Commentary had brought her notice; Hunter's interest made her hip, happening, and a nascent political guru.

It had set up a battle of wits and words between them which they carried on to this day, sporadically trading faxes and E-mails of equal and nasty one-upmanship.

They'd hung out together, she and Hunter, and she'd watched the girls at school fall over him with sardonic amusement.

There was just something about guys like Hunter. They always got everything: good looks, wealth, supreme confidence, achievements, close family ties. Love . . .

But she hadn't ever thought about him in *that* way. She'd recognized early on that pining for someone like Hunter was futile. It was easier to be his buddy, his conscience, his pal. That way, she could share in his triumphs and successes without any emotional investment.

And she got to make fun of him too, which was especially satisfying since within a year and half of obtaining her graduate degree in economics from the University of Chicago, she'd become the new conservative media darling. Her rise had been meteoric, straightforward—and a carefully planned three-pronged attack, the mission statement of which was: Get Noticed.

Slender women got noticed. She lost thirty pounds.

Blondes got noticed. In spades. She dyed her hair blond.

Outrageous opinions got noticed. She'd made sure she wrote letters and op-ed pieces to every possible paper, journal and magazine while she still was in graduate school, until her excesses came to the notice of the powerful and the pundits.

From there on, it was pure luck and some fortuitous timing.

And the blond hair. She was sure of it. People treated her differently. They spoke to her. They smiled at her, and told her things, and then she made the story.

Her first op-ed for the *Times* generated a mountain of heated mail which had led to an invitation to do another piece and then another.

She reveled in the controversy. Deliberately, she took the least popular stance on any given question, researched it thoroughly, prepared thoughtfully, and then she lit the match, stood back, and gleefully watched the conflagration.

People had gotten angry. People had strong feelings about certain subjects, and she knew, with her blondeness and her shimmering intelligence, exactly how to set them off.

And as she'd planned, she got noticed, and *Cityscape* magazine offered her a weekly column.

Six months later, everyone was talking about her, and the local political talk show on early Sunday morning had offered her a one-time, on-camera opinion piece.

She'd generated ratings and fury in equal amounts and now she was a biweekly commentator on the show.

And there was the possibility of a cable news show slot in the offing.

And now Hunter, in the news again.

Anyone that spotlight hungry was worthy of a Leslie Gordon skewering.

"I'll fax him," Leslie said decisively. "See if I can get a rise. Maybe I'll do an endcap on him. I *don't* think he deserves a full column."

"You could do more than that," Natalie said tantalizingly.

"I could? Is it worth the effort, Nat? I mean, until the next stunt?"

"See what *you* think. He's a sponsor of the Diamonds and Dust Ball this year, and they're auctioning dates for charity. He's on the block, Leslie. Doesn't it just make your mouth water?"

Leslie's emerald eyes narrowed as her imagination spun twenty scenarios from that offhanded statement.

"You don't expect me to . . ." she started, and then lost her train of thought. It was too irresistible. Even *she* could see that, and Natalie's devilish grin only reinforced what she was fantasizing.

But she was nothing if not hardheaded. "How much?" she asked.

Natalie sent her an innocent what-can-you-be-talking-about look.

"I can't imagine what you mean. I thought the glory of the story would be enough."

Leslie held out her hand. "You obviously have *something* in mind, Nat. And you mustn't forget, I'll need a sumptuous day at the spa to prepare. And a gown commensurate with the kind of guy I'm bidding on. And money, pots of filthy lucre, because I have a feeling the sky's going to be the limit on him."

Natalie grinned. "Don't you just love it?"

She was going to do it. She was really going to do it, Leslie thought, and she felt a moment of pure panic. She hadn't seen Hunter in years. And the only place he could have seen her in her new bimbo-babe guise was on *New York Rising*, a talk show that aired at six A.M. on Sunday mornings. She couldn't imagine Hunter ever got up that early. But what did she really know of the Hunter Devlins of the world?

It appeared, she thought mordantly, she was about to find out. She squelched her misgivings, and rubbed her fingers together. "How much, Natalie?"

"Anything for a story, Leslie dear. Whatever your little greedy heart desires. Charge it up to me, and *Cityscape* will foot the bill."

"I do like an editor with imagination," Leslie murmured, swiveling back to her computer. "Watch this." She exited her file, brought up a 36-point font and wrote across the blank screen:

*Nominated as clothes*horse *of the year, did they say?*
Or was it—stallion?

And with the stroke of a key, she gleefully E-mailed the jibe to Hunter Devlin's office.

Hunter Devlin did not consider himself extraordinary in any way. He thought of himself rather as an entrepreneur for whom any regimentation at all was absolutely counterproductive.

And so he'd arranged his life so that he was never bored.

He was at home everywhere and anywhere. He'd had a childhood that anyone would envy: the most imaginative and adventure-loving parents who adored their only child; the best of everything at his fingertips; the world as his playground; the most expensive education to round him out; and finally, the wherewithal, from an extensive trust fund, to invest, invent and create as his fancy led him.

He had parlayed that into nearly a billion dollars in assets in high-profile businesses, including a film studio, a publishing house, restaurants, theaters, a half-dozen small newspapers, and a New York fashion house, which he ran under the aegis of an umbrella company he called Rogue's Gallery.

The risk of his investments kept him on his toes and interested. A gallery of society debutantes kept his libido healthy, and intermittant correspondence or dinners with old friends kept him grounded.

Otherwise, titles like "Media Lion" and "Best Dressed Hunk," or "Tenth Most Fascinating Person of the Year" would have surely turned his head and made him insufferable.

Thank God Leslie Gordon had settled in New York. Every couple of weeks, he could count on a scintillating comment from Leslie, cheerfully calculated to deflate any pretentions or ego he might have cultivated in the interval.

He was delighted by her success, even if he hadn't quite had the time to follow it. He did try to read her column in *Cityscape*—he managed that about once a month. Everything else was hearsay, but that didn't mean it mattered less.

The E-mails were short, sweet, pithy, and more appreciated than Leslie would ever know, coming as they did at odd, quirky and sometimes critical moments in his busy day.

He had one today, in fact; he pulled it up with great anticipation, read it and laughed out loud. He gave it moment's thought, and then he typed his response:

So . . . what do you think—no one will marery me now?

And he flicked it back to Leslie's computer with a smile still creasing his face.

Oh, man—she hadn't really thought through all the ramifications of this idea, Leslie thought ruefully, as she contemplated her schedule of what she needed to accomplish before the Diamonds and Dust Ball.

It looked like a battle plan, and she was not cut out to be a general. Too many details. Too little time.

The dress—that was of paramount importance. *The dress* . . . she bit her lips as she fantasized about it. Long, slinky, form-fitting, glittery, low-cut . . . oh, sure—

No bosom to speak of there. A little mystery and a lot of draping would suit her better, she thought, doodling on her pad of notes. But it could be low cut in *back*. She liked that idea. On the other hand, that kind of dress would place a lot of importance on her hair.

Oh God, her *hair*. She scrambled to look in a mirror. Damn. She needed a touch-up. A trim. It was right in that awkward stage when it was growing out, and it was so impossible to style, that you just wanted to cut it all off.

Whose stupid idea was this?

How many days until the damned ball?

Dear God—only *two weeks?* And a column due, and an appearance in two days on *New York Rising*. How stupid was she? Her plate was full all right, and made of paper, and soggy to boot. And already leaking all over her shoes.

Shoot. Okay. She had her budget, spectacularly generous by *Cityscape* standards. The bulk of it she had earmarked for the bidding war. That left about five hundred dollars to spend on her dress and hair.

Forget the spa. Forget Dead Sea mud wraps and soaking in seaweed while focusing on her *chi*. No time to sweat off three inches so the bulge in her tummy wouldn't show.

It was Nordstrom's for her, and preferably the sale rack. If she even had time to shop.

What have I gotten myself into?

"Natalie!" she moaned into the phone. "This *cannot* be done in two weeks."

"Sure it can," Natalie said cheerfully. "Work at home. Take some time. Do a thousand words instead of two this week. If you have to. I wouldn't prefer it. But I'll compromise for the cause."

"There is no cause," Leslie barked.

"Come on now, where is that calm, clear-sighted Leslie Gordon sensibility? You're acting like a teenager getting ready for her first date."

Bingo! Exactly . . . how nice of Natalie to pinpoint it so tellingly. Her first date, if she should win the bid. With Hunter. A man who was the stuff of women's fantasies. How did sharp-tongued, quick-witted, not-too-cute Leslie Gordon live up to that?

That was the thing she hadn't considered when she'd leapt at the chance to "buy" a date with Hunter. That absolutely defined the misgivings she'd felt.

And there, in a nutshell, was the thing no woman would ever want to admit. She was scared to go face-to-face with Hunter. Removed, by fax or E-mail, it was perfectly fine. Easy, in fact, to trade insults and quips.

She'd already sent back an answer to his reponse to her foray. It was the most back-and-forth they'd had in months.

*Mare-ry? Who's Mare-ry? Are you dating some-
one named Mare-ry? Anyone we should know
about? You sly thing . . .*

Easy to write as long as she didn't have to look
him in the eye. She was excellent at twisting
words. She was funny as hell with words. She was
incisive, wrenching and wonderful with words.
Just look at that witty response. On paper, she was
a love goddess.

But in the flesh—oh, baby . . .

She hadn't seen him in years, and she'd seen
enough of him on TV and in the papers to know:
he hadn't lost one ounce of that magnetism; he
was still loaded with charm and charisma, and
was still irresistible.

The Hunter Devlins of the world did not date
women like her. She wasn't flashy enough, rich
enough or full-blown enough. The only thing he
would respect about her in the morning was her
intellect.

And if she even won the bid, she'd be a charity
case in more ways than one.

"Hell, anything for a story," she muttered, returning to her list. Her impossible list. Twenty impossible things before next Sunday.

She scanned the list again. No problem. Piece
of cake. She couldn't let Natalie down.

And herself?

Full speed ahead. And damn the Bismarck. It was
just a matter of following through on her long-

standing philosophy about him: no investment, nothing to lose.

She was going to buy that date with Hunter Devlin, and she'd make sure she enjoyed the consequences.

Chapter Two

The dress ... the dress ... the dress ...

She was driving herself crazy over what to wear. She was driving Natalie crazy until her friend finally put her foot down. "I refuse to spend another lunch hour in the stores. You are a maniac, and you're starting to invest this with something that is suspiciously unhealthy."

Oh, hell—that stopped her short. Natalie pinpointing reality as usual; Natalie never sugarcoated anything, least of all herself. She was plain, foursquare, and as straight-shooting as anyone Leslie had ever met. *And* she was the best editor, and the best friend.

Leslie threw up her hands. "You're right. When

you're right, you're right. And I'm violating my own basic rule about Hunter."

"I'm always right," Natalie said acerbically. "What rule was that? Hysteria on the frontlines equals a good story?"

"No investment. No *emotional* investment. Let me tell you about Hunter. . . ."

"You have told me about Hunter."

"Well, let me tell you again. Maybe *I* need my memory jogged. This is guy is lethal. He is magic. He is as unpretentious as he seems when you see him on TV. He's always been confident and charismatic, and he never goddamn fails. He turns lemons into lemonade. I don't know what it is. He thinks differently or something. And he lives his life like that—he turns on a dime and goes in the other direction just when you least expect it. He hasn't changed in all these years. Everything I've ever seen or read about him—he's just the way he was when I knew him in school.

"So-o-o . . . I don't know quite what I'm expecting. I mean, if I have the successful bid, he's got to honor the committment, right?"

"Exactly. You could be wearing sackcloth and ashes, and it shouldn't make a difference."

"That's just what I mean," Leslie said more light-heartedly than she felt. "Actually, sackcloth and ashes sounds very trendy. Fits in with all that new spirituality."

"He's an honorable guy, right?"

131

"A regular knight in shining armor."

"And it's all for charity."

"Exactly."

"And the story, of course."

"Mustn't forget the prime directive," Leslie murmured.

"So you could wear any wear any old dress in your wardrobe and save the company some money," Natalie finished in a triumph of logic.

Leslie glared at her. "I'm going shopping."

"Black," Natalie said, eyeing her critically. "Or brown. Gold, if you must—but don't. And make sure you buy it today, you hear? I've had enough of this nonsense and I'm beginning to regret ever having suggested it to you."

"And thanks for your support too," Leslie said airily as she grabbed her bag. "I won't let you down."

"Providing," Natalie called after her, "*you* don't freeze up."

"The Diamonds and Dust Ball is this weekend, Mr. Devlin," Hunter's secretary said as he laid his mail on his desk that Monday morning.

"Oh, hell—" Hunter muttered, and caught himself. It didn't do to show emotions in front of the hired help. "Thanks for reminding me, Arthur. I'm sure I'd forgotten."

"And the auction," Arthur ventured helpfully.

Auction? What auction? There was nothing up for sale that he was interested in. He'd already put in his weekly call to Sotheby's . . . "Auction?" he murmured.

"At the ball."

"At . . . the ball?" Hunter said faintly, inviting Arthur to elaborate.

"You—um—agreed . . . yes, *agreed*—" Arthur knew just how it sounded, and just how much attention Hunter had probably paid at the time he'd been approached. "—that is, it was agreed that—to—raise some more money, a group of eligible gentlemen would let themselves be auctioned to thehighestbiddertotakeonadate," he finished in a rush.

"Oh," Hunter said blankly. "All of us at once?"

"One at a time."

Light dawned. "I see. I'm one of those *eligible* men. . . ."

Arthur let out a breath. "Yes, sir."

"They're going to bid on *me?*" Hunter sounded outraged.

Arthur was not so sure of his response now. "Yes, sir."

"I see." That dismissive tone Arthur hated. It meant Hunter was bored and wasn't going to do anything he didn't want to do.

"You committed to it over a year ago," Arthur reminded him.

Hunter sent him a scorching look. "So what?"

"Well—" Arthur fumbled over his words. "They've been advertising it, sir. Trumpeting it—I mean, all the names of the participants. The response has been . . ."

"Overwhelming," Hunter supplied dryly.

"Yes, sir. It's been reported that sales of formal gowns have increased ten percent, sir. It's a ripple effect. A trickle-down, as it were."

"I'm blessed to be able to contribute to the economy," Hunter said, pulling his calendar in front of him. *Saturday. Saturday.* He was hoping he had *something* pencilled in—and he did: Diamonds and Dust, 7 P.M. Plaza Hotel.

Damn.

Diamonds and debutantes, he thought, already bored. He couldn't remember ever having said yes to it.

He took the invitation that Arthur extended to him and scanned it. His name was there, larger than life, and in *Town & Country*, the *Sunday Times* . . . and . . . he didn't want to see any more promotion of the event.

"See to my tux, Arthur." God, he hated the thing. He was sure he hadn't worn it in a year. Maybe he'd been wearing it when they'd come to him about the Diamonds and Dust Ball. Maybe his collar had been so tight, and his neck had been so constricted, he hadn't known what he was doing.

No matter. He was committed, and that was that.

And Hunter was a man who always honored his committments.

* * *

Thank God for hair extensions.

Leslie stared at herself in the mirror, a stranger with whipped blonde curls piled on her head and exquisite make-up applied by the hand of an aspiring Hollywood makeup artist.

And thank God for designer hair dressers who know what to do with hair, face, body and soul.

Her hands shook, just a little, as she pulled the plastic away from *the* dress, which was hanging like temptation on her closet door.

Seek and ye shall find. Not everyone was a size two. Six. More like ten–twelve. She just knew her competition, the bidding budding debutantes, would be a size zero.

But this dress—this dress made her look a size . . . four.

She'd found the dress in Bloomingdale's. On the sale rack. A subtle beaded brown-and-black animal print that had been slashed in price because of some unravelling along the hemline. An easy fix for a dress that turned her into a goddess.

It had a high neck with a thin chain attached that dangled down her exposed back, calling discreet attention to the drape of material that framed it.

It weighed, she thought, about twenty pounds. It could have weighed a hundred: she would have killed for that dress. She'd had to wrestle it away from someone else who was interested, in point of fact.

And now Natalie was on her way over to help her get ready for the event.

She caressed the shimmering beads that were handsewn on the silk underdress. How lucky could a girl get?

The doorbell rang. "It's open," she called, and Natalie let herself in.

"So—let me see what my shopper dollars bought," she said, coming into the bedroom.

"Ta-da," Leslie crowed.

"Oh, my God," Natalie breathed, touching the shimmer. "Lord, that must weigh a ton."

"I said I needed help."

"Get down on your knees, lady. We're going to dress you the old-fashioned way."

"Whatever works for you," Leslie murmured. "It's beautiful, isn't it?"

"Killer," Natalie said. "Come on, on your knees, right by the closet. Where's the zipper?"

"There isn't one."

Natalie's eyes rounded. "Oh. I see. Okay. Well, just come up under the hem here, and I'll slip the thing over your head."

"Carefully."

"I love your big hair, darling."

"So do I," Leslie said trenchantly, as Natalie slowly lowered the dress over her head.

"Big hair for a swelled head."

Leslie ignored her. "Hold on—I have to get my arms in the sleeves . . . okay, take it off the hanger." She raised her arms, and Natalie gently slipped the body of the dress over her head.

She'd been born to wear this gown, she thought, as the silk underdress molded to her and the weight of it settled sleekly against her body. It was amazing, slenderizing and flamboyant both, erotic, and it fit like a second skin.

Slowly she turned to face Natalie.

"Goooo-ood lord . . ." Natalie breathed. "Unbelievable."

"Are you saying *I'm* unbelievable?" Leslie demanded. "I'd better be very believable in this thing."

"No one can touch you, my dear. You look—you look . . ."

"Words can't describe it, right?" Leslie muttered, turning toward the full-length beveled mirror on the back of her bedroom door.

Her mouth fell open. "Oh, my . . ."

She had never considered herself a *femme fatale*. At best, after she'd lost the weight and dyed her hair, she'd thought she projected an air of healthy atheticism, which she'd enhanced by learning to play a passable game of tennis, and by joining the company softball team.

But this . . . this was the stuff of fantasies. This was diamonds and fairy dust. Elegant. Extravagant. Sensual, even faintly erotic. And a part of herself she never had known existed.

"I think I'll just . . . keep my mouth shut, and maybe I can preserve the illusion that this is all real," she murmured, turning sideways to admire the golden chain that caressed her bare back like fairy fingers.

"It'll never happen," Natalie said. "Besides which, you're going to be very up-front with Mr. Wonderful. Aren't you?"

"Absolutely," Leslie said, her gaze riveted on the exposed expanse of her back. Had her skin always been that creamy, or was it the dress, the color, the light? You could never trust the light. What she needed was a harsh fluorescent bulb right in her closet to bring her back to reality.

She just didn't *look* like this.

Except she did.

"All right. So here are the little nothing shoes," Natalie said, dropping the dull gold sandals on the floor so she could slip into them. "*How* high is that heel?"

"Three inches?" Leslie guessed.

"Bought from . . . oh, let me figure it out—the highest priced shoe salon in the East fifties."

"Something like that," Leslie murmured. "But worth every penny."

"If you break a heel, I will break your neck. *Cityscape* owns those shoes."

"Gotcha."

"And that bag—it isn't what I think it is, is it?"

"What were you thinking?" Leslie asked guilelessly.

"Oh, it kind of reminds me of that famous designer of little glittery bags in the five-hundred to thousand-dollar range."

"Nah. It's a knockoff," Leslie said. "Fooled ya."

"Bet you didn't," Natalie muttered. "Are you about ready? It's six o'clock and it's going to take time to get across town. What about jewelry?"

"Bracelet, earrings, and watch, so Cinderella can escape Prince Charming at midnight before she turns back into the scullery journalist that she is."

Natalie eyed her critically. "Those earrings are gorgeous. I can't wait to see the bill for this."

"I promise you, I was a conscientious shopper. I'm spending most of your money on prime hunk."

"Whom you are about to stake out. Okay, I guess it's time. Your limousine awaits to whisk you away to Camelot."

"Is that how it's done? I don't get beamed up and reassembled in the palace?"

"Not at the price that ensemble costs, you don't. Come on, Leslie. You're stalling. I'll ride over with you, and make sure you're pointed in the right direction on the yellow brick road."

The hotel, on the park, was lit with floodlights and strobes intersecting a hundred feet in the air, which gave it the ambiance of a big Hollywood opening.

News vans crowded the surrounding streets and the entertainment reporters for the evening news were stationed along the sidewalk at the entrance to the hotel; the driveway was reserved for the ongoing line of stretch limousines which drew up and discharged passengers with the precision of a swiss watch, and a noisy crowd of passersby and celebrity seekers were contained, for the moment, behind the police barriers blocking 59th Street and Fifth Avenue.

There was a Master of Ceremonies parading up and down the red carpet who introduced each incoming guest to the camera which was taping the event for the charity's publicity machine, as they were cheered by the impromptu audience.

Natalie's incisive gaze swept the crowd. "Oh, my—all the big guns are here, my dear—from the entertainment networks to *People*. And they're going *in*. I hope your competitive juices are flowing, Leslie. It could be a bloodbath. In fact, I wish I'd been smart enough to buy a ticket for myself. I would bet Hunter's presence is responsible in no small part for this turnout. But—no use repining now. And anyway, here we are. . . . Good luck."

Leslie smiled wanly and opened the door. Immediately a light played over her as she extended her leg. Her boneless leg that she was sure wouldn't support the weight of a jellyfish right now.

This stuff was out of her league, even if she had come from a family with money. It wasn't Big Money, the stuff of contributions that totaled in the millions and philanthropy that would last for generations.

It was comfortable money, a small fortune that her father had inherited from her mother's family, which was earmarked, she was certain, for her successful older brother who was even now somewhere in Chicago making money hand-over-fist in the stock market.

Daddy had done everything to further Brad's career; but Daddy had only been willing to finance her private school and college education, because it had basically kept her out of his way.

When she hadn't gotten married after graduation, she was of no use to him. She'd wound up working her way through graduate school, and to this day, she had no idea if he even knew of her success and notoriety.

Ah! No use thinking about that now. Or the pots of money it cost Daddy to maintain a mansion in the poshest suburb in Virginia now that he was retired.

Thank God Mother had had money.

Mother would have understood this. And maybe it was that side of Leslie that was responding so strongly to it.

She shifted her weight and eased into a standing position as the Master of Ceremonies held out his hand.

"Leslie Gordon, conservative commentator and would-be heiress . . ."

She unleashed her hundred-watt smile on him and turned toward the camera as he introduced her, no prompting needed. She was the daughter of a prominent general and the well known debutante daughter of a Main Line Philadelphia family. And she was making news on her own.

She fit right in. She was one of them, *really*, though she'd never thought of herself that way at all.

He asked her all the prime and proper questions before he let her go, and she sashayed up the red carpet to the sound of enthusiastic applause, and over the threshold into the candlelit, glitter-dusted ballroom . . . heaven.

This was the worst idea in the world, Hunter thought, as he prowled the fringes of the crowd, looking for a stiff martini. Too many people, too many cameras. Too many damned *women*.

And too many everybody else's who knew him.

He supposed, technically, that he was a victim of his own well-oiled publicity machine. He loved the spotlight, and he wasn't loath to admit it.

And he *was* a charitable man, but in quiet and subtle ways. This kind of ostentation wasn't for him. That, given his public persona, made him an anomaly, he thought wryly.

He didn't like these big glitzy affairs, although this one was the most famous of the lot—which was why, in a moment of weakness, he had agreed to be a sponsor. And he *had* participated early on in convincing the hotel to host it, and donate the space that had once been home to a well-known uptown caberet.

He just didn't remember the auction thing, and as the hour crept unrelentingly toward the time when it would begin, he felt more and more discomfited.

A man didn't like to be trapped like that. Especially him, who had a horror of being confined and regimented.

"Hi, how are you? Good to see you. Thanks for coming. A fabulous party, you're right. They do it right, every year."

He shook a hundred hands, hugged a dozen opulently gowned women whose names he didn't know. Conferred with two members of the Board of Directors. Accepted champagne from a passing waiter. Smiled and waved at another two dozen people he didn't know as he made his way back across the cavernous room and slipped into the prep rooms next to the kitchen.

It was a moment's respite, even though he walked into the pure chaos of the preparation of the evening's buffet dinner.

He leaned against the wall and sipped his champagne, and watched the orchestrated frenzy.

He heard the opening strains of the dance music. There would be a half hour or so of that before the buffet would be set out. Then an hour allocated for dinner while music played. A half hour of big-name entertainment, which would be followed by the auction, scheduled to start around 9:30 P.M.

Nine-thirty was too late. Damn.

He set aside his champagne flute. He couldn't

hide in the back rooms all night, although he devoutly wished he could.

All right. This could be fun, if he didn't let himself get so sticky about it. And it *did* feel good to dress up once in a while after living his working life in tweed jackets, oxford shirts and jeans.

The food would be wonderful, judging by the presentation, the champagne was excellent, he was an expert at avoiding bad company, and—hell, it might be fun to be the pursued instead of the pursuer for a change.

Even though there wasn't a woman he'd met tonight he'd be interested in getting to know.

No matter. It was the price of admission, and he'd accept the consequences. Sometimes a jolt of the unexpected was a gift.

He eased himself out of the prep room and back into the ballroom. The lights were down and the orchestra was playing. Christmas lights, tucked into drifts of tulle meant to represent clouds, twinkled like stars. There were candles everywhere, in wall sconces, on the little tables that ringed the room, and a foggy billow of dry ice wafted across the dance floor. Couples swayed all around him, to the old-fashioned lilting strains of a waltz, and on the sidelines, knots of people murmured in intimate conversation.

In the next room, the maitre d' was directing the setup of the buffet stations, and in the reception area, guests were still arriving, fashionably late.

He wandered across the dance floor, nodding

here and there to an acquaintance, when his attention was caught by three men and a woman huddled in a corner in deep conversation that was obviously very amusing.

She caught his eye in that shimmering column of a dress, with the long graceful line of her neck, and the thin gold chain that glittered on her bare back.

Blond, elegant, intelligent, he thought as he sauntered past them. And then, as she turned, and he glimpsed her translucent skin, her dark winged eyebrows, the pure straight line of her nose and chin and her firm lips, he almost stopped because he thought he recognized her—but . . . maybe not—how could that be? Surely not—not here. She was probably just on his mind because of their recent E-mail exchanges.

He kept looking back at her as he made his way across the room, still not certain.

Leslie . . . ?

Chapter Three

Bong, bong, bong. The clock struck ten.

Do it again—hickory dickory dock . . .

The crowd shifted closer to the dais where already three of the six eligible bachelors on display had strutted across the stage and been snapped up by eager bidders.

Leslie hung back, watching, waiting, her nerves strung surprisingly tight. *Oh, get a grip. This is Hunter, for God's sake.*

But then she saw him, and she knew she had avoided seeking him out the entire evening, until this one moment.

And the reason why was obvious. The sight of him hit her like punch in the solar plexus. He was more impressive in person—but he always had been. And he was a decade more mature, which meant a decade more experience, a decade more danger.

Oh, lord, what have I gotten myself into?

He moved with the grace of a panther, though taller than she remembered and tanned, his dark hair streaked with gray, sophisticated, and elegant.

Gorgeous.

Has he always been that compelling? Or have I just been so naive? The man is goddamned lethal.

He didn't smile, which made him look like the predatory businessman he was; and he stepped reluctantly up onto the dais, taking his place behind the remaining two men.

The auctioneer, that well-known New York gossip columnist, waved her hand and introduced the next competitor: a thirty-five-year-old stockbroker who admitted he was a workaholic—and a baseball fanatic, which he hoped leavened that negative.

The bidding for him was hot and fast. There was something about a man who liked to make money, obviously, but who was more bottom-line oriented than Hunter? Leslie wondered, as the lights played over the crowd and picked out the successful bidder, who was then joined by her date.

The next bachelor up was a manager in a major Fortune 500 company who liked hiking and camping in his off-hours.

Oh, here there was a difference. The ladies

didn't like to rough it. He priced out slightly below the previous man, captured by an aggressive red-headed debutante who didn't look as if she were going to hike anywhere with the guy except maybe down a theater aisle.

And then Hunter.

Oh, jeez . . . Hunter.

The gossip columnist had a field day with him. "What can you say about Hunter?" she trilled. "Who doesn't know Hunter Devlin and his Rogues' Gallery? Hunter is a man of many parts, many talents, many interests. He is a challenge, ladies. You know him. A man of impulse, moods and mastery. Always on the move. Always on the make. He has the attention span of a five-year-old—"

Hunter protested—futilely.

"You'd better be imaginative, spontaneous, smart, strong and maybe a little reckless to hold *his* attention. Am I scaring you off, ladies? Who among you is adventurous enough to bid on the last bachelor—and I do mean that literally—Hunter Devlin?"

The band emphasized that introduction with a musical sting, and then faded away into dead silence.

And no one moved. No one shouted a bid.

The gossip columnist looked nonplussed. Hunter was impassive.

I should—Leslie thought, and then: *They're scared. They're all as scared as I am. He scares them to death because he's too perfect, he's too what he is, and they don't know how to handle him.*

And then the surprising notion: *But I do . . .*

She stepped forward, raised her hand, shouted out, "I bid one thousand dollars," and she was stunned when the crowd erupted into applause.

Hunter was distinctly uncomfortable. To have no one interested in bidding on him was humiliating on a grand scale. Especially here. It wasn't the worst moment he had ever experienced, but it was up there.

It was better that he couldn't see them all beyond the glare of the footlights. Damned sheep. Not an original thought, idea or action among them. But he knew how to disguise his contempt. He was just counting the minutes until he could jump off the stage and get the hell out of there.

The silence was deafening, disheartening as if all the excitement of the evening had been sapped away.

He didn't understand it. He wasn't that kind of guy.

But *they* thought he was. And so he was forced to stay up on stage like a ventriloquist's dummy while Ms. Gossip was so confounded, she didn't seem to know quite what to do to remedy the situation.

Another minute and he was gone. He clenched his fists and schooled his expression. This had gone beyond a joke, beyond even what was rude.

And then a clear strong voice sliced through the

uncomfortable silence: "I bid one thousand dollars," and then the applause, for what reason he couldn't begin to imagine, but whatever it was, whoever *she* was, she had gambled, she had opened the floodgates, and the bidding began in earnest.

Cattle, Hunter thought uncharitably. *Following someone else's lead. In business and in life, no one wants to make a decision unless someone else makes it first. Damn them all. Well, whoever wins this date, I want to meet that opening bidder, bless her warrior's heart.*

He turned his attention to the dollar figure that was ping-ponging back and forth between two bidders.

"Four thousand."

"Forty-two fifty."

"Forty-five."

A preemptive strike: "Five."

He recognized the voice: the first woman.

"Fifty-two fifty."

"Six!" She wasn't fooling around, this one. Hunter liked that.

"Do I hear sixty-two fifty?" Ms. Gossip asked coyly. "The bid is with the blonde in the back. Do I hear sixty-two fifty?—you, ma'am, in the white dress . . ."

Ms. White Dress considered it, considered *him,* as the light played over her perfect features and glossy dark hair, and then she shook her head.

The light picked out the blonde in the back.

Hunter could just see her over the spotlights, a distinct shadow, tall and resolute, an angel in disguise.

He only knew from the voice that it was the warrior princess who had initiated the bidding and he was surprised by his strong desire to have her win him.

Win him . . . There was something inside him that liked the sound of that.

"Anyone else?" Ms. Gossip asked. "Anyone else bidding on the man *Fashion Forward* magazine has named the fashion hunk of the year? Anyone brave enough to outbid the lady in black? Do I hear . . . do I . . . ?"

Silence again.

"Well then, sold to the blonde in the back of the room for six thousand dollars. Hunter, go meet your date."

Thank God. He vaulted off the dais and followed the light toward the woman who stood as still as a statue, waiting for him as music played and the crowd applauded.

It was the woman in shimmering black that he had noticed earlier, the blonde with the bare back who was elegant as hell.

Maybe this wasn't going to be too bad. If they'd only get the damned light out of his eyes.

And then he was face-to-face with her and he could clearly see her luminous face, her dancing eyes.

"Hi, Hunter," she said lightly, extending her hand.

He took it. "Oh, my God. Leslie. Of course. It *had* to be you."

Well, she hoped so. Or it was nice that he thought so. In any event, Leslie liked hearing it, but of course it was meaningless. She thought she would forever after think of it as her rescuing Hunter from a fate worse than abandonment.

And as a bonus, she was good company besides.

"Come on, let's get out of here," Hunter said.

"Nooo," she protested. "You wouldn't deprive me of a supreme moment of triumph, would you? Too mean, Hunter."

"What moment is that?"

"Saving your sorry behind, my friend. Anyway, where's that mysterious Mare-ry you wrote me about?"

"You're a piece of work," he growled, taking her arm.

"*I* thought it was funny. I thought she'd be the one to rescue you. Ah well, we can't always choose our saviors, can we?" She was talking too much, she thought. She had to stop bulldozing him, and slow down and savor the moment. He still looked a little shell-shocked.

"Here, have some champagne." She grabbed two flutes from a passing waiter as the band began to play.

"Rest assured our favorite columnist will have a

field day with this tomorrow," Hunter muttered darkly.

"Well," Leslie mused, "then I'd really love to be that *mysterious* woman in black who saved your reputation."

"You? *Mysterious*?"

That hit hard in a place that really hurt. But what had she expected? He didn't know *this* Leslie Gordon.

She slanted a coy look at him. "Don't you think?"

He stepped back from her a moment. It was Leslie, and it wasn't. The clear, clean features, the voice, the quick wit, all that was Leslie. But the hair, the body. . . .

He watched as she turned slowly to show off her dress, her figure light years from the dumpy freshman he'd left at Loyola.

And then she threw him a shimmering glance over her shoulder that was pure Eve, green-eyed and elusive, and he thought, *I don't know her at all*, and he felt his interest quicken.

She sensed it, and that this was the one moment in which she didn't have to fill the silence with words. *All I have to do is keep quiet. Just rein in my runaway mouth, and it'll be okay.*

She turned to face him again with a slightly uncertain smile.

But what he saw was an alluring woman with a knowing look in her eyes, so utterly un-Leslie, he was immediately intrigued.

"Well, you bought me."

Her mobile mouth twisted humorously. "I guess I did. You are *not* a cheap date, Hunter, but I'll be damned if I know what to do with you."

"I'll be happy to make suggestions," he murmured.

That notched things up to a different level. She gave him a long considering look. *What exactly is happening here?*

"How about we just dance?" she said. That would put him at a safe distance, and in a crowd, how dangerous could he be?

Wrong. Damned dangerous—and too damned close.

Hunter never did anything by half. He pulled her close, too close, and he held her—damn him— just the way she liked to be held, with his arm firmly around her waist, and her body leaning into his, every curve and angle in perfect apposition.

And his hands were huge—and hot and dry.

And enveloping.

Had she known about his hands?

Off-limits, Leslie, she scolded herself. *It's just a damned slow dance. Too slow. Too long. Hard to breathe. He's holding me too tightly. I didn't know he was so tall, so broad. When did* he *grow up?*

On the other hand, it's probably the tux. Every man looks six feet tall in a tux.

Only Hunter is.

How the hell did he bungee jump onto a TV set?

Even in the dim light, he caught the scrutinizing

look in her eyes. This was the Leslie he remembered, quick, curious, penetrating, trenchant, the girl with whom he had been in perfect harmony for all those years in school.

But in the flutter of an eyelash, that look disappeared, and it was replaced by the tantalizing gaze of a temptress.

It rocked him. He couldn't wrap his mind around the idea of Leslie as a come-hither blonde when he remembered her as a sharp, funny, intelligent nerd.

She was neither—and both. And she had a body that didn't quit. He felt every inch of her clinging to him as he slowly maneuvered her around the floor.

How did she do that? He could swear it wasn't deliberate. And yet he was so aware of her, of the sway of her hips, the press of her leg against his, the line of her neck, the curve of her cheek. And that sad, affectionate look in the depths of her eyes when he caught her unawares—

"Let's get out of here," he whispered against her ear. Did he never notice the delicate shape of it in that other life? Or her beautifully defined cheekbones? Or the sweet quirk of her firm lips?

She tilted her head back to look at him, a bewitching smile playing around her mouth. "Ohhh, I don't think so, Hunter. You don't get out of this *that* easily. You've noticed people looking at us and making the high sign? It seems everyone thinks I'm a regular heroine for taking you on."

"What do *you* think?" Hunter asked huskily.

"I feel like the ringmaster in a circus. And of course, I've always been a heroine."

He pulled her closer. "And heroines always walk right into the lion's den."

"Stumbling, eyes wide open, where fools fear to tread," Leslie murmured. "It's so *me*."

"And it's the only way to achieve success."

She shot him a questioning look, but he was dead serious, and she thought maybe it was something she didn't want to pursue, not here anyway.

And then the music ended, and they stood there, his arm still around her, while everyone applauded gently, and then moved off of the floor almost in one body toward the buffet tables.

"We can go out to dinner," Hunter said.

"Hunter, you are not getting it. I want to be *here*."

"Damned if I know why."

"Hey, I'm the evening's celebrity and I'm going to milk it for all it's worth."

"Then you're damned lucky you're not a stranger," he muttered, moving her, with a subtle pressure of his arm, in the direction of the crowd.

Whoa—that was an intriguing comment. "What if I were?" she asked curiously.

"I'd have been gone an hour ago."

Her eyebrows quirked. "Then you're lucky I'm so fascinating."

You are, he thought, as they queued up along one of the serving stations, and he watched with interest as she exchanged quips with the couple in front of them.

A different Leslie, socially adept, self-deprecating and funny. And blonde. He couldn't get over the blondeness, and how well it suited her.

She brought him into the conversation as effortlessly as the best society hostess, as the line moved forward, and he suddenly found he was enjoying himself immensely.

"This is better than Windows on the World," she murmured, as they huddled against a wall, balancing fine china dishes, heavy silver-plated knives and forks, and gold-rimmed goblets.

"I wouldn't have missed it for the world," Hunter said, and again, he was surprised that he meant it.

She smiled beatifically. "Of course you wouldn't. Everyone knows that." She scooped up the last of her sirloin tips in wine sauce. "*I* am ready for dessert."

He liked a woman with a robust appetite. He wondered, as they handled off their plates to a passing waiter, where she put all that food. There was certainly no room in that dress for one extra ounce.

And yet she honed in on a slice of rich chocolate cake—with whipped cream over it—without any coy hesitation. He liked that too.

"Come on, Hunter. This is absolutely decadent."

"I don't believe in chocolate."

"Oh! Hunter! You Philistine. You *have* to believe

in chocolate. It's one of the *verités* in life. Taste this. It will change your whole perspective."

He was watching her eyes. He didn't know whether she remembered his philosophy about sweets and desserts—he never had them, he believed sugar was the root of most evil, and he drank his coffee black. But he could see by that devilish glint, she was determined to break him.

"A crumb."

"That wouldn't nearly do it justice, my man. Go on. Your HDLs won't die."

"I might."

"Yeah, of joy. This stuff is . . . *sexual* . . ." Oh, dear God, why had she said that? Hunter was obviously a man who didn't like to be pushed. Even by an oddity that attracted him for an hour—or two. The oddity, of course, being her. She didn't delude herself about that. If she didn't have a mouth, she wouldn't have been standing with him for five minutes let alone a couple of hours.

Hunter, she thought, *was a man who was easily bored*.

It was the strangest sensation, operating on a level with him, in his world, and feeling the enchantment of owning him for the course of the evening.

Because of that, she felt reckless, powerful. She handed him the plate; she wasn't going to cram the cake into his mouth like a combative newly-wed.

He forked off a reasonable mouthful, and lifted

it to his lips, his eyes holding hers, diving into the mystery of the glimmering humor in them.

He closed his mouth around the morsel of cake, and let the sensations bombard him. *Rich, melting, sumptuous, seductive—with the faintest hint of something tart . . . like sex. Like Leslie.*

He swallowed hard. This was getting way out of hand. "My HDL's are committing suicide. It's wonderful." *You're wonderful . . .*

"Exactly," she said triumphantly, but she wasn't looking at him. She was digging into the slice of cake with the eagerness of a ten-year-old. "God, I love chocolate." She licked the fork, and the joyous innocence of the movement jolted him like an earthquake.

And he understood why: there was nothing artificial about her. She was exactly the same as he remembered, but now there was an overlay of sophistication, maturity and—*blondeness.*

There was just something about a blonde. . . .

He abstractedly swiped a dollop of frosting from the plate, clamping down on the severe urge to rub it on her lips and then lick it away.

Or lick it off a half-dozen other parts of her body I could think of—

"I've created a monster," Leslie murmured.

She'd read his mind. "Ummmph?" He paused in mid-swipe.

"That's the fourth mouthful. I think you just overdosed."

On you . . . "Let's get some coffee," he said

gruffly, wiping his fingers on the linen napkin she held out to him.

"You're going to be off the wall at this rate, drinking caffeine after chocolate. You're living dangerously tonight, Hunter."

"Not as much as you," he murmured.

But he took his coffee strong and black, while she doctored hers with sugar and cream, and she was more likely to be swinging from the chandelier than he was, as he pointed out to her while they scouted out a small table at the far edge of the ballroom, away from the band, the noise, the heat.

"So—what next?" he asked, cupping the fragile china cup in his hands. "What about this date you bought for that outrageous sum of money?"

Uh, oh—time to pay the piper. And she had been enjoying herself so much. Too much. She looked at her watch. It wasn't close to midnight. Maybe she didn't need to grovel in the ashes—yet.

"Well . . ." She bit her lip. "True confessions time, Hunter. *I* didn't buy you."

"Oh?" Now what? It was always the same: the minute he was ready to fall, something always tripped him up.

He kept expression carefully neutral. "How's that?"

"The magazine fronted the money."

His heart stopped racing. "Gee, that was novel." God, he should have known. Leslie didn't have that kind of money, not to burn, anyway. He ignored the little pricking feeling that told him to get out, *now*.

He could rescue this, he could. Leslie wasn't unreasonable, and she was enjoying herself. And he wasn't bored—yet.

He eased into it gently. "But of course, being the journalist of integrity that you are, you're *not* going to *write* about this so-called date, are you?"

Shoot. Clearly time to back off.

"It never entered my mind, Hunter. How could you think that?" She thought she sounded properly indignant. Of course, when she eventually revealed this conversation to Natalie, she'd be properly *dead*. But that was days away. *Years* away, maybe. Maybe she wouldn't have to tell Natalie at all.

"But the stunt you pulled on the *Today* show *is* fair game," she temporized. "And all that *hunk* business."

Dismissed as easily as that, he thought. *God, she was good on her feet*. And he liked that, too.

"I don't suppose I have enough inside pull to kill those stories, do I?"

Oh, you have inside pull, Hunter, my boy. You could pull me right to the edge of oblivion and I would volunteer to jump.

"I'll consider any and all offers," she said. "Make it a handsome bribe, Hunter." *As handsome as you—*

"I'll take you anywhere you want to go on this date, providing you *don't* write about it."

161

Her eyes sparkled; he envisioned a hundred ideas bursting across her fertile imagination, and it amused him to think that they ranged from the grandiose to the mundane.

She eyed him consideringly. At least she'd be getting something out of this. Only she didn't want to be too greedy. And she didn't want them in a situation where he would feel forced to give more than he wanted to.

"Take me skiing in Vermont." *There, that was a good compromise, with enough bone-wearying exercise to put a damper on the most uncontrollable libido.*

Hers, not his.

He started laughing. That was so Leslie. Take her to Vermont. Not Vail. Not Lake Tahoe. Vermont. Every other woman of his acquaintance would have demanded the Swiss Alps.

"Don't you dare laugh at me, you monster. You're probably a world-class skier, aren't you?"

"You should know."

"I don't know the half of it," she grumbled. But she knew he'd do it. He could do anything, she was absolutely sure of that.

He shrugged. "I've been down a few slopes."

"I thought so," she said smugly. "You'll know just where to go. And you know damned well my family wasn't the type to just take off for a weekend in Vermont or Vail."

"Vail is possible."

"Vermont will be fine."

"When?" He couldn't wait.

"Don't you have to clear your calendar?"

"Oh, that . . . not a problem—"

Ha, she thought. *He is probably booked up in meetings until 2002.*

"Name the day," Hunter said, knowing he hadn't fooled her a bit.

Those telling eyes gleamed with mischief. "Next weekend, then. Make some magic, Hunter. Move a mountain."

He felt like a superhero because he wasn't only going to move mountains for her, he was going to rearrange his whole jam-packed schedule just to accommodate her express wish.

Chapter Four

"We're going *where?*"

"St. Moritz," Hunter repeated. "You have a problem with that?"

Leslie turned away from him to stare out the narrow window of his private jet. They were waiting for clearance to take off and she was still a little shell shocked.

Private jets and weekends in Europe were not words in her lexicon when she thought about a weekend getaway. And one part of her was just a little disappointed. She hadn't wanted grandiose gestures from him.

"Yeah, I didn't have enough time to buy a new wardrobe. And anyway, what about Vermont? And where did you get my passport?"

He grinned at her and he looked about seventeen years old. "Oh, I can do anything I want to, Leslie, but I expect you know that already." And he had, more than she'd ever know. He'd juggled a month of meetings to clear off the weekend, and then he'd enlisted Natalie Balter as his co-conspirator. And Natalie wasn't easy to charm either. He'd had to outflank and outmaneuver her—and agree to the damned interview to boot.

Well, that was for later; now he could see that Leslie thought he'd been high-handed as hell. Anybody else he knew would have killed for a weekend in Europe. But not Leslie. *She* would have been perfectly happy to have gone to Vermont, and he knew it.

Sometimes money made a man just a little vain, he thought. Sometimes a man overthought the impression he wanted to make and then it was too late for second thoughts.

Leslie would just have to suffer through the weekend.

Only in truth, she wasn't suffering at all, and she had to work very hard to galvanize any irritation at all.

It was just like Hunter, she thought grumpily, as she braced herself for the upward surge of the plane. *You want to ski—you hop on a plane to Switzerland. And you sweep everyone along in your path. How many people live that way?*

Who wouldn't love to live that way?

Hunter lived that way, and that was the problem. She was as out of his league as a first-year rookie in the final game of a World Series with bases loaded, a full count, and two men down.

She was going to Switzerland, for God's sake. *What is wrong with you, Leslie? Anyone else would be whooping it up and figuring out how to make the most of these forty-eight hours.*

She knew she had to rescue the moment, or it would set the tone for the rest of the weekend. Especially since he *had* done it to please her, and it would probably be the one and only time she'd ever get to be with him on any kind of a date.

"You didn't have to do this, you know," she said gently.

"I just figured that out," Hunter said, leaning toward her, his direct dark gaze never wavering from hers.

She broke into a grin, not hard to do, given his slightly woeful look. "But, man, it is too *cool* for words. You know what? You're nuts."

He grinned back. "Mixed or party?"

She gave him that shimmering green gaze that utterly entranced him.

"You're a cashew, my man—expensive, sweet, crunchy and so delicious you can't stop at just one."

I can't stop, period, he thought as the jet lifted into the air, and she turned to watch out the window with the glee of a first-time traveller. *And I think maybe I don't want to . . .*

* * *

Love Sessions

A car had been waiting for them; Hunter did like comfort and it was a three-hour drive to the hotel, which was an elegant century-old timbered building nestled right on the slopes. He had booked two separate rooms, a courtesy for which Leslie was grateful, and dinner awaited them in the dining room after they unpacked and changed.

Everything was efficient, everything was there for the man who could snap his fingers and buy the hotel five times over. Her father, the General, would have thumbed his nose.

She liked this scenario so much better.

And she loved her room, which was sumptuously appointed with a king-sized bed, a skirted vanity table with every accoutrement a woman of the world could desire, a fireplace, and a jacuzzi virtually the size of a swimming pool. A palette of subtle colors—pastels and creams in silk and moiré stripes—decorated the walls, the bedspread, the curtains and carpet.

She felt a little like a fairy princess as she made her way down to the dining room. She felt like Cinderella.

It was late, so the dining room wasn't crowded. The international après-ski crowd was in the lounge with the live entertainment, and the muffled sound of the plaintive song stylings of a well-known vocalist filtered through to the dining room, underlying the muted conversation.

She was shocked that she was feeling strangely reticent. She barely knew what to say: *thank you* didn't seem nearly adequate. On the other hand, this kind of thing was probably so commonplace for Hunter that anything she could say would seem superfluous.

So she said nothing, she toyed with her wine, she watched his face as covertly as he watched hers.

"You know," he said suddenly, "there's a shop in the hotel where we can fill in anything you need in the way of equipment or clothes."

Her eyes widened just a fraction. "No, no. No. The cost of one item in that place equals about a year's salary for me. I'm fine."

"I meant," he said gently, "I would . . ."

"No!" Damn, she had said that too abruptly, with just a hint of anger. Consciously, she tempered it. "No, you won't. No more grand gestures, Hunter. I want to enjoy this weekend, not be in debt to you forever. Think how it would look on my credit report."

"I always cover for my friends," he said.

"And I never inconvenience mine."

"Your cheapskate editor should have given you an allowance," Hunter muttered.

"Hey, we were buying a story. And you were a good sport. So, it works out fine: *Cityscape* gets a tax deduction and I get St. Moritz. What more could a girl want?"

Me, Hunter thought. He smiled disarmingly. "Me," he said.

"That goes without saying," Leslie said instantly. *Good footwork, Cinderella. Just watch the time so you don't turn into a mouse at the witching hour.*

His brows lifted inquiringly. "What time do you want to get started tomorrow?"

"I'm a crack of dawn kind of girl. What about you?" But she knew: Hunter probably monitored investments all night, in between catnaps, and was on the phone checking the overseas markets by four in the morning.

"Breakfast at six then," he said without answering her directly. "Here or in your room?"

"Oh, here." *Better safe.* "I love the view."

"You can't see the view."

"I know I'll love the view," Leslie amended. "The room is so spectacular, everything else must be too."

"What a tap dance," he scoffed.

"Oh, I've learned a lot of new skills since you last saw me," Leslie said airily.

"I can't wait to hear."

Whoops . . . runaway mouth. Why did I leave myself open for that?

"Well," she said consideringly, "for one thing, I learned to be blond."

"And you do it *really* well," Hunter said warmly.

"Do you think so?" she murmured. "I always worry about my roots."

"Your roots are fine," Hunter assured her.

He held her eyes for one long fraught moment, and then she looked away. There were too many levels going on here, and she didn't want to dig anywhere below the topsoil. He could bury her otherwise. *He could.*

"I knew you'd think so."

"Know me so well?" he asked idly, toying with whatever was on his plate; at that moment, he had no idea what it was. He felt like dining on *her*.

"Oh, I'm sure you've learned a lot of new skills, too," she said, for want of something to say, and just pitched right into the quicksand.

"I can't wait to hear what you think they are."

Sinking fast . . . "Let me see . . ." *You couldn't tap dance while you were being sucked into the maw of your own unruly mouth.* "You obviously learned how to dress, since you're the fashion hunk of the year. And bungee jump. And enjoy chocolate. Am I getting warm?"

"Warm-*er*," Hunter said. He liked this game. He liked her mobile mouth with its rueful twist, and the humorous gleam in her eyes. It seemed to him that glimmer was always there, as if everything she saw, everything she encountered, fascinated her and was worthy of her interest. And he liked that, too.

"We-e-ll—" She pursed her lips. "Let's see. You learned how to run a movie studio—although it's not breaking even yet; you just added the Guest Host Hotel Suites to your Rogues' Gallery, and I do believe you tried to cut an album to no great success. At least according to my sources."

"Super-hot, Leslie." She was up to the mark on everything. "That's awesome."

"And you speak German and French like a native," she went on. "I heard you. . . ."

"That, too."

"Ummm—you invested in that theatrical production that was twenty million dollars in debt because you're a fan of the composer. . . ."

"That's not public knowledge," he said sharply.

"I know. I hope it works."

I hope we work. He shook away the thought. He kept forgetting she was a reporter and that by nature she was nosy. But she was too sharp, too perceptive. Too, too tenacious. Skills. Things he didn't want to know about unless he wanted more from her.

And suddenly he wasn't sure.

She sensed his retreat and reached across the table to grasp his hand. "I'm sorry. I overstepped the bounds there."

"No hard feelings," he said easily as he signaled for the check. "I think we'll just leave it under the table, and concentrate on getting that early start in the morning."

She was a vision in purple and pink, and she didn't miss the expression on his face. It was more than horrified, it was more like dumbstruck.

"Don't you like it? I thought it was terrifically *haute couture* when I bought it." She turned this way and that, and then popped on the matching helmet. "Now you can get the whole effect."

"I don't think I want to," Hunter muttered. He tended toward black with strategic neon stripes himself. And no helmet. Leslie looked like a character in a sitcom the way she was prancing around as they made their way to the lift wait station.

"Did I tell you my limit is the bunny slope?" Leslie asked, as she flapped her arms to keep warm.

"Not today it isn't. Anyone who pays six thousand dollars to go skiing with me can't be considered a rank amateur. I'm going to make sure you get a thorough workout."

And he did. He was smooth, flawless, effortless and he made her shoot the slope first so he could keep his eye on her. For a variety of reasons. And he was inordinately pleased that she was better than she had said she was; and perhaps, she thought as they completed the first run, better because he expected it.

Whatever it was, she felt both exhilarated and empowered by the end of the day, and she wanted nothing more than to kick back, relax and soak in a hot bath.

Hunter had other ideas. Hunter was the night owl, an adrenaline junkie just as she'd thought, who lived by the pulse and beat of the latest trendy night club. He couldn't sit still for five minutes. Yesterday's dinner was his limit, obviously. He was easily bored—but she'd always known that— and he was still a challenge.

She showered and changed into an evening dress in a half-hour, and of *that* at least he approved. And even though it was an *old* dress, it was one of her best, a column of drapey black crepe that ended in a halter-neck bodice banded in shimmering stripes of metallic gold and copper.

"No big hair?" Hunter asked, feigning disappointment.

"Oh, Hunter, I don't know how to tell you this," Leslie said melodramatically. "But—that ol' big hair was all *fake*."

"Oh, my God," he breathed. "I never would have guessed. It's really true: blondes will do it to you every time."

"Blondes don't do anything to attract attention," Leslie said severely. "Now, are you going to feed me, or are we going to stand around making jokes all night?"

He fed her, wining, dining and dancing her around every club floor in the whole of the town, and when they were done, he took her back to the hotel, where they checked their coats and boots to be reclaimed in the morning, and went into the fireplace lounge for a nightcap.

There, at three in the morning, there were still a dozen stragglers who didn't want to end the night, and a guitar player strumming soulfully on stage.

"Brandy?" he asked as they slipped into a leather banquette near a window, where, by the intermittant outdoor torchlight, they could see it had started snowing again.

She smiled a little ruefully. "Hot chocolate."

"A novel choice." *A Leslie choice.* "But why not? It's all about warming up after all . . ." But he was too warm already, stoked up by the feeling of Leslie in his arms, Leslie on the dance floor, Leslie in conversation with strangers who fell immediately under her spell.

Leslie pensive, and, rare as it was, quiet. And Leslie the woman . . . beautiful, curvy, sassy, sexy, smart, lean, leggy . . . elegant. . . .

The waiter came with their drinks. Hunter cupped the snifter in his hands to warm the liquor. "What time tomorrow?"

"Not six A.M.," she said, taking a tentative sip from her mug. "I don't pull all-nighters any more. But I bet you do."

"You have some crazy notions about me," he said, staring at the light reflecting in the liquid. But no crazier than the ones he'd had about her when she was only a name on a fax and light years past their school days.

"It's an exercise in imagination, Hunter. In my off-hours. You do know I have a couple of jobs."

"I've heard about them. I read your column occasionally, but I haven't caught *New York Rising* yet."

"Well, you see—now I can really appreciate how busy you've been. I've only been on the show a year. And I'm up for a commentator's spot on *Belt-*

way Forum on the Capitol News Network. I *think* that's a cable news service you *don't* own."

"I'll buy it tomorrow," he jibed. "When will you know?"

"Later this month, I guess. I have another guest slot next Sunday. If you watch, it'll push the show up another ratings point, and that could only help."

"I could do that," he said, setting aside the brandy from which he'd barely taken a sip. He was drinking in Leslie leaning back against the banquette, her eyes sparkling, her mouth glistening from the hot chocolate.

Hot, rich, succulent, smooth . . . Leslie.

He wanted to kiss her in the worst way.

What would Leslie taste like? Sweet, melting, hot—like honey . . . or chocolate. . . .

But Leslie didn't look like she wanted to kiss him. She looked tired and she was fidgeting—just a little.

"Come on, sleepyhead."

"You run a mean race, Hunter."

"And I always win."

Well, she knew that. She obediantly allowed him to lead her to the elevator, down the hallway to her room, and to take her key and open the door. Hunter was a gentleman, plain and simple.

Except Hunter was looking at her with a predatory gleam in his eye.

"Leslie . . ." He moved closer to her.

Her heart sank. "Do we have to?"

He cupped her chin. "I think so."

"You're going to spoil a really nice friendship." God, she was shaking like a teenager.

"Maybe not." He slanted his mouth over hers.

Something fierce and hot attacked her vitals as he touched her lips ever so gently, ever so experimentally. Her whole body twinged, and then a stream of pure desire poured through her, pulling her deeper into that quicksand where she was already in above her head.

Dangerous. She'd always thought he was dangerous. And when he swiped her lips with his tongue, tasting the residue of chocolate there, she thought she would melt.

This is not supposed to happen with Hunter.

It was happening. . . .

He pressed her gently to open her mouth to him.

"This is a really *bad* idea," she whispered against his lips.

"How could anything that tastes so good be so bad?"

When he put it that way, it made sense to her.

"Hunter . . ." She had to protest but she didn't know why. She liked his kisses, his heat, the firm way he held her, his restraint.

"Shhh . . ." He brushed his fingers over her mouth. "Shhh . . ." He wanted to cradle her, rock her, bury himself in her, and make her moan.

Instead, he seduced her luscious, willing mouth every way he knew how, first with soft kisses, gentle kisses that eased into a light, compelling pressure for her to open to him. And when she complied, he took her deeper, harder—down, down, down into the hot swirl of his need, his desire.

It was like conflagration, from a place he didn't even know there were embers, bringing him to life, to love, to capitulation . . . even as he coaxed her, enticed her, mastered her lips, her mouth, her tongue.

Who was surrendering to whom? Even she didn't know, but she was too far gone already, lost in the heat and wonder of him. All she had to do was hold on tight and let him take her for the ride.

She wound her arms around him and leaned into the kiss. He backed her into her room and closed the door.

"Leslie?"

"Ummm?"

"Yes or no?"

"Do *I* have to decide?"

"I think so."

"I think so too," she whispered, and she lifted her hands to her shoulders and slipped off the straps of her gown. The dress slithered down her curves and pooled at her feet, a swath of black and shimmery gold.

She smiled a quirky little smile. "I always wanted to do that."

She was naked underneath.

But he had known that just from holding her, and maybe that was what had enhanced his desire for her. Everything about her was natural, perfectly balanced and perfectly shaped. And when she gave, she gave everything.

She wrapped herself around him, aligning the soft alluring parts of her against the hard pulsing angles of him.

"Is that a yes?" he murmured, lifting her and seating her against his swollen length.

"I think you could read it that way."

"Good." He moved then, carrying her toward the bed.

God, he was strong. Her excitement escalated as he lowered her to the bed, and with quick, economical movements removed his jacket, his shirt, his shoes.

Slowly he climbed up over her, and sank his weight against her body.

"We don't have to do anything else," he whispered against her mouth.

"This is nice," Better than nice. She liked the feel of her nakedness against his clothed torso. And the scrape of his chest hair on her breasts as he shed his jacket and shirt. His mouth, millimeters from hers, taking light, licking, breathtaking kisses from her too-willing lips.

And she liked it that Hunter was in no hurry. Not at all. She felt as if he would have spent the night just exploring her mouth if that was all she wanted.

And she wanted. There was something utterly enchanting and arousing about being connected to him just like that. She couldn't get enough of his kisses. She felt the welling inside of her, the swell of mounting desire. Maybe her mouth was the most erotic part of her body.

Oops. Maybe not.

He cupped her breast, his thumb rubbing her nipple, and she swooned as the sensation of molten gold coursed unerringly from that taut pleasure point to every part of her body.

She arched against him, seeking more. More of everything, kisses, caresses, that incredible movement of his thumb against her nipple. Just that. Just there. Centered, focused on one point, one pleasure, generating an incredible heat that spiralled down, down, down between her legs.

He squeezed then, tightly, sensitively, his fingers in control of the depth of her pleasure. The sensation was unspeakable. His mouth penetrating hers, his fingers pulling, rubbing, squeezing lightly, lusciously, escalating her excitement, prolonging the sensation to an almost unbearable pitch.

She dug her fingers into his muscular back, and wound her legs around him, grinding against the bulge of his erection, seeking him, begging him.

He didn't let her think. He kept up the pressure, permitting only that one erotic connection between them, and his tongue in her mouth.

"Oh God, Hunter . . ." she breathed as she gyrated her hips against him.

"I like it, too," he murmured.

"Don't stop . . ."

He pulled out of a kiss. ". . . wouldn't dare . . ."

She nipped his lip. ". . . better not—"

They rocked together in an undulating rhythm set by her movements and her erotic little back-of-the-throat moans. Hunter's fingers, Hunter's mouth. A gorgeous dream she never wanted to end.

He closed his mouth over her sensitized nipple and the golden heat pooled in that precious place between her legs. She felt his movements as he impatiently ripped off his pants, and she groaned as he aligned his naked body tightly against hers.

He was so hot, so tense, near to boiling. He felt himself coiling up, his body frantic to possess her. But he was going slow, he reminded himself, going slow. He was dynamite, and no matter what she did, she could light the fuse.

She was ready. He loved the fact that so quickly she was ready and reaching and demanding his weight. If she touched him, he would blow, and Leslie wasn't shy. He felt her hands at his hips, on his buttocks, squirming between their bodies, seeking his heat.

"Let me . . ."

". . . let *me*—" He lifted himself over her, knowing she would grasp him in his most vulnerable place. His body buckled as he felt her hands surround him. Gentle, knowing hands. Appreciative hands stroking him, reveling in him, making him hers.

"Lord, Leslie . . ."

"I know . . ." she whispered, and he caught the joyousness in that word.

She *knew*. He wanted her to hold him like that forever. She knew. She loved it. She was prepared for it, and simply and without embarrassment, she prepared him, and then guided him toward her in mute supplication.

Hunter *there*, Hunter at the breach—she could just feel him nudging her. He tensed, he thrust and he buried himself to the hilt.

Heat . . . voluptuous wet enfolding heat . . . luscious, deep, joyful . . . joyful . . . and she fit him like a glove.

He felt breathless with it. He encircled her head with his arms and pecked at her lips. "What do you say now, sassy mouth?"

Her words caught in her throat as he rocked against her. "I like this sex business. I like you."

He settled his mouth on hers. "It's a start."

It was more than a start; every movement of her body almost tripped his control. She felt so good, so tight, so right.

And he felt so good, so tight, so right. He drove exultantly into her welcoming body and into the heat. Again and again, pumping, thrusting, cramming himself into her as deep as he could go.

All there. The locus around which her whole world revolved. All she wanted, all she needed, right then, right there.

His body wracked with shudders as she held

him, and he held himself in check as he rooted in her, pushing her further and further toward the edge.

Oh, the edge. *Not yet, not yet.* She resisted it mightily. Tried to distract him. Gave him her mouth, her hands, her roiling body in reciprocal demand. But nothing she did deterred him. He wanted her to explode.

He had infinite patience as he primed her, and whispered encouragement between the hot hard kisses he took from her mouth.

"Now, Leslie, now . . ."

She centered her body and bore down on him.

"Now . . . come to me, now—"

She met every thrust. *Now* . . . she felt the tension building. *Now* . . . he had it just right. *Now*— it gathered inside her, knotting up just above her pubic bone. *There*—the feeling settled lower and lower, rippling purposefully toward her center.

Unstoppable now. She gave herself up to it, fighting it, riding it, bucking it, and finally sliding irresistibly down into the undertow of his wrenching drenching release.

Chapter Five

She was having one incredible dream. She was floating on a cloud of sumptuous pleasure, enveloped by an uncommon warmth, and the sense of someone naked in bed beside her . . . and loving the feel of his hair and his hot, rough skin against her body, just loving it . . . because it was so familiar, so known, so *Hunter*. . . .

NO! She jolted awake in a panic. *No* . . . It wasn't even dawn.

No . . . She reached out in the dark . . . *Oh, God* . . . snatched back her hand . . . *Oh no . . . nono-nonono—*

Oh, yes—She was in bed with Hunter Devlin; she was actually sleeping with Hunter. . . .

Oh my God, oh my God . . . violating my absolute cardinal rule . . . how dumb. Stupid!

And anyway, wasn't he supposed have gone back to his room?

Oh God oh God oh God. She scrambled around the room picking up clothes, and rummaging for her sweatpants and a shirt. Dear God . . . how could she have let herself *do* that?

How could she not?

Sex with Hunter. The last thing on earth anyone in her right mind should ever do—

She crept into the sitting room of the suite, flopped onto the couch that was backed against the window wall, and stared pensively out into the dark.

You were NOT in your right mind, obviously.

And he was too good.

But I always knew he would be.

I won't think about that.

I WON'T think about that. We'll do the slopes again today, and then I'll go home, and when the clock strikes midnight, Hunter will disappear back into my computer.

I need some coffee. Or chocolate. I've got a packet of chocolate somewhere. I've got my coffee pot . . .

She was mentally babbling, but it didn't matter. Chocolate she could *do* something about.

She managed to lift the items from her maintenance kit in the bathroom, run some water, and get it boiled without making too much noise.

And then she curled up on the couch, warming

her hands on the mug as she sipped lightly and tried not to think about Hunter.

Stupid, stupid, stupid. . . . She'd gotten carried away like some hormonally hysterical teenager. Too, too easy—even when you didn't have any feelings for the man . . .

Or do I?

Long pause. Her heart pounded painfully. Did she?

Honestly?

Maybe . . . ?

Oof—a kick in the gut—worse and worse . . .

What a disaster—how did I get myself into this?

I need to keep this light and airy. I need for it not to matter at all.

I can do that.

In fact, that's all I can do.

Right. She knew how to hide feelings. She'd been doing it most of her life, mainly because it was one way she could maintain control.

Cover your behind, always. . . .

Only she'd uncovered so much much more. . . .

Idiot! *Get real*. This was a fairy tale, plain and simple. The handsome prince had swept her away for a make-believe weekend where nothing was real. And as long as she understood that, she would be fine.

She was fine. Just fine.

But oh lord, he was so fine in bed . . .

And for her own peace of mind, she thought, she'd better bury those feelings too.

*   *   *

Hunter stood on the threshold between the bedroom and sitting room, just watching her and thinking that he would forever associate Leslie with the scent of chocolate.

It permeated the rooms and it was the second thing he had become aware of when he'd awakened—after the fact that Leslie was not beside him.

And there she was, quiet and pensive, in the dim light of sitting room, her knees drawn up to her chin, staring out the window as if there were answers to her most profound questions in the dark.

He suspected this was a side of Leslie that had never been visible to anyone who had ever known her. It scared him a little, after the intensity of the night. Leslie was the night, Leslie was home. And he'd never thought to find that in any one woman.

It was a lightning bolt to his soul. He wanted everything to be perfect for her.

And he didn't like that she looked as if she was thinking. *Hard*.

There was only one hard thing he wanted her to concentrate on.

Him.

He had to act, now.

"You're overthinking this," he said softly as he stepped into the sitting room.

Her mouth twisted in a wry smile. "Noooo—I think the problem is I *didn't* think about this."

He sank onto the couch opposite her. A soft

down-pillowed couch. About ninety inches long. Nice and commodious. There was snow drifting down outside. And Leslie was kind of soft and warm and cuddly.

"So don't. Let it be." He reached out and cupped her chin. "Let it happen."

"I want to know I am not the kind of girl who jumps into bed with just anyone," Leslie said severely.

"And God knows, I'm not just anyone."

"Exactly. That's the problem."

"There is no problem, Leslie. There's just you and me enjoying each other's company."

"You call *that* company?" She gestured at him. "That isn't company. That's a downright sex-drenched invitation. *No one* has the right to look like you do this early in the morning. How do you get your jeans to hang around your hips like that?"

"Leslie . . ." He leaned forward. "You're talking too much."

His mouth was an inch away from hers. "You scare the hell out of me," she said desperately.

"I'm scared too," he murmured. "Why don't you kiss me?"

"That's not going to help."

"That'll help." His lips touched hers. "I can't tell you how helpful . . ." He deepened the kiss, and then pulled slowly away, "that is. I love the taste of chocolate on you." He swooped down on her again, and she opened her mouth to him and took him wholly deep inside.

Too irresistible. She was only mortal after all. And she loved the way he kissed. She could live on his kisses. And she didn't know if he pushed her or she pulled him down into the soft cushions of the sofa.

All she knew was that she needed to feel his weight.

What happened to scared?

She wasn't scared of his kisses, or his hands, or the heat of his body or his sex. She loved the way he enveloped her, so tall and lean and stoked up like a furnace. And she loved the fact that she made him that way.

And the rest she forgot as his body pulsed enticingly against hers.

"I love your nightwear," Hunter murmured against her ear as he nipped the lobe lightly.

"Victoria's Secret," she said breathlessly.

"Very arousing." And in a way it *was* enticing to imagine her delicious curves under all that locker room gray. For about thirty seconds. And then he had the sweatpants on the floor.

Better. Much better. His free hand shaped one long silky leg from her ankle to her thigh. And then between her legs.

Her breath caught. He probed deeper. She made a sound. He thought she begged for more. He gave her more.

"Oh, Hunter . . ." she breathed, canting her body against the expert exploration of his fingers.

"Scary," he murmured. "Or was that sexy?"

"You," she whispered, seeking his kiss. "Both."

He sank himself into it for a long, long time, holding himself in check, exerting the faintest pressure of his invading fingers just to heighten her awareness that he was there.

He was born there; she was utterly entranced by him there, and when he slowly withdrew from her there, she moaned in protest.

He reached across her hip to take her cup from the coffee table.

"I want some chocolate," he murmured, holding the cup in his palm thoughtfully. He tilted it, and poured a stream of the warm liquid onto her belly.

She felt the trickle from her navel to the juncture of her thighs and the thought of what he meant to do made her breathless. She closed her eyes and her body stiffened as she felt the first swipe of his tongue, swirling the chocolate from her bellybutton.

And then the hot wet trail of his tongue as he painstakingly sucked and licked the wash of chocolate from her skin.

Oh oh oh ohohohohoh . . . she undulated against the firm, succulent pressure of his mouth as he got closer and closer . . . yes, closer . . . his mouth rooting in her feminine hair, and then lower, still lower, seeking and ravishing now with erotic intent between her legs.

Mindlessly, she eased his way, stretching to give him access, bearing down as he touched the chord of her pleasure. There and there and there—amorphous at first, and then firmer, stronger, harder, just the way she wanted, the way she had always wanted . . . and *he* knew—he just *knew* . . .

She gyrated her hips wildly as he pulled at her erotic center, wringing her pleasure from deep inside her, hot, frantic, sucking that one telling point of sensation until . . . until—lightning crackled inside her, bolting all over her body, flashing hot and fast between her legs, on and on and on, hard and sharp and keenly *there*.

"God, you taste good," he whispered as he eased himself up and over and into her, and cradled himself between her legs until the tumult of her climax eddied away. "Leslie *au chocolat*. . . ." He smoothed back her hair.

She had no smart answer for that; she was still riding the storm of her culmination, and feeling him there, centered in her like the rock of her being.

And that was too close to the bone.

He held her, rocking gently, barely moving in the cradle of her hips.

A moment of stillness. Silence. Communion.

Leslie was frantic suddenly to get away.

And then the jarring chirruping sound of a phone.

"Damn—" Hunter muttered. "Damn and damn and damn—" His cell phone. And in the bedroom. And no way to get it without leaving her. He wasn't going to leave her. The caller would have to wait.

The chirrup was irritating, insistent. Whoever it

was didn't want to leave voice-mail. Cursing under his breath, Hunter eased himself away from her, caressing her cheek as he broke the connection between. "Jesus—I'm sorry."

"It's okay." It was; it had saved her from a moment that had been about to get fraught with complications.

He returned with the phone glued against his ear. "Jesus, Cal, why tonight? What about tomorrow night? Yeah, I know all about commitments. I thought everything had been taken care of. . . . Oh, not this? Since when? You know, I'm a mild-mannered man until someone screws up. I'm hearing screw-up, Cal, and I'm not happy." He listened a moment. "Okay. All right. I'll be there by nine tomorrow morning. You just get them there. Jesus. Just do it. Fine." He clicked the receiver shut, his mind already on the problem of the day.

She saw it clearly; it was like cold water doused on the moment, the magic, the time. This was the real Hunter, the man of business, the man of action, ready to move on a dime.

His mind and body responding instantly and in concert, all his attention focused on the problem at hand.

It was beautiful to watch, and terrifying in the aftermath of a soul-sapping orgasm.

She struggled to her elbows, leaned over the couch and rooted around for her sweatpants.

He sank down beside her. "Hey . . ."

She schooled her expression. "Hey, yourself. You have to go."

"Yeah." He didn't want to go. He wanted to stay and wrap himself in Leslie's warmth and scent forever. But he didn't know quite what to say. He hadn't been in a situation where he wanted business to take a backseat to his personal life for a long, long time. But he wasn't quite ready to put the stamp of importance on this cataclysmic joining of body and mind.

So he grabbed his jeans and flipped open the phone and paced around the room while he made arrangements. Arrangements were good, because he could solve problems and take care of Leslie too.

"So I gather I'm staying here tonight," she said when he finished.

"God, I'm sorry." He hunkered down next to the couch. "I have to leave tonight. Meeting in Tokyo first thing in the morning."

"It's okay."

"It's *not*," he said, and he was shocked at the ferocity he felt. "It just *is*, and I have to deal with it."

"Not good at delegating?" she asked lightly.

"Too good. Sometimes the people you trust aren't quite as capable as you'd like. But that's my problem. In any event, I booked you first class on Swissair tomorrow morning. The limousine will call for you at nine. Flight's at two, and you'll be picked up at Kennedy."

"I'm *not* a cheap date," she said whimsically.

"Between the two of us, I think we're looking at ten to twelve thousand between the trip and the auction. However—" he levered himself to his feet, "you do get the article, Miss Leslie. So that should be some consolation."

She wrestled with a storm of mixed feelings and decided to play it for laughs. "Oh yeah, I get the consolation prize?"

"Hey—I'm the one who deserves the sympathy," Hunter said, touching her cheek. "I have to leave you, and I don't want to go."

Good line, she thought; nicely modulated. She almost believed it. Part of her wanted to believe it.

But the cynic in her wouldn't allow it. Guys said things like that all the time. Hunter was no exception, plus he had the excuse of a jet set global business life; he could say anything he wanted and sound as sincere as a father confessor.

"I'll help you pack," she said cheerfully. *Good scout, Leslie. Best girl pal.*

And it didn't take long either; Hunter was organized and efficient. This was his life, after all, and he had structured everything so he could be up and out at an instant. She wondered how anyone could live like that. She couldn't.

"I'll call you," he said as he swung his suitcase into the hallway.

Guys always said that.

She gave him a shimmering smile. "Of course you will."

"I will." He cupped her chin. "Give me your kiss, Leslie."

That she could do, one last kiss to cap off the abortive weekend that she could tuck away like dried flowers in a decrepit book of memories.

Ah, well . . . what a kiss. It was deep with a suppressed longing, even regret. She liked that, even if it was only of the moment.

He pulled away reluctantly. "I'll call," he said again, and then he was gone.

"So you're the guilty party," Leslie said, wheeling her desk chair around as Natalie came into her office Monday morning.

"I'm it," Natalie agreed. "Had to get value for my money. What's a little petty thievery on top of that? And you never blinked twice when I suggested you should keep a suitcase and your passport in the office because there was a breaking story I might have wanted you to cover."

"So, I'm a gullible fool," Leslie muttered.

"But he's going to let you write about him."

"From a distance," Leslie countered. "He's in Japan."

"Nope. He's back. He just bought Kenoji Electronics. Billion dollar deal. They're signing the papers at Somayama Bank this afternoon."

Leslie whistled. "He's a fast worker. I feel like he only just left me in St. Moritz. By the way, let me tell you about the wonders of travelling first class. And having a limousine meet you at the airport. I got very used to luxury in those three days."

Natalie held up her hand. "I didn't hear that."

"I didn't hear *you*," Leslie said grumpily. There was something naggingly pedestrian about going back to such a mundane job after a such a glamorous weekend and then hearing that Hunter had negotiated a newsmaking takeover in the space of twenty-four hours.

She wondered where she had gone wrong.

Ah, well . . . she wasn't the type to be swept away; it was, in fact, the last thing she wanted.

Only—maybe . . . once in a while . . . it wouldn't be—*bad*. . . .

"Earth to Leslie, earth to Leslie—are you there?"

She shook herself. "Actually, I'm not. I'm planning a billion dollar takeover of *Cityscape*."

"Ha ha. Look, don't forget *Capitol Forum* this Sunday. You're flying out to Washington Friday morning."

"First class, I hope. I can't accept anything less."

"Bill CapNewsNet, sweetie. Anyway, it's unrestricted seating."

"With the peons, for heaven's sake," Leslie grumbled. "When do I get my fifteen minutes of fame?"

"Hopefully," Natalie said, "on Sunday."

Leslie made a face. "You have no idea."

"I'm waiting to hear." Natalie perched on the corner of her desk. "Think of it as a confessional. Tell me all and I'll absolve you of every sin."

"What makes you think we're talking about sinning?"

"You're grumpy. You're always that way after you sin. Makes perfect sense. It's the curse of women. You give your heart and you get back garbage. So what happened?"

Leslie shook her head. "Nothing. Nothing worth talking about. We skied. We danced. We dined. We connected. He left. You understand, he's the kind of man who lives his life on the edge, and over the next horizon. That deal probably could've waited, but I'll never know. Maybe he's been working on it for months; he *said* someone messed up. So that's where he went. And I came home."

"I see," Natalie murmured.

"Don't see. I'm on top of things, Natalie. I'll do the interview with him. I'll be in Washington Sunday. And . . ."

"What's this?" Natalie interrupted as one of the secretaries knocked softly on the door and handed her a foil-wrapped vase. "For me? . . . Nope. Shoot." She set it on Leslie's desk. "For you, my fairy princess. Apparently you weren't ships that passed in the night. I'll leave you to contemplate life and lilies."

"Thanks," Leslie said. *Lilies . . . death—damned symbolic* . . . She closed the door behind Natalie before she tore the foil from around the floral arrangement.

Lillies, arranged in a shallow golden bowl, with an Oriental touch.

Beautiful.

She pulled off the card, which was thick ivory vellum, engraved with his initials.

. . . and the memory lingers on . . . she read.

She could almost believe it. The tone was exactly right. But she knew what it really was: a thoughtful consolation from a man who was an expert at doing it, and who had—face it—already moved on.

Absence made the heart grow . . . angry, Hunter thought, as he logged onto his laptop and pulled up the day's E-mail. But there was nothing from Leslie and he felt . . . what? Irritation? Disappointment? Both?

He had expected a barrage of notes from her, amusing commentary on the abortive weekend. He didn't understand her silence.

But then, he didn't understand a lot of things, like his great crashing realization that a woman he'd known for fifteen years was the woman he wanted to spend the rest of his life with.

He didn't know quite when that had happened either. Maybe when he was walking out the door of the hotel in St. Moritz, and he had almost turned back.

Maybe when he had found himself thinking about her all during the flight to Tokyo. Or during the negotiations for Kenoji. Or all the hours after.

He didn't know. It was all tangled up with the old Leslie who had been sharp, intelligent, amusing, a pal; and the new Leslie, who was all of that *and* sexy and smart and funny, and how she felt in his arms and how she kissed and made love . . . and those glinting, knowing eyes—Leslie knew him, and she had a healthy skepticism about him too.

And above and beyond all that, Leslie had never been boring. And that alone was a treasure beyond price, and something he'd never felt about any other woman he'd ever known.

He was not going to let Leslie get away from him.

He stared at the blank computer screen. He had never been deterred by a setback. But he also had to keep clearly in mind that Leslie didn't need big gestures.

Leslie needed *him*.

It was a new thought, to be tenderly nurtured. He wasn't sure what it meant to give Leslie *him*. But he was open to new experiences.

And for the first time, he thought, he was open to love.

Chapter Six

At the very least, a thank you note was in order. Leslie wrote it out with great polite and politic care, covering all the bases, from the auction to the weekend to the flowers, and she mailed it just before she took off for Washington.

She had learned how to divide her attention, and set emotions and problems aside so she could focus on more important matters at hand. And a weekly spot on *Capitol Forum* was damned important.

Career making, in fact, and nothing could get in the way of that.

And anyway, what did she think was going to get in the way?

Oh—memories of hot kisses and hotter sex . . .

no! This wasn't the time to moon over ships passing in the night.

She determinedly caught up on her reading during her economy-class flight down to Washington. *Nothing like a private jet . . .* She squelched the thought before it went any further.

The network put her up at the Ritz-Carlton Hotel, and the producer called an hour after she arrived to make arrangements for Sunday morning, and sent a car for her—early—so she could have breakfast at the studio and spend some time going over relevant areas for discussion.

And then, she and the other guests were settled on the set, given a last makeup check and the producer began the countdown.

There was something about that red light. It seemed demonic. Her inhibitions loosened the minute it came on, and the camera focused on her.

She was like a naughty child, aggressively taking the least popular stance, combatively making cogent arguments, and holding her own against telejournalists and pundits who were louder and far more experienced than she.

Lord, she loved it. The ideas. The wordplay. The competition. The challenge. And she got in the last point too, just under the moderator's final words and the producer's countdown, ". . . and two, and one—and out . . ."

The music came up and the lights went down.

"Clear!" the control room called, and the lights

shifted on again and everyone got up and shook hands.

"Great show. Just great. Leslie . . ." The producer came forward, holding out his hands. "You were *on* today. Great job."

She grinned. "Thanks."

"You were wicked."

"That's the best compliment. Thanks, Jim. Hey, Sam—" she said to the moderator, "thanks for your patience."

He shook his head. "You took no prisoners, Leslie. Keep up the good work."

"Great. Thanks." She stepped off the set and around the cameras and cables, saying a word or two to the other guests as they passed.

And then she stopped short and her heart started pounding.

Standing in the shadows by the curtains was Hunter, his arms crossed, his expression one of complete bemusement.

She took a tentative step forward. *Okay. My legs still work. Now let's try for the voice.* "What are *you* doing here?"

She thought it sounded like cracked ice, and not particularly gracious, but he either ignored it or didn't hear it..

"You are something else, Leslie."

"Back atcha." *Move, Leslie. Step by step.* "Have business in Washington?" *There, that was good. Just the right tone of interest and friendliness.*

"Yeah. You."

Her knees went weak. He shouldn't have done this. She didn't want him to do this. And he looked too good in that tweed jacket and turtleneck underneath. Anyone else would have wanted him to do this.

"What is this, a takeover?" *Keep it light*.

"How about a white knight?"

She took his arm because it was the nearest thing to hang on to, but that was a big mistake. Touching him. Feeling his heat. His strength. *Damn*.

"Could be hostile."

"You don't look hostile. You look rather full of yourself, actually."

"Well, the show was good, wasn't it?"

"It was a brawl and you instigated it. You are some piece of work, Leslie."

"Don't tell *them*," she whispered dramatically. "They believe it."

"Me too. You're scary when you're on set."

They'd reached the studio door and he held it open for her. As they emerged into the corridor and started walking toward the exit, station personnel kept coming up and congratulating her on the show, interrupting any further conversation until they'd reached the parking lot and he'd signalled for his limousine.

Lord, this man knows how to live. "So, what *are* you doing here?" she asked again, as he opened the door for her.

She climbed into the posh interior and settled

back against the leather cushions. *I can get used to this.*

"I thought I'd be there for you," he said, sounding almost as if he were trying out the words. "You said this was important for you."

She stared at him. "Hunter, are you ill or something? This isn't like you."

"What isn't?"

"Being there. You're not a *there* kind of person."

"And yet here I am," he said, a little stung. "And what do you mean by that, anyway?"

"I mean the only time you're ever *there* is when it affects your bottom line."

"Don't tell me you're not a set of numbers, Leslie. I've seen very well you are. Thirty-four, twenty-eight, thir—*What*?"

She smacked his arm. "That's *not* what I mean."

"Fine. Tell me what you mean. I have a feeling this is going to be good. Just remember there aren't any cameras on you."

Okay. You didn't obfuscate around Hunter. "Okay. You're too absorbed in your business, your life, your self."

"God, Leslie, why don't you just *say* what you mean?"

"So—why did you say you were here?"

He gave up. "I just had a meeting with the President, and I wanted company for lunch."

"Okay. I believe that. And what's on for this afternoon?"

"I'm flying to California. Want to come?"

Yes. No. She had a thousand other things to do. Damn him, she couldn't live like that.

"Let's do lunch, Hunter. It's about all I can handle right now."

He took her to the trendy West Wing Cafe, where they were seated at a prominent table by a window. It was a place you had to know someone to get in: lunch was booked three months in advance, so obviously Hunter knew someone. Or rather, as it turned out, everyone knew him.

"Did you really have a meeting with the President?" she asked curiously after he'd ordered the wine.

He buried his face in the menu. "Nope."

"Oh." She opened hers. *Oh, lord.* One of those places that charged the earth for the entree and then the moon for the side dishes. She *hated* restaurants like that. "Are you going to California?"

"Yep." He lowered the menu. "Come with me."

There he goes again, turning on a dime. She felt her misgivings all the way to her toes. "Can't."

"Okay." He regrouped. "Let me take you back to New York then."

"I bought round trip, Hunter. Besides, why take you out of your way?"

"Right." Up with the menu. *She didn't like the restaurant either.* By his count, he was at strike four, and no wiggle room in sight.

Not a problem. He'd been in tougher spots than this. "Why don't we order?"

Oh, brother, this is worse than that moment on the jet. "Sure," she said, scanning the menu again. "You know what I want, Hunter? I want a thick juicy steak is what I want."

He eyed her warily. "You sure?"

"Yep." She put the menu down emphatically. "I'm feeling carnivorous today."

"Bloodthirsty, judging by your performance this morning," he muttered. "Okay. I'll join you, and"—he looked up at the hovering waiter—"the house salad." He handed off the menus and the waiter withdrew. "I'll share it with you."

"Sounds good." *Damn it, this was too awkward. Too—scary. If he even meant what he had said . . .*

Maybe she should find out.

She sipped her wine thoughtfully. It was excellent, like everything else. She decided on a full frontal assault.

"Hunter, what do you really want?"

Whoa. Blindsided right in the middle of power lunch heaven. But that was pure Leslie and an extension of her television persona. The question was, how candid should he be?

Well, he was a risk-taker, first and always. He looked her straight in the eye and said, "You."

She burst out laughing.

God, he was going down for the count.

"You're kidding." She had to believe that—and more important, she had to play it like that, or she'd be in big trouble.

"Ah—no."

She stopped laughing. "Oh."

The steaks arrived, and the salad. She stared at the sizzling slab and then looked at him. "I'm not a commodity."

"God knows."

"And my mother always told me, you can't always have everything you want."

"That's funny, mine told me I could have anything I want."

She believed it. "How about this: I'm deeply flattered but . . ."

"Bullshit. Eat your steak."

She cut into it ferociously. "All right, how about thanks, but no thanks?"

"Why?"

Well, she supposed he had a right to launch a counterattack, she thought grumpily. But it still wasn't fair. A girl should have a right to say *no* to Hunter Devlin.

"Because you're off to California and I'm going to New York." She read the protest in his expression and she knew what he was going to say. Which was what always happened if you didn't spell things out.

It was painful. "Because I can't live out of a suitcase, and with someone going in and out of my life at the ring of a cell phone," she amplified.

He absorbed that while he ate. The silence stretched, enveloping her and making her very uneasy. She'd already lost her appetite, but she tackled her steak gamely, mainly because there was nothing else to do.

"Okay," he said at last.

"O-kay? Okay what?"

He shrugged. "Okay, I understand. But don't expect me to give up."

"You're nuts."

"No," he said simply. "I just always get what I want."

She believed him too. But when she was finally back in New York and safe in her small apartment in the West Village, it all seemed very far-fetched.

Man, you leave your environment and the craziest things happen to you. There is just no place like home. And sanity.

She and Hunter together would be *in*sanity.

In her wildest dreams, she had never thought it would come to that.

He called her from California. "Maybe it's a New York thing."

"I was just thinking that," she said. "And it *was* thoughtful of you to come to the show."

"I know. I can do thoughtful."

"And being *there*. It's just I don't think of you doing the warm fuzzies."

"Shows how much you know. I'll see you when I get back."

"I—" she started to say. But he'd rung off. "I don't want to see you," she told the dial tone roundly. "That'll just make things harder. And guys like you shouldn't always get what you want. And how futile is this?" She slammed the handset down.

Hunter would do whatever he wanted. She was just going to make sure she stayed very far out of his way.

Talk about futile. Friday afternoon, he walked into her office.

Her heart plummeted. Soared. "Hunter . . ."

"Hey, I owe you an interview." He sat down by her desk.

"Natalie's been on your case."

"Nope. I never forget an obligation."

"Oh right, that little *quid pro quo* with my passport. Why don't you go chase Natalie? I'm busy."

"*No one* is too busy for me," Hunter said severely.

Too true. Only her. The only person in the whole wide world.

"Send me an E-mail."

"Smokescreen, Leslie."

She gave up. "You're right. Okay. We'll do an interview."

"Good. What do you want to know?"

"What don't I know?"

"Where do I start?"

"Let me set up the tape. With your permission of course." She had it at the ready in her right-hand desk drawer. He nodded; she removed the

208

tape, snapped it in the cassette and started it rolling.

"You're just doing this to humor me," Hunter said.

"No. Everyone wants to know about you, Hunter. Why don't you comment on why you seem to promote yourself with these over-the-top stunts like the one you pulled on the *Today* Show?"

"Ouch. How about to get attention? Think about it, Leslie. What won't a person do to get attention? Dye her hair blond? Argue unpopular opinions in front of millions of people? Is anybody fooling anybody?"

She snapped off the tape. "Certainly not you. I think we're done here."

"Shortest interview of my life," Hunter murmured. "You'd better do some more research, Ms. Gorgon—uh, Gordon. And call for an appointment next time. I don't know when I'll be free again."

Natalie drifted in after he'd left. "Umm—what exactly happened here?"

"I don't know." *Liar.* She felt like crying. She'd handled him abominably. And she didn't account for the fact that Hunter knew her too well. And she knew him, and it just proved that together they would be a disaster, and that she was right.

She was.

She *was*.

* * *

The problem was, Hunter decided, that he was so used to doing things in a lavish way that it was hard to think about scaling down. But if he wanted Leslie, and he did, he would have to live his life on a smaller canvas.

Okay. He understood that, and with his entrepreneur's mind, he analyzed what was needed.

The first thing was, none of this flying off into the sunset stuff that he was so used to doing at the drop of a hat. At least not until he'd won her. So that meant delegating even more. Or downsizing his business life as well.

Hmmm. That did have some appeal. The thing was like an octopus as it was, with so many arms, it was possible to get too wrapped up in one to the detriment of everything else.

Note: where can I divest?

Then: Leslie didn't like big sweeping gestures. No. Check that. She probably did, but at this stage of the relationship, anything like that probably seemed gratuitous and insincere.

Note: look at the smaller picture.

And: he had to remember Leslie's roots. She came from an army family; she liked certainty and control. Unlike him, she had never felt her childhood was an adventure. Or that she had the unqualified ongoing approval and support of parents who idolized her.

On the other hand, having led that kind of life might well have turned him into an arrogant, self-centered, self-aggrandizing pig—but he didn't think so. And neither did his adoring parents.

And anyway, he was having too much fun. So was Leslie, in her way, on her comfort level. So what he needed to do was bring her up to his.

That was good, he thought. Change was always good. He'd made his reputation and a fortune on ringing changes on his various enterprises.

He could do change. In point of fact, he was doing a lot of things he'd never thought about doing. He was adaptable.

And now, Leslie was going to have to be.

Note: do big things on a smaller scale, and small things on a big scale.

The best thing was how good they were together. And that was the thing that drove him, the goal to keep in sight. They had unfinished business, Leslie and he. He couldn't stop thinking about her. He wanted her all the time.

Note: love sessions for Leslie, long and slow . . .

Chapter Seven

Leslie got the news the following weekend after her stint on *New York Rising*: she was going on *Capitol Forum* as a biweekly guest, and her agent was doing some hard negotiation to keep her on *New York Rising* on alternate weeks.

Oh my God, oh my God, oh my God . . . Her knees were weak. For one fraught moment, she didn't think she could do it. This was the big leagues, the shark tank, the piranha parade that could eat you alive.

Fine, she thought, summoning her courage, *bite me. I'll devour you all.*

She called Natalie. "Do you know what this means?"

"More visibility for *Cityscape,*" Natalie said, "because of course they always mention it when they introduce you."

"Fiend. That's all *you* care about. Meet for lunch, my treat."

"You bet. I can get free at one."

"The usual place." Leslie put down the handset. She had a million people to call. She started writing down names, and then she picked up the phone. And stopped.

She wanted to call her father, and her brother. *Never mind. Sometimes friends were better than family.*

She dialed, heard the reassuring ring on the other end.

And Hunter's voice, brisk and to the point: "Devlin here."

Damn, how did that happen?

Her voice caught. "Hunter . . . ?" It sounded as if she was crying on the best day of her life.

"Leslie." He was instantly alert. "What's the matter?"

"I got *Capitol Forum*."

Long silence, proving that she was going be eaten alive no matter what she did. She just didn't have the instincts.

"God, Leslie, that's *huge*."

"Yeah," she said. She was shocked that there were tears in her eyes.

"We'll celebrate tonight. Dinner. At eight. Don't say no. Think of the luster you'll add to my image."

She laughed. "You're nuts. You've lucked out:

this is the one night in the world I will let you buy me dinner."

"I am *really* proud, Leslie. You killed them that Sunday."

"I know. Thanks, Hunter."

Long pause. "Why don't you call your dad?" he said, carefully, softly.

"That's all right. He wouldn't be interested. I'll see you later."

She put down the handset slowly. It had been the right call to make—for all the wrong reasons. And too late to recant now.

She consulted her list and began dialing again.

Big gesture, small scale. Perfect.

He had planned it to the smallest detail. They drove, in the limo, from her apartment to the helioport, where he had a helicopter on standby, and they flew out to Montauk, to a small inn on the ocean where he had a dinner reservation in the quiet, intimate dining room with its stone fireplace and roaring fire, and champagne chilling on the side.

He could tell by her expression that she liked this place. It wasn't too expensive. And it was elegant, quiet, romantic and brimming with charm.

Like Leslie, tonight, seated opposite him, her eyes lit with joy, and dressed in a black tea-length dress with some kind of lace overlay that made her look like a Victorian heroine.

"A toast first," he said, lifting his flute. "Slice 'em and dice 'em next Sunday."

"Just call me Freddie." She sipped the excellent champagne.

"You can do anything," he said.

"I should've grown up in your house," she retorted, and then stared at him, wide-eyed. "Sorry."

"Don't be. The General wasn't—isn't—an easy man. I remember him very well."

"Well, it's stupid to let the fact that *my* family won't share in my sucess spoil it."

"Think of me as family then," he offered.

She shook her head. "Not hardly."

That was good. That was an opening. "So what *do* you think of me as?"

"The enemy."

One step forward, ten steps back.

"And still you called *me*."

She was still wrestling with that one. It had been almost as if her fingers had dialed him up of their own volition. She couldn't deny it. "Yeah—I did, didn't I?"

"And here we are."

She threw him a bone. "No one else I'd rather be with."

He smiled. It was heart-stopping smile. An I-knew-you-couldn't-resist-me smile. And maybe she couldn't. One of his best qualities was the fact that she knew him so well; there didn't need to be those torturous mazes of trying to figure out what to say and how. She could speak her mind. She could be vulnerable.

And to think, not two weeks ago, he had been only a presence on a computer screen. But still— private school days—he had always been in her life.

"I know you mean that," he said. "Ah—" He held up his hand as the waiter approached. "Let's order."

It was a peaceful, quiet dinner at the very moment she needed peace. The surroundings were perfect, the waiter attentive, the noise at a minimum, the conversation low.

And Hunter didn't press her, didn't challenge her, didn't make conversation for the sake of making it.

She liked sitting across from him, liked how he looked in the black business suit he affected. There was something about black; it made a man taller, more commanding, more elegant. And he was all of that to begin with.

And he knew when to leave her alone.

"Think about this," he said over coffee. "Just think. Two weekends a month you're going to be on the go and living out of a suitcase."

Wham . . . just when she'd been feeling all soft and fuzzy about him . . . She should have known he had meant what he said.

"So?"

"Oh, something about not being able to be in a relationship with someone who travels a lot . . ."

"*Who* said that?" she asked in mock severity.

"Someone I know who's fighting real hard not to give in to her feelings for me."

"No kidding," she murmured in awestruck tones. "You mean someone can put up with you? Tell me about her."

He grinned at her. "Well, she's blond. And stubborn. And sharp, and funny. And soft and warm. And prickly as hell. Know anybody like that?"

God, he was irresistible when he was like that. And he was *there* for her to boot. And she *was* going to have to learn how to be a beltway commuter. Damn him.

"Nope. Not a soul comes to mind. So tell me, Hunter, are we flying back to Manhattan?"

"Hell, no. I don't want the evening to end that fast. We're driving back. Just the two of us. And you can cuddle up and go to sleep if you want, or we can listen to music and talk. Or not talk. Whatever you want."

Oh, she hated him. He understood too much. And if he kept it up, he would get to her. And all the wisecracks in the world wouldn't keep her safe from him after that.

Love sessions. He understood now what it meant, and it had nothing to do with sex. What it meant was quiet moments like these, driving his high-powered rental car down the ribbon of highway toward the city, the music low, Leslie wedged next to him, her head on his shoulder.

It meant no words when words might have been superfluous. It meant companionship with the person you cared for. And it meant the feeling of supreme well-being that permeated his soul.

And he knew she felt it too. She was just a harder sell. But he was the best in the business at making the sale.

Note: more quiet time like this.

They drew up in front of her apartment more than three hours later.

"Don't invite me in," he said.

She was grateful for his restraint. "That must be a first for you."

"Or you," he countered. "But I do want a kiss."

She did too. She turned her head and waited breathlessly as he settled his mouth on hers. Sunk himself into her, softly, gently, heatedly, on and on and on, keeping himself in check until she wound her arms around him and pulled him in deeper still.

Then . . . oh, then—it was her hunger that fed his desire. And still he contained himself. Kisses were enough, for now. They were. And her sweet generous mouth. And her suppressed need.

He had to forcefully pull himself away from that or he would have taken the kiss further than he had meant to.

"I think . . . you'd better go in," he whispered against her lips as she planted soft nibbly little kisses all around his mouth.

"I think so." But she didn't stop.

"Hey—I'm the enemy, remember?"

"Not when you kiss like this . . ."

"You'll hate yourself in the morning."

"I won't care, if *you* respect me—"

He set her away from him then. "Leslie . . ."

She swallowed her rising lust. After all, it wasn't his fault that she had said no to a relationship with him. Or maybe she'd gotten temporary amnesia and forgotten what a wonderful kisser he was. She would have to remind herself of that from time to time, especially when he was playing at *being there* for her.

"Okay. You win. It was a lovely evening."

He walked her inside, chancing a parking ticket, but he didn't care.

"I'll see you soon." He meant it and she knew it. *Note: more kissing, less talking.*

Whistling, he drove uptown to return the car.

He was there when she made her debut on *Capitol Forum.*

"You didn't have to do this. And who's running all your enterprises if you're here?"

"It's all covered." He took her arm. "C'mon. We're going sightseeing."

Big gesture, small scale.

From Mount Vernon to the Vietnam War Memorial, he showed her everything, because of course he was very conversant with the city.

"You do too have meetings with the President," she accused him.

They took a tour of the White House to prove he didn't.

"He's hiding. You're involved in something covert."

That night, they dined at a small out-of-the-way restaurant in Georgetown, and *he* took her back to Manhattan, with silence and music laying between them on the four hour drive.

Two days later, he took her ice skating at Wollman Rink.

Small gesture, small scale. And the big-city woman with a small-town heart just loved it. The last time she'd skated was at Dumbrille when the gym classes went out on the frozen ponds behind the school.

She looked like a damned Rockette with her fur trimmed hat and her long skirt. She looked like something out of Currier & Ives.

He liked making her happy.

Note: small works.

He met her Friday evening for a quick drink at P. J. Clarke's.

"Don't you have a trip or something?"

"No. I have you."

"Don't you start, Hunter."

He invited her to a charity event the following Saturday at Morgan Library. She wore a teal green suit that was classic and spectacular. He immediately decided he wanted her to be the mother of his children.

But he'd been inching that way all along.

"Doing good deeds is an excellent way to meet nice people," Leslie said in passing as she turned to converse with another knot of people she didn't know, but was going to, soon.

Note: take Leslie to these events more often.

Wednesday, he took her to a hockey game. He didn't know if she liked hockey from hula, and here too he was admittedly loath to give up his box seats. *She* would just have to make the best of it. A man couldn't enjoy hockey up in the rafters.

Or at least he didn't think so.

And he was pleasantly surprised at how much she knew about the game, and at the ferocity of the arguments she got into with the surrounding crowd.

A woman who likes sports is a treasure.

"Hunter, I cannot believe you don't have to hare off someplace this week," she said as they toured the opening of an art show.

"I delegated."

"It feels more like you divested."

"Actually, I did that too."

"You are not a homebody."

"I'm enjoying it a lot, if you want to know the truth. I haven't sat still so long since before I left school."

"Great. I can see it now—they're going to blame me when your stock plummets."

"No to worry, we're doing fine. It's gone up two points since I took on a partner to run Kenoji."

That stopped her. *When did he do these things?*

221

"Oh. Well. So . . . are you going to buy this artist?"

"Nope. I'm going to buy you dinner."

Love sessions. That meant truly *being* with the woman you cared about. It meant putting off sex. It meant not rushing off *ever* when business called. It meant putting her first, and sharing your life and your friends.

It sounded like damned close to committment to him.

Except that Leslie was nowhere near in step with him, and he wondered what it would take to bring her around.

He thought of one thing. *Note: Don't put off sex.*

She didn't know why she felt so restive. Maybe she did know. Hunter was getting too close.

But worse than that, she was letting him.

Bad move. It had been three months now since the auction; five Sundays as a regular on *Capitol Forum.* Everything was going swimmingly. Numbers were up everywhere, the show, the magazine, *New York Rising,* because of her national exposure on the cable show.

And Hunter was everywhere.

Maybe that was the thing. He was just not known for staying in one place longer than it took to consummate a deal. Even the gossip columnists had taken note, and now, whenever they were in the public eye, there was always some mention in local tabloids.

Hunter Devlin—not on the hunt anymore. Seen

at Lutece (or the Four Seasons, Lincoln Center, the Met) with gorgeous blonde Leslie Gordon, media mouth with a conservative bent who scribes for Cityscape *magazine and who's been making waves and garnering wows on* Capitol Forum *and* New York Rising. *Is something else rising, Hunter? You want to run it up the flagpole?*

"You're the best publicity machine this rag ever had," Natalie said, dropping that puerile paragraph on her desk. "Are you sleeping with him or something?"

"Oddly enough, I'm not," Leslie murmured as she scanned the column.

"It *must* be love."

That jolted her. It was *not*. "Hell, no. He's using me for my news value."

"You are the power couple of the season, honey. Wake up and smell the bridal bouquet."

Leslie tossed the newspaper on the floor. "I'm not going to listen to this. Nobody's said a word about love. Nobody's said anything."

"Maybe somebody's waiting until the other body is ready."

"I'll never be ready. Who can live like that?"

"Well, you are, for one," Natalie pointed out. "You're the one on the road these days. And Hunter's been the homebody. What about that?"

"What about it?" Leslie snapped. God, she was getting cranky. And she knew why too. Because Hunter was *being there* for her, being perfect in every way, up to and including exerting no pressure on her whatsoever.

A man ought to pressure a woman *sometimes*. All he did was rouse her up with those kisses, and then leave her hanging.

And to add to that frustration, she had another Washington weekend upcoming, and what she'd been doing was driving down and then staying overnight at an inexpensive motel for the last three shows.

Why spend that lovely compensation on a luxury hotel? Or airfare.

But it was definitely wearing on her. And she'd missed Hunter. God, she loved it when he came down to the studio.

The problem was, she wasn't telling him any of this. She was still rock-bottom scared. And she still hated that kind of life.

Which she nevertheless would put up with for the run of the contract.

So she was standing in quicksand and sinking fast. She didn't have a leg to stand on, and she knew it, and Hunter knew it.

He'd been supremely patient while he'd rearranged his life, watched the gossip columnists have a field day with him—them—and he'd let her have time and space.

But she had a feeling he would be patient no more. And that this was just how he pursued a business deal: with unrelenting persistence, logic, patience and control.

And full, abiding knowledge of just what it took to please her. On every level.

Damn his hide.

"Leslie?" It was Natalie's voice, drawing her back to the matter at hand. "Can I be your best man?"

Leslie ground her teeth and tore out the offending paragraph from the paper and crumpled it in her hand. "Hunter's a friend, nothing more, nothing less."

"Well, maybe considerably less than you'd like him to be," Natalie said, "but this is a man in love. And you're acting like a woman on the fence. And if you don't climb down on one side or the other, one of those pickets is going to maim you for life."

"Natalie-e-e-e . . ."

"Go. It's time for you to leave anyway. Go do your thing for the good of the American public, and while you're down there, think about doing something for the good of Leslie Gordon."

"And just what do you think that should be?"

Natalie gave her a hug. "Give poor Hunter a break."

225

Chapter Eight

She was feeling so out of sorts about the whole thing, she decided to fly down—early. She'd heard enough about Hunter.

Too much.

She would just go have dinner with someone whose initials were not H.D., and she'd prep for the show, and think about everything else later.

Easily done. What blonde couldn't get a dinner companion at the snap of her fingers? She discovered that Mickey Cooke, her political nemesis, was in town early as well, at the same hotel, and available. They arranged to meet in the restaurant.

"You're not carrying any concealed weapons, are you?" he asked, as she came toward the maitre d's station.

"I'm a teddy bear when there's no camera around, Mick. You know that."

"I don't know that at all. I think the maitre d' should watch his back. He's signaling us."

"Good, I'm starving." She let Mickey seat her, they ordered some wine, and she settled her napkin on her lap and grabbed the menu.

"Want to gnaw on a bone for your appetizer?"

"I'd rather gnaw on your outrageous statements tomorrow," Leslie said, quickly scanning the day's specials. "Ummm—the veal looks good."

"I'd recommend the shrimp remoulade." This was a new voice, and her heart plummeted to her toes.

Hunter. *How*?

"Hi, Hunter. What are you doing here?" *Four hundred miles from New York and looking like four hundred feet of towering fury in that black power suit.*

"I came to have dinner with a friend," he said silkily.

"What a coincidence. Me too." No glossing over this. "This is Mickey Cooke. Mickey, *the* Hunter Devlin."

They shook hands coolly. Leslie kicked Mickey under the table to keep him from suggesting Hunter join them.

"I guess you'll want to go back to your friend," she said brightly.

"You've got it wrong, Leslie. I've come for my friend, and now my friend is going to come for

227

me." He walked deliberately behind her chair and pulled it out. "Don't make a scene."

She was dumbfounded. She looked at Mickey. He shrugged, so she stood up. "Fine. No scene."

"Good." He lifted her in his arms. "Nice to meet you, Cooke."

"Hunter!" she hissed as he made his way out of the restaurant holding her high in his arms. "You put me down."

"I'm not letting you loose anywhere in this town."

"This is ridiculous. Everyone's staring. The gossips will have a field day . . ." She kicked her legs.

"I don't care."

"Hunter-r-r-r-r—" She pounded his chest.

The maitre d' was smiling. People clapped.

He strode through the lobby to catcalls, applause and cheers rooting him on.

Note: women do *love to be swept away . . . sometimes.*

They went into the elevator and a crowd of hotel guests.

"Hunter," she whispered fiercely. "I'll bite you."

"Sounds encouraging."

"You're impossible."

"Never denied that."

"Put—me—down."

"I don't think so."

"Newlyweds?" someone asked, grinning from ear to ear.

"Possibly," Hunter said.

"Not likely," Leslie growled simultaneously. "Take me to my room!"

Hunter looked around at the smiling faces that surrounded them and smiled smugly.

"*You . . .* !" Leslie smacked him. The elevator rose ominously. Third floor . . . fifth . . . tenth . . . "*Hunter . . .*"

"Almost there," he said cheerfully.

Twentieth . . . twenty-fifth . . . she felt doomed. The elevator was empty now, and the last stop was the dreaded PH. The door slid open and he carried her into the elegantly appointed anteroom, off of which there were three doors. Doors in which you inserted real keys.

And he did it so expertly, she thought irritatedly. The door swung open to reveal the luxurious sitting room furnished with oriental rugs, plump sofas and chairs, gold-framed paintings and subdued lighting.

"Hunter . . . This is *not* my room."

He didn't break stride. He carried her straight into the bedroom and set her down on the silk-draped king-sized bed. "No, it's not. It's the bridal suite."

"The bridal suite . . . now, wait a minute—" He climbed onto the bed next her. "Don't you get any ideas."

"I've got plenty of ideas." He came closer. "And you"—closer still—"talk"—pushing her down into the pillows—"too"—hovering over her now, inches from her mutinous mouth—"much"—

229

slanting his mouth over hers for one breathtaking moment before he claimed it.

Swamped. She was too susceptible to his kisses. Oh, those kisses. She had been living on those kisses for the last two months, wanting more, not wanting more, scared of more. Terrified of more . . .

"We have," he whispered against her lips, "unfinished business."

"Until your phone rings with some *other* unfinished business," she muttered, catching the moment to try to shift away from him.

"I won't answer it." He levered himself into a sitting position, straddling and capturing her wriggling body. "You will." He began unbuttoning his jacket. "Where did we leave off?"

"With you on your way to Japan."

He shucked his jacket. "I didn't hear that." He ripped off his tie. "Besides, this is the bridal suite. What happened to romance?"

"Hunter, you are no proponent of marital bliss."

He shucked his shirt and reached for her, pulling her to a sitting position so that they were face-to-face. "With you, I advocate *martial* bliss. You just don't know how to be quiet."

"You are the most high-handed—"

"I'm left handed, actually. . . ." He drew her closer, his mouth grazing hers as he began undressing her.

His heat seduced her, and she supposed it always would. And the touch of his hands. And those featherlight kisses that wreaked such havoc with her senses. He knew just where. With touch and scent, and succulent little kisses on her neck, her shoulders, her mouth, between her breasts as he bared them, and a quick little suckling kiss on each pointed tip.

"She's speechless," he breathed in awe. "A miracle."

But *he* was the miracle, all long and strong, and muscle, all male. And relentless.

How did a woman tame a hurricane? She didn't—she let it sweep her up and away and she gave herself to it willingly. Gave herself naked, into his hands, his mouth, his erotic vision of her, of them.

She opened herself in the most intimate way to his demands. He seemed to know her every pleasure point, her every need; all she could do was hold on tight, take him deep within her, and ride the whirlwind.

Stone-hard, he centered himself in her, pushing, pushing, pushing, to root himself to the utmost in her heat.

"I think this is where we left off," he whispered, rocking urgently against her.

She made a futile little sound. She felt him so keenly. This was getting too serious. Just this, just now. If she surrendered, she might lose her soul. Hunter didn't *do* commitment. And in her heart of hearts, she couldn't bear to ever relinquish this mystical joining of body and mind. She didn't know how men did it.

She felt like she was on the edge of a precipice, and Hunter could push her right over. But then, she had nowhere else to go.

And he was in command. He moved against her, and every rebellious thought dissolved into a soft focus that centered on the way he was undulating his hips against the very pleasure point between her legs.

You tart, she thought fuzzily. *One erotic moment and you throw every principle out the window.*

And then she didn't care. His delicious gyrations became purposeful; her bodily hunger took over in that eruptive moment of the drive toward culmination.

There was nothing else; just the hard heat of him thrusting, thrusting, thrusting—the crowning point of her world; she was hanging there by a glistening gossamer filament. The heat of it twisted through her body like thunder. It twined down, down, down, knotting in her vitals, priming her to explode.

She felt it coming; she set her body to cushion the moment, and then her body caved, and everything went out of control and the light fractured as she rode him home.

They could neither of them move. He still lay on top of her, enfolded in her, his hands entwined in her hair, his face buried in her shoulder.

She felt as if she'd just survived a force of nature. He was amazing, and compelling. And so *there*.

There for you, as he said, in every way. She brushed the thought away. The moment was too perfect to be spoiled by reality.

"Will you be the mother of my children?" he murmured from the depths of her shoulder.

Don't do this, Hunter. This will lead to something disastrous.

"Sure," she said. "But why did you say that?"

"What do you mean? You think I don't want sons and heirs?"

"I don't know. Do you?"

He levered himself up onto his elbows so he could see her face. "I do."

Hunter, a father? "Oh."

He cupped her face so that she couldn't turn away. "With you."

That stunned her. *He can't be serious.* "You're joking."

"Leslie, don't be dense. Why do you think I corralled you in the bridal suite? What do you think I've been doing for the last two months?"

"*What?*" she asked faintly.

"Courting you."

"Courting . . . ?" She was absolutely floored. "—*That's* why we haven't had sex?"

"Abstinence works," he said smugly. "Yes, courting you."

"You're not serious."

"Dead serious. Why is it so hard to believe?"

"Because I don't see you with a home-grown honey. You belong with one of those jet-setting, high-flying models or something."

"Nope. I belong with you. Get used to it. You can't wedge a suitcase between us any more, now that you're commuting to Washington. So I don't see any just impediments to—"

And there it was: that annoying birdsong of reality—the chirrup of his cell phone.

He withdrew himself from her gently. "You take it."

It was on the dresser, a little nightmare, the call to adventure in other places, most of which would never include her.

She swung her legs off the bed and reached for it, sending him a puzzled glance.

"Hello?"

"Leslie?" The voice was rusty, gruff.

"Ye-es. Who is this?" But she thought she knew and she felt her whole body go cold. "*General*? Is that you?"

"*Harrrrrmph* . . . I'm calling to say . . . *harmmmph* . . . that I've been reading your columns and . . . *ah-umm* . . . watching you on that *Forum* show."

Her voice caught. "Have you really?"

"*Harrrmmmph* . . . Just want to tell you . . . *harrrmmmmph* . . . I'm proud of you, Leslie. Yes. Proud. *Harrrrrummmph*. Just want to say that. And that I'll . . . I'll be watching tomorrow. And . . . *ahhh-ummm* . . . that I'll see you . . . I'll see you . . . *ah* . . . soon."

It was the most he'd ever said to her in her whole
life about her work. And the first time time he'd
ever praised her.

She held the phone to her ear long after he'd
disconnected, tears streaking her cheeks. And
then she turned to Hunter.

"You did this."

He gave her a deprecating smile. "If we are going to be a family, we are *all* going to be a family.
No estrangements. No one abandoned. No one
outside the circle."

"Oh God, Hunter—" She climbed into his arms.
"I love you."

Note: it's okay to solve problems—sometimes.

"Thank God, Leslie—I love you too."

Proud of her . . .

She stepped up onto the set of *Capitol Forum*
loaded for bear. If the General were watching, she
wanted to give him a show.

And Hunter, too.

Because she hadn't really given Hunter an answer yet, and she was feeling a little guilty about
that.

What he had done for her. She couldn't get over
it. Hunter got things done. Hunter wanted *her*.
And she was the one running this time.

Time to stop running.

She was not the Leslie Gordon of ten years ago.

That was a lifetime ago. And he had seemingly drastically altered his life in the last two months so that he could spend that time with her.

Courting her. How old-fashioned could a hip and happening guy get?

But maybe that was what he wanted, the kind of wondrous old-fashioned adventuresome marriage his parents had. Maybe, though he had loved his peripetetic childhood, he wanted hearth, home and continuity after a life that had contained none of those.

And it would balance. She yearned for love, safety and stability, and he could give her all of that, and spontanaeity besides.

What wouldn't work? She was lively, funny, energetic, and pretty smart. And reasonably nice looking. And being blonde didn't hurt.

Being the only woman on the panel today didn't hurt either. It meant she had to fight harder to jam in her points. She had to be on her toes this morning, feinting this way and that to stave the barbs and wit of one famed loudmouth pundit who was determined to take over the show.

She had to show her mettle.

And Hunter knew it. He stood by the curtains behind the wheeling cameramen and just smiled and smiled.

Leslie was amazing. Leslie was *his*. She hadn't said yes yet, but that was a matter of another cataclysmic night, and she would be, forever.

But meantime, she belonged to the camera, to the viewing public.

The floor director was counting down—*"five minutes . . . four . . ."*

Leslie was making a point. The loudmouth pundit interrupted her. "It isn't a question of . . ."

She blasted right back, "But it is a question of— *Hunter!* YES, I'LL MARRY YOU!" just as the lights went down and the music swelled up.

There was a moment of stunned silence, and then everyone on set started clapping and hooting wildly.

Hunter loved it, just loved it. A million viewers witnessing her commitment. To him. Forever.

She couldn't get out of it now.

She didn't want to. The only place she wanted to be was with Hunter, and she had already spent one hour too long away from him.

She saw him standing there, beyond the cameras, waiting.

There. Always there, ever there.

When Hunter made a commitment, he made it for life; and he would make it work because he made everything work.

That was the way Hunter was, and maybe that was the only thing she'd ever needed to know.

She knew it now.

She vaulted off the set, across the studio floor, and, jumping over cables like Flo-Jo, she hurled herself straight into Hunter's outstretched arms.

Promise
Me
Pleasure

CONNIE
MASON

Chapter One

She could feel his eyes on her. Dark. Sexy. Bedroom eyes. He wore one of those Speedo bikinis that revealed more than it concealed. He'd been watching her for well over an hour. His deliciously naughty gaze warmed her clear through to her bones. He was darkly handsome with the kind of charisma that attracted women. His raw, lusty magnetism penetrated her deep depression and made her feel alive again.

Cara Brooks shifted her slim, bikini-clad body on the deck chair, adjusted the back to a reclining position, and tried to ignore the sensual perusal of the intriguing man sitting at the edge of the pool with his feet dangling in the water. Cara had no desire to engage in a shipboard romance with a strange man, although she couldn't deny that the thought was a tempting one. After what Gil had done to her, she was more than ready to throw caution to the wind and do something daring, something far removed from her normally conservative behavior.

Cara tilted her straw hat to shade her face more completely and rummaged around in her bag for a bottle of suntan lotion. Without protection, her fair complexion would look like a lobster at dinner tonight, although why it mattered escaped her. She'd been abandoned and tossed aside like so much unwanted baggage.

Cara's bright blue gaze shifted unconsciously to the man at poolside. He was without a doubt the most disturbingly handsome man she'd ever seen. She could feel his narrowed gaze on her as she slathered generous dollops of lotion on her arms, legs, upper torso and back as far as she could reach. Then she flipped over on her stomach to tan her backside.

Cara closed her eyes and dozed as the the gentle rotation of the ship and sound of the waves slapping against the hull soothed her frayed emotions. She was almost asleep when she felt a shadow pass between her body and the sun, cooling her skin. It was a cloud passing over the sun, she reflected listlessly, thinking no more of it until she felt a splash of something wet glide over the sun-heated flesh of her shoulders and down her back. The sudden warmth of a large hand upon her flesh startled her and she attempted to rise.

"Don't move." The deep, sensuous voice had a jolting effect, like being struck by lightning. He spoke English with a British clip, flavored with just a hint of an unfamiliar accent. French? Italian? Greek?

"What are you doing?" Cara asked, craning her neck to look up at him.

His broad shoulders blotted out the sun. He was deeply tanned and muscular, as if he worked out on a daily basis. The prominent thrust of his sex beneath his Speedo was embarrassingly masculine and she shifted her gaze upward, gazing at his handsome features with avid interest. His hair was black as sin. The bold slash of his eyebrows, seductive dark eyes and generous mouth curved into a friendly smile caused a strange flutter inside her.

"I'm just doing a fellow traveler a favor," the stranger said as he massaged lotion onto her shoulders and upper back. "I noticed you couldn't reach your back, and since you had no one to do it for you . . ." He shrugged. "I hope you don't mind." His hands moved in lazy circles over her smooth skin. "You're awfully tense."

Mind? It felt wonderful. She could lie there and let him massage her forever. And she had a right to be tense. She was supposed to be on her honeymoon. Instead, she found herself on a solitary journey to despair. "Thank you. Have we met before?"

She knew they hadn't.

"Not yet. My friends call me Dom."

"Is that short for Dominic?"

"You're very perceptive."

Cara started to ask if he had a last name when she felt his hands on the tiny back strap holding her bikini top in place. She gave a small cry of surprise when he released the hook. "What in the hell do you think you're doing?"

"Spreading lotion on your back," he said, giving her a smile that belied his innocent intent. "Lie still, Cara. I'll be done in a moment."

Cara's breath caught in her throat. She had the oddest feeling that Fate had had a hand in this meeting. He knew her name and she didn't know a thing about him. "How do you know my name?"

The warm hands stilled on her back and he gave another one of those careless shrugs she found so compelling. "I saw you board in Athens and asked the purser for your name. You're a beautiful woman, Cara. What red-blooded man wouldn't want to know who you are? I also learned you're traveling alone, that your traveling companion failed to show up. I was hoping we might become friends."

His hands boldly skimmed the sides of her breasts and she exhaled sharply, stunned by the sensations this stranger created within her at the merest touch of his fingertips.

"You presume a lot for someone who never saw

me before I boarded the *Odyssey* yesterday," she said with a hint of censure.

His fingertips grazed her breasts again and she nearly jumped out of her skin.

"All done," he said, removing his hands before she could reprimand him. "Shall I refasten your top?" His eyes twinkled with wicked humor. "Or would you rather I left it unhooked?"

"Fasten it, please," Cara said, wishing he'd go away. She'd had enough of men like him to last a lifetime. Handsome, assured, suave, everything a woman found attractive in a man. Unfortunately, Gil had proven that men couldn't be trusted, and she wasn't ready to take the plunge again.

"Do you have a dinner partner?" Dom asked.

"I didn't know I needed one."

"You don't, but it's much more pleasant when one has someone compatible to dine with."

Cara flipped over on her back and stared up at him. "What makes you think we're compatible? I don't even know you."

Dom stared pointedly at her long, tanned legs stretched out before her and smiled. "You will." His smile held a wealth of promise.

Cara couldn't deny that this man turned her on in a way that Gil never had. Dom's quiet confidence and bold, impertinent manner was too suave to be sincere but she certainly admiried his savoir faire. He knew what he wanted and was honest about it. There was no pretense, no beating around the bush. He wanted sex from her.

"About dinner tonight," he reminded her when she failed to answer his question. "I have a table for two at the late seating, all to myself."

"I'm not looking for a relationship," Cara contended. She wanted to be as candid as he had been.

"What about a shipboard romance?" Dom teased, undaunted. "I'm damn attracted to you, Cara. We're both adults, both unattached. We have two weeks to see where this attraction takes us."

"To hell," Cara muttered beneath her breath.

"I take it your last relationship ended on a sour note," Dom said as he pulled up a deck chair and sat down beside her. "Want to tell me about it?"

She wanted to tell someone but she was still too raw and torn up inside to talk about it. "No."

He touched her hand. "Sometimes it's best to get it out in the open. Who better to tell than a stranger who doesn't know enough about you to judge?"

Cara felt heat pulse through her hand where he'd touched her. She couldn't ever recall feeling like that with Gil. She and Gil had been good together, but looking back on it now, she realized Gil had never totally committed to their relationship. She had known he had secrets and thought she could live with them. It hurt to think that he cared more for his ex-wife than he did for her.

"There's not much to tell," Cara said, with a lack of emotion that belied the turmoil whirling inside her. "I was engaged to be married. I truly believed Gil loved me. We were to have a shipboard marriage and spend our honeymoon on the *Odyssey*. A huge reception to be held in Miami was planned for family and friends after the honeymoon."

"Obviously no marriage took place. What happened?"

Cara paused to gather her thoughts. It was still so damn painful. Here she was, nearly thirty, and one would think she was old enough to know when a man loved her. She should have recognized the signs of discontent. She'd been living on her own for a very long time. Hip, knowledgeable and astute in her business dealings were words peers used to describe her. As an editor of *Fashion Wise* magazine in Miami, Cara dealt with problems every day of her life, but nothing had prepared her for the dissolution of her comfortable relationship with Gil Tallman.

Cara's fiancé must have been mad to let her get away, Dom thought to himself. Cara was not only beautiful, she had a sexy body most women would die for: firm, round breasts, long, supple legs that seemed to go on forever. Her flat stomach accentuated the slim dimensions of her waist and her tiny bikini displayed all those attributes to perfection. Her hair was the color of a summer sunset and her eyes were as blue as the Mediterranean upon which they sailed. It didn't surprise him that he wanted her.

Cara had always been one to keep her innermost

thoughts, her disappointments, to herself, but something about Dom inspired confidence. She'd been intrigued with him the first moment she'd set eyes on him, vitally aware of every subtlety of his character, every gesture. Dom excited her. She'd known Gil a whole year and had never felt this way about him. And obviously he'd never felt strongly about her despite their plans to marry. How could she have been so damn naive?

"I can almost feel the anguish churning inside you," Dom said when the silence became oppressive.

"If I tell you about my abortive attempt at matrimony will you tell me something about yourself?"

His dark eyes became hooded but his hesitation was scarcely noticeable. "It's a deal."

"I met Gil Tallman a year ago. He's an importer of fine antiques. His store is located in the Art Deco district of South Beach in Miami. He's quite successful at what he does and spends lavishly. We met at a party and hit it off immediately."

"Did you become lovers?"

A light flared in her blue eyes. "That's none of your business."

"We're not living in the dark ages, Cara. If I were Gil I'd want us to become lovers. It usually happens when two people care about one another. And even when they don't," he added as an afterthought. "Finish your story."

Cara's gaze wandered past the people milling

around the pool, then lifted upward to watch the seagulls darting in and out of the waves left in the *Odyssey*'s wake. The Mediterranean cruise had seemed like a fantasy come true when Gil had mentioned it for their wedding and honeymoon. Though normally a practical person, Cara had always harbored a secret desire of being swept away by a dark lover—like in the pirate romances she was so fond of reading in her spare moments. She knew it was pure fiction, but what girl didn't dream of dark, mysterious lovers and magical sex? Gil wasn't exactly the dark lover of her dreams, and their sex had never been earthshaking, but Cara had hoped this cruise would fulfill her secret fantasy.

As it turned out, her fantasies had been destined to remain unfulfilled. Gil had ditched her and her fantasy had become a nightmare. At least she had thought so when she first realized she was to spend two weeks on a romantic cruise by herself. She gazed through lowered lashes at Dom and suddenly the next two weeks appeared less bleak than they had that morning.

Cara reined her thoughts back to the present. Her words sounded as if they had been forced out of her. "Gil and I were to be married by the ship's captain our first night out. Gil made all the arrangements. It was to be my fantasy wedding."

"What happened?" Dom prodded.

"Gil was to meet me at the airport. My luggage had already been taken aboard. Then he called me at the airport on my cell phone and said he'd been unavoidably detained. Business, he'd said. He promised to meet me in Athens in plenty of time to catch the ship. He apologized profusely and hoped I would understand."

"Gil never arrived in Athens," Dom ventured.

"Exactly," Cara concurred. "I boarded the ship, expecting Gil to arrive momentarily. A message arrived moments before sailing. Gil's ex-wife had arrived on his doorstep unexpectedly. She wanted to reconcile. Gil decided he needed time to consider his options. It was obvious to me that Gil loved his ex-wife more than he did me. The ship sailed without him and here I am. I cancelled the wedding arrangements and decided to see the cruise through to the bitter end." She took a deep, steadying breath. "Gil dumped me and it hurts like the very devil."

"He must be a damn fool," Dom contended.

"Enough about me," Cara said, pulling the pain tightly inside her. "Tell me about yourself. Why isn't an attractive man like you married or attached?"

"I *was* married," Dom admitted. "It didn't work. I wanted children, she didn't. She left the marriage a wealthy woman."

"What are you doing on a romantic cruise by yourself?"

"My father is one of the owners of the cruise line. I'm traveling incognito so I'd appreciate it if you didn't reveal my identity. Periodically members of the board travel aboard ships of the line to check out the staff and services. We've had a few complaints recently and the board of directors asked me to investigate. So here I am."

"I know who you are now!" Cara said, recalling the articles she'd read in the tabloids in recent months about the wealthy playboy who was on the prowl again after dumping his French actress wife. "You're Dominic Domani, son of Aristotle Domani, the Greek shipping magnate."

"I'd prefer that you keep that to yourself," Dom said. "I booked passage under the name Dominic Nessi. Nessi being my mother's name. I'm half Italian."

"Where did you get your British accent?"

"I picked it up in England, where I attended college. Now you know everything there is to know about me. Tell me more about yourself."

"I'm an editor at *Fashion Wise*, a magazine for women about women, and live in Miami. My parents live in Atlanta, where I was born. I haven't visited them in ages but intend to soon. I have one sister, one brother, three nieces and one nephew. I'm just an ordinary woman. My wants are simple: marriage and children someday, nothing spectacular. But after Gil, I'm not convinced those goals are obtainable."

His smiled at her. His gaze was so intimate the red glow crawling up her neck had nothing to do with the sun and everything to do with Dom's perusal. Cara thought him the most gorgeous creature God had ever created. But she was certain he knew that. She recalled reading about his romantic escapades and was surprised she hadn't recognized him immediately. He was one of the beautiful people, a jet-setter who traveled the globe in search of love and excitement. He'd scaled the highest mountain in the Andes and spent a year with a group searching for the tomb of King Tut's son in Egypt. And he'd dated the most beautiful women in the world.

"I'd say those goals are not only attainable but commendable in this day and age."

Now that Cara knew who Dom was, she felt intimidated by him. What would one of the world's most eligible bachelors want with her when he could have any woman he wanted?

"I'd better get out of the sun before I burn to a crisp," she said, swinging her long legs to the deck.

"What's your cabin number? I'll escort you to dinner tonight."

Cara's answer was forestalled by the arrival of the deck steward. "Miss Brooks?"

"Yes, I'm Cara Brooks," Cara answered.

"You have a ship to shore telephone call. You can take it on the portable phone," he said, handing her the receiver."

"Thank you," Cara said, turning away to take her call.

"Hello."

"Cara, is that you?"

"Gil. I have nothing to say to you. You have some nerve calling me."

Gil's voice crackled in her ear. "I have plenty to say to you, Cara. First, I want to apologize. I was a fool. I don't know what got into me. Lisa means nothing to me. I was surprised to see her and was confused for a time. I want you back, Cara. I'm going to fly to Barcelona to meet the ship when it docks. We'll fly home together and have a romantic wedding on the beach."

"I don't think so, Gil. You ruined everything when you left me high and dry in Athens."

"I'm not going to take no for an answer, Cara. I'll see you in Barcelona."

The phone went dead.

"I take it that was Gil," Dom said.

Cara frowned at the receiver. "He wants to reconcile," she said.

Dom's eyebrows shot upward. Cara was too good for the man. "What do *you* want?"

"I don't know. Gil is going to meet the ship at the end of the cruise in Barcelona."

"He doesn't deserve you, Cara. He's disappointed you once, what's to say he won't do it again?"

"I know you're right. God, I'm so confused."

"There are men more deserving than Gil."

She stared at him, wondering if he was one of those deserving men to which he referred. "Why should you care? We just met."

"Can you deny the attraction between us? I felt

it the moment I saw you boarding the ship in Athens. I'm not going to let you go back to him, Cara. Come on, I'll walk you back to your cabin."

"Let me don my cover-up first," Cara said as she slipped on a sheer shirt over her bikini. Then she gathered her book and lotion and placed them in her bag while Dom pulled a tee shirt over his speedo.

Cara offered no objection when he curled a tanned arm around her waist and guided her toward the stairs.

"Where is your cabin?" Dom asked.

"Upper Deck. Number 802. Gil booked a deluxe cabin for us."

They climbed two flights of stairs to the Upper Deck and preceded along the passageway. Dom held out his hand for the key when they reached Number 802. Cara fished for it in her bag and handed it to him. He opened the door and followed her inside.

"Thank you," Cara said, expecting him to leave.

He didn't. "I'll come by for you at seven-thirty," he said, closing the door behind and leaning against it. His tone brooked no argument and Cara gave none. "Do you like champagne?"

"I love champagne."

"I'll see that a bottle is properly chilled for us. I want to make this cruise memorable for you, Cara, despite its disappointing beginning."

"That's not necessary. I don't want your pity."

He pulled her against him. "Pity?" Laughter

rumbled through his chest. "What I'm feeling now is far from pity. What *you're* feeling pressing against you has nothing to do with compassion and everything to do with wanting to be inside you."

"We've just met," Cara said, both thrilled and appalled when she felt the bold thrust of his sex against her. Never in her life had she gone to bed with a man she'd just met and scarcely knew and she wanted to make sure he knew it. "I'm not a one-night stand and never have been."

"I know that. You're one foxy lady, Cara." He sent her an incredibly sexy smile that turned her bones to water. "It's going to take more than one night to satisfy me."

The tiny Speedo stretched across his loins didn't begin to contain his enthusiastic response to her own bikini-clad body. Cara couldn't recall when she'd been so aroused by a man's body. How could that be? Basically all men were made the same, yet something about Dom excited her beyond measure.

Before Gil there had been Frank and Scott. Except for Gil, those brief affairs had been extremely disappointing. On the whole, Cara found men to be selfish and indulgent to their own needs. So far she'd found no man—Gil had come the closest— who wanted the same things she did. For a modern woman she had old-fashioned values. Home, family, a faithful husband, all those things most men avoided. She'd truly thought Gil was the one man with the qualities to become the kind of husband she wanted. Perhaps he still was the man for her. She hadn't made up her mind yet.

"You're thinking about Gil," Dom said, his displeasure apparent. "When I hold a woman in my arms I want her to think of me."

His arms tightened around her. Cara caught her breath, aware of the sexual energy pulsing from every inch of his gorgeous six-foot-plus frame. His mouth hovered scant inches above hers, and suddenly she wondered what his kisses would taste like. Would they taste of arousal and sin? Of danger and mystery? All of those and more, she suspected.

Then his mouth closed over hers and she found the answers to all her questions. He tasted of peppermint and maleness, of sun-baked skin and sexual arousal. His tongue probed against her lips and she opened her mouth, enjoying the intimate kiss more than she thought possible. She was enjoying it so much, in fact, that she wasn't aware that Dom had opened her shirt and released the hook on the back of her bikini. Full realization came when she felt the heat of his hands against her bare breasts.

"Dom! What are you doing?"

"Your skin is so soft," he whispered against her mouth. "I want to taste you all over. He lowered his head and took her pink nipple into his mouth, flicking the jutting tip with his tongue then drawing it deeply into his mouth.

"Oh, God, Dom," she breathed in erotic ecstasy. "Don't do this to me. I'm too raw right now. Too vulnerable. I can't bear to be hurt again."

He drew back slightly, affronted. "I'd never hurt you, Cara. I can promise you pleasure, and that's what you need right now. But I won't pressure you. I'll wait for you to realize we have something special together. Think of me while you're getting ready for our dinner date tonight. I'll be thinking of you."

Cara's gaze followed the progress of Dom's long, muscular legs as he strode from the room. Anticipation of her evening with Dom brought an eagerness that surprised her, given the dismal beginning of her honeymoon cruise and a wedding that had never taken place.

She even hummed a little ditty as she peeled off her shirt and bikini bottom and stepped into the shower.

Dom whistled a spritely tune as he walked to his own cabin.

Chapter Two

"Why are you staring at me?" Dom asked. "Is something wrong? Is my fly open?"

He wore a tux. Cara thought it a sin for a man to look so good. His dark lashes were so long it seemed almost indecent to see them on a man so blatantly male. Dom had appeared at her door promptly at seven-thirty, looking as if he'd just stepped out of a fashion magazine.

"You look wonderful," Cara said.

"Tonight's the captain's reception. Formal dress is required." His dark gaze swept the length of her and back, apparently pleased with what he saw. "You look smashing. Turn around."

Cara smiled as she whirled for his benefit, pleased with his reaction to her black sequined minidress. It fit her like a second skin, held up by two skinny rhinestone straps. She'd bought it to impress Gil. It wasn't the type of dress she usually wore and she had felt wicked and somewhat decadent when she'd bought it. She'd decided that her honeymoon was a perfect time to wear something a bit more seductive than her usual attire. She rather liked the idea of flaunting her sex appeal before Dom, who by all accounts dated beautiful, sexy women.

"You have a great figure, and that dress displays it to perfection," Dom complimented. "I'll be the envy of every man at the reception tonight."

And I'll be the envy of every woman, Cara thought but did not say.

"Are you ready? Shall we go?"

"Do I need a wrap?"

"It would be a damn shame to cover up that dress . . . and what's in it," he added with a sinful grin. "The night is warm; I don't think you'll need a wrap."

"Then I'm ready," Cara said.

Yesterday had been the worst day of her life, and then Dom Domani walked into her world. Cara knew she was going to wake up soon and find she'd dreamed the whole thing, but she was determined to live this fantasy to the fullest.

They walked along the passageway to the wide, sweeping staircase whose rich, hand-rubbed mahogany railing and thick carpeting added a touch of elegance. The crystal chandelier hanging from the ceiling above the main lobby was so stunning Cara stared at it in awe as Dom pulled her along with him to the ballroom, where the reception was being held.

There was the inevitable reception line, the tiny cucumber sandwiches, champagne, soft music playing in the background, the works. Cara made appropriate small talk with some of their fellow travelers, hardly aware of what she ate, drank, or said. Dom seemed to have the strangest effect upon her. She was in a room filled with hundreds of people yet she was aware of no one but Dom; his hard body, his heat, the way he looked and smiled at her. His incredible sex appeal. Looking into his dark, knowing eyes, she realized he was aware of the attraction between them.

He continued to charm her thoughout dinner. She ordered from the elaborate menu, ate, drank the properly chilled champagne, the dessert wine, conversed, laughed, drank some more, basking in the heat of Dom's gittering gaze. His eyes held a wealth of worldly sophistication, making Cara acutely aware of her own shortcomings. But as long as this was her fantasy, she could be anything she wanted to be. When she woke up tomorrow she'd be just plain Cara Brooks again, a woman who had been left standing at the altar, and Dom would have moved on to another woman.

After dinner they strolled arm in arm on deck, enjoying the stars and moon and fresh balmy breezes. When they reached a dark spot, Dom pulled her beneath the shadow of a lifeboat and kissed her. He tasted of heaven; he tasted of sin. He tasted like more. She wound her arms around his neck to show him just how much she enjoyed it.

Dom groaned and deepened the kiss, teasing the soft insides of her mouth with his tongue. He loved her taste, her scent. He'd been attracted to Cara from the first moment he'd laid eyes on her. She was beautiful, but he'd had women lovelier and more cosmopolitan than Cara Brooks. Debutantes, actresses, even a princess or two. But simple Cara Brooks with her girl-next-door good looks and lithe, supple body had taken his fancy as no other woman had in a very long time. He'd become so jaded that those pale-skinned, chain-smoking women who traveled in his crowd bored him to tears.

Cara had looked so sad yesterday that something had compelled him to cheer her up. But a strange thing had happened as he spoke with her. He'd found himself unaccountably drawn to the titian-haired beauty. Had the man who'd jilted her been onboard the *Odyssey* he would have beaten him to a pulp and felt no guilt about it. He wanted Cara sexually, that much was clear to him. And judging from the fervor of her kisses, she wanted him too. He'd promised her pleasure and he planned to give it to her in abundance. For some unexplained reason he wanted to give Cara the romantic honeymoon her fiancé had denied her.

"Listen," Cara said, breaking off the kiss. "Music. It's been so long since I've danced."

He tucked her arm under his. "Then we shall dance the night away." They strolled along the deck to the lounge.

"This is by far the best fantasy I've ever had," Cara said, feeling like Cinderella. "Maybe it's the romantic night, or the moon and the stars, or the sea . . ." She paused, turning to gaze up at him. "Maybe it's you. You're the kind of man a woman dreams about but never meets personally. I've read all about your escapades, and the glamorous women in your life."

Dom felt the weight of her disapproval. Even if she hadn't meant it to sound like disapproval, the inflection in her voice was unmistakable. For the first time Dom regretted his playboy reputation. He knew the world regarded him as a man who discarded women as often as he changed his soiled shirts, and truth to tell he had worked hard to give the world that impression, but it wasn't really him. He was searching, always searching, for the right woman. One with the values he admired.

He leaned forward and placed a gentle kiss on Cara's lips. "If you let me, I'm going to fulfill your every fantasy."

Cara sighed. "I'm not usually so sentimental. I guess being jilted did a job on me. Gil wants me back, though. That takes some of the pain away."

Dom didn't know where the anger came from.

He didn't know Gil, and hardly knew Cara, but the thought of Cara returning to Gil made his blood boil.

"Forget Gil. I don't want to hear his name mentioned again in my presence. I intend to keep you so busy you'll have no time to dwell on the bastard."

Dom held the door open and Cara stepped into the lounge. The orchestra was playing "Memories," which Cara thought was appropriate. She intended to store enough memories from this fantasy cruise to last a lifetime. Though she didn't mention it to Dom, she supposed she'd forgive Gil and become his wife. At least Gil had no objections to having children.

Her thoughts scattered when Dom took her into his arms, gliding with her onto the crowded dance floor. He held her close, humming into her ear as they swayed in time to the music. Cara thought him a wonderful dancer. They moved in perfect harmony, until the set ended and the band launched into rock and roll.

Dom effortlessly moved her through steps that had them both laughing and panting from the vigorous workout. "You're a great dancer," Dom said as he twirled her out and then back into his arms.

"So are you. But then, I'd expect no less from an international playboy."

Dom winced. Coming from Cara, the title sounded offensive. Though he'd probably earned the reputation, there was much more to him than

Cara knew. He *did* jet around the world, but it wasn't strictly for pleasure. He worked as hard as he played. Sometimes harder. Unfortunately, the tabloids reported only the part of his life that might be seen as sensational, rarely mentioning his work or involvement with various charities. The paparazzi could be brutal.

"Shall we rest a moment?" Dom suggested, spying an empty table in a secluded corner. "I can use something to drink. What about you?"

The waiter appeared and Dom ordered a bottle of champagne.

"It's noisy in here," Cara said over the din of loud music and laughter.

"Too noisy," Dom agreed. "I've got a better idea." He tucked the bottle of champagne beneath his arm and held out his hand to her. "Come on, let's get out of here."

"Where to now?"

"You'll see. We'll take the elevator," he said, guiding her through the lounge. They entered the elevator and Dom pushed the button to the Sky Deck."

"Are we going to the Sky Lounge?" Cara knew there was nothing on the Sky Deck but the lounge and two penthouse suites.

"Better than that," Dom said with a twinkle. The elevator stopped and they stepped out. "This way." They walked down a short passageway to a gilded mahogany door. "Here we are." He produced a key, unlocked the door and pushed it open."

"This is the Dynasty Suite," Cara said, stepping inside the room. Her fantasy just kept getting better and better.

Dom entered behind her and closed the door. Then he placed the champagne bottle down on the table beside two champagne flutes. "Pretty swanky, isn't it?"

The soft glow of indirect lighting reflected off the polished tabletops. Swanky hardly described the suite, Cara thought as she nearly sank down to her ankles in thick white carpeting. Chocolate leather furniture added a touch of elegance to the suite. So did the paintings by famous artists decorating the walls and the lavishly draped and curtained windows.

Her gaze finally found the room beyond the sitting room, where the open door provided an unrestricted view of the bedroom, and the enormous king-size bed.

"Do you like it?" Dom asked.

"It's magnificent. I never imagined such elegance aboard a ship. My cabin is nice, but nothing like this."

"Champagne?"

She nodded and walked over to the set of double windows while he poured, surprised to see that they weren't windows at all, but a set of French doors opening onto a private veranda.

"Open them if you'd like," Dom said.

Cara pushed open the doors, lifting her face to

the soft, scented breeze. "I've probably had enough to drink tonight."

"Not nearly enough," he said in a low, husky voice. He handed her a champagne flute and raised his in a toast. "Here's to romance." Cara took a sip of champagne, feeling an unaccountable urge to giggle. Then he said, "I want to fulfill all your fantasies tonight."

"You already have," Cara said softly. Then she flushed and looked away, searching for another subject to explore. "You have a fantastic view."

"Amazing," he agreed, staring at her instead of the undulating moonlit sea.

They clinked glasses and Cara raised her flute to her lips, enjoying the bubbles tickling her nose. Suddenly "Candle in the Wind" by Elton John wafted through the open doors.

"I put in a CD," Dom said, answering her unspoken question. He took her empty glass and set it down on the railing with his. "Shall we dance?"

She went easily into his arms. It seemed so natural. "Are you trying to seduce me, Mr. Domani?" she teased.

"Is it working?"

More than you know, she thought dreamily, enjoying every minute of his seduction. Her entire future with Gil couldn't have been half as exciting as this one night with Dom. He was a foreigner, which was intriguing; he was worldly, which was erotic; he wielded power; and if that wasn't enough, he was sexy as hell.

"I'll tell you later," Cara said when she realized Dom was waiting for her answer.

Dom's smile oozed raw sensuality as he bent his head and kissed her. She melted against him, breathing him into her pores, tasting his arousal. This man knew how to kiss! She savored the feel of his mouth on hers, so caught up in the moment that she was scarcely aware that Dom had unzipped the back of her dress.

Dom was as intrigued with Cara as she was with him. He loved her taste, her scent, the way she responded to his kisses. He wanted her naked beneath him so badly he hurt. A groan slipped past his lips. He wanted to make mad, passionate love to her, to prove he was a better man than Gil. He wanted to fulfill her fantasies, and at the end of two weeks he wanted to . . . His thoughts skidded to an abrupt halt. He had no idea what he wanted at the end of two weeks.

In all probability, Cara would leave the ship in Barcelona and he would report back to the board about conditions found aboard the *Odyssey*. Doubtless Gil would be waiting for Cara, ready to whisk her off for their wedding, and that thought bothered him.

He captured her face between his hands and stared into her eyes. "Are you having a good time?"

"The best."

He licked the seam of her kiss-swollen lips until they parted; then he thrust his tongue into her mouth. His kiss was hungry, demanding, seeking deeper intimacy. Cara knew what he wanted and couldn't find it within herself to deny him. Fantasies were supposed to be a little bit naughty, weren't they?

He caressed her throat with gentle fingertips, slowly drifting downward to cup her shoulders. She drew in a shuddering breath when he placed his thumbs beneath the tiny straps holding up her dress and pulled them down her arms. Her dress slithered to her waist and stopped, held in place by her hips. She wore no bra.

"God, you're beautiful," Dom breathed against her lips. "I want to worship you, Cara mia. Your body is made for loving." His hands skimmed her ribs, brushing the full undersides of her breasts, but he didn't touch them, no matter how desperately she wanted him to.

He gazed into her slightly dilated eyes and slowly, carefully pulled her dress past her hips. It puddled on the floor and she stepped out of it. She stood before him in black lace bikini panties and high-heeled sandals as Dom looked his fill.

"If you're going to say no, do it now," he said in a voice made hoarse with need. "Once I get you in bed it will be too late."

Cara was drawn headlong into his glittering gaze. She didn't want to say no. She wanted Dom. She wanted *this*. She had never been one to make a fool of herself over a man, she was too practical for that, but Dom had promised her pleasure and she expected nothing more. Pleasure was what fantasies were all about, wasn't it? Guilt might follow, but she'd confront that later.

"I'm not going to say no, Dom. No matter what happens at the end of two weeks, I want this. I want you."

"I hoped you'd say that," Dom said as he swept her up into his arms and carried her into the bedroom. He placed her on the bed and turned on the bedside lamp. "I want to see you. All of you."

She sat up, crossing her arms over her breasts. "That's no fair—you've still got on all your clothes."

He laughed. She loved the way his eyes crinkled at the corners, producing tiny little lines. She recalled reading an article that gave his age as thirty-five and thought he looked younger.

"I wouldn't want to disappoint a lady." He peeled off his jacket and tie. Then he removed the gold studs from his shirtfront and cuffs, yanked off his cummerbund and pulled the shirt from his pants. He flung it away, unzipped his pants and pulled them off with his shoes and stockings.

His body is incredible, Cara thought as she watched him undress through half-closed eyes. He had the physique of an athlete. All strong, sculptured muscles and rippling tendons. His hips and waist were slim; there wasn't an ounce of fat anywhere on his body. Her gaze roamed freely over him. He still wore bikini briefs but they hid nothing. His erection filled the front, stretching the material to its limit.

The mattress sunk as Dom lowered himself onto the bed beside her. His arms came around her, pulling her against him, letting her feel the hard ridge of his sex.

"Tell me what you like, Cara. Tonight is for you."

Cara's breath caught in her throat. Gil had never asked her what she liked. He'd always assumed she liked what he liked and proceeded from there. Consequently, she had no idea what to tell Dom.

"Surprise me," she said, almost giddy with anticipation. Being a little bit tipsy helped dispel her inhibitions. This was one fantasy she wanted to remember, to look back on and savor.

"Suppose we start by just kissing and touching," Dom suggested. "I want to memorize every inch of your flesh."

Cara offered her mouth and he eagerly accepted her offering. His kisses turned her brain to mush, just as they had the first time. His passion thrilled her; his heat scorched her everywhere he touched, and suddenly he was touching her everywhere. His caresses grew bold, invasive, as his mouth worked magic on her senses. She felt her breasts swell, felt her nipples harden as his mouth left hers and dipped down to take an aching nipple into his mouth.

She moaned, writhing upward against him in wild abandon as he licked and suckled her nipples, moving from one to the other with the expertise of a man who had done this countless times in the past yet never tired of it.

"Let's get rid of these," Dom said huskily as he pulled off her bikini panties and high-heeled sandals and tossed them aside.

"And these," Cara said, yanking down the waistband of his briefs.

"Now where was I?" Dom asked as he skimmed off his underwear and kicked them away.

It didn't take him long to find his place again as his mouth returned to her breasts and nipples. She tasted so sweet he could go on suckling her forever. He liked it that there was no pretense to her response. Dom was experienced enough to know that her emotions came from the heart—unlike those women whose artificial responses left him cold. Superficial women no longer aroused him. He saw through them too easily. He supposed that was the inevitable result of bedding women indiscriminately.

His hand drifted down her flat stomach, sifting through the reddish-brown hairs at the tops of her thighs. He kissed her belly, felt it quiver in response. He cupped her heat with his palm, then inserted a long finger inside her. She sighed and he smiled, pleased that he had pleased her. He worked another finger inside her and moved them in and out as her breathing quickened and her hips arched upward.

"Oh, God, Dom, you're driving me mad!"

"I'm going to take you with my mouth, Cara mia," he whispered as he lowered his mouth to that warm, moist place between her thighs.

She heaved upward, panting, whimpering, her hands digging into his shoulders. She yanked on his hair.

"If you don't stop I'm going to shatter!"

"Let it come, Cara. I promised you pleasure. Don't be afraid to take it. This time is for you." His mouth returned to the tender pink flesh between her thighs.

She felt the heat of his mouth, the rough texture of his tongue parting her, tasting her deeply, and the thread of her sanity snapped. It began deep in her core and spread throughout her body, and it wouldn't stop. Spasms racked her. Her contractions were so violent she felt as if a giant wave had slammed into the ship and turned it upside down.

"Are you all right?" Dom asked, raising his head and staring at her.

"More than all right," Cara gasped on a lusty sigh. "Do you always keep your promises?"

"That's not the half of it, sweet. We've hardly begun."

Cara thought that if he gave her any more pleasure she'd die of it.

He raised slightly, grasped her thighs and placed them on either side of his hips, opening her for his entry. She stared down between their bodies, her eyes widening when she saw the size of his erection. She'd thought men were all built pretty much alike, but Dom had just shot that theory all to hell.

"Wait!" she said when she realized he was preparing to enter her. "Aren't you going to use—"

"—protection?" he asked, finishing her sentence. "Of course. I assume you're on the pill."

She hesitated. Dom must have taken her silence for accord, for he said, "Ah, I see, you're worried about disease. I took precautions earlier, though it isn't necessary. I'm disease free."

He reached into the nightstand drawer and removed a condom. He ripped open the package and handed it to her. "Do you want to put it on me?"

She did. Oh, God, she really did want to. She took the condom from his hand. He sat back on his haunches, presenting himself to her. With only a slight hesitancy, she grasped his sex and rolled the condom in place. By the time she finished they were both more than ready to continue. He came over her again, kissing and caressing her, but she was more than ready. His smile was almost feral as he thrust into her.

"You're so tight," he said, sounding surprised but pleased at the same time. "Do you like it fast and hard or slow and easy?"

"Yes," Cara said. *Yes, yes, yes. Fast and hard and slow and easy.*

Dom chuckled. "A woman after my own heart." He buried himself deep, grasping her hips, raising them to meet his thrusts, his own hips pistoning back and forth in a rhythm older than time.

He groaned and prayed for control. It was too soon to spill himself, far too soon. But nothing had prepared him for the sweet, taut heat of Cara's passage. He felt his climax coming from deep inside him. He felt heat gathering in his loins and his juices rising.

His face contorted with pleasure and pain as he desperately clung to sanity. "Hurry, sweet," he gasped through clenched teeth. "Hot. So damn hot. I'm burning. Come with me. Come now."

Her breath pounding in her chest, Cara met his thrusts with frenzied enthusiasm. She was almost there. So close she could feel tiny ripples of pleasure overtaking her. She closed her eyes, gripped Dom's shoulders and let herself fly. A ragged cry left her throat.

"Thank God," Dom groaned. "Hang on, Cara, we're going to fly together."

Together they soared to that high place above and beyond mere pleasure. He stayed with her until he softened inside her. Then he rolled away and hugged her against him. Savoring the closeness, Cara snuggled against him and drifted off to sleep.

Much later, Cara awakened with a start. It took a few moments to gather her wits enough to realize she was in Dom's bed. She made as if to rise. Apparently Dom felt her move, for he grasped her around the waist and pulled her back into bed.

"Dom. I thought you were sleeping."

"Just catching my second wind. Not thinking of leaving already, are you? The night is still young."

"I thought . . . well, nothing could top what we've already done."

"You think not?" She could hear the smile in his voice. "We've just begun. You deserve a wedding night. Come here, sweet." He pulled her on top of him, letting his erection speak for him. Cara gulped and forgot why she wanted to leave.

Chapter Three

The sound of water splashing against the shower
stall awakened Cara from a wonderfully erotic
dream. She opened her eyes, stretched, and remembered. . . .

Gil had jilted her and she'd spent her wedding
night in Dom's bed! Surprisingly she felt no guilt.
She felt—besides having a slight hangover—mar-
velously alive.

Thinking naughty thoughts, Cara rose naked
from bed, opened the bathroom door and stepped
inside. The shower door was bathed with steam
but she could still see Dom's powerful body out-
lined against the glass. Broad shoulders, slim
waist, narrow hips. He had the kind of inherent
sexuality men would give an arm and leg for, and

he had used his prowess last night to give her un-speakable pleasure.

Abruptly the shower door opened and Dom stuck his head out. He was grinning at her. "Are you going to come in? Or are you going to waste both our time standing outside looking in?"

"I'm coming in," Cara said, hesitating but a moment before making up her mind. She'd come this far, why turn shy now? After their fabulous night together Dom probably knew her body more intimately than she knew it herself.

Dom pushed open the shower door so she could enter and moved aside to allow her room to stand under the spray.

"That feels wonderful," Cara sighed.

"I'll wash your back." He soaped a sponge and applied it diligently to her backside. "Turn around." She did. He stared pointedly at her breasts before spreading suds over her upper torso.

Cara assumed he was finished, but it seemed he had only just begun. She gave a start of surprise when he reached between her thighs and spread her with his fingers, massaging the slick folds of her tender, inner flesh, intentionally arousing her as he took her nipple into his mouth and suckled her. It was too much for her. She cried out and shattered, convulsing violently around his fingers.

"That's it, sweet," Dom encouraged. "Don't hold back. I love the way you respond to me. It's re-freshing after the practiced response I'm accus-tomed to from women who would rather pretend than exert energy for an honest response."

"Dom. Oh, God, I don't know what got into me. You must think I'm terrible. I don't usually act like this with men I hardly know."

"I'm what got into you, sweet," Dom teased as he turned off the water and wrapped a fluffy towel around her. "And if I have my way I'm going to get into you again in a very few minutes."

He carried her to bed, pulled the towel from her body and slowly, with great relish, began to arouse her again. Within minutes he was reaching for protection. Seconds later she was on top of him, taking him deeply inside her, bringing them both to an explosive climax.

After another shower and short rest, they agreed to meet on the pool deck for a late breakfast before going ashore to explore Santorini Island. The ship had docked earlier for a ten-hour visit, and according to Dom they had plenty of time to explore the whitewashed village perched high on the ochre-and-pink-striated cliffs that rose above Santorini Bay.

Wearing a short sundress that left her shoulders bare and a wide-brimmed straw hat that shaded her delicate complexion, Cara walked down the gangplank with Dom. She glanced at him from beneath lowered lids, thinking he looked quite splendid in tan trousers and white polo.

"The Lost City of Atlantis is said to be buried beneath the waters nearby," Dom said. "We could go diving if you wish, but I have a better idea. I'd like to take you to the village of Thera. You can only get there by donkey or cable car. It's truly a dazzling sight."

"I prefer cable car," Cara said, laughing. "I'm not much of a diver, and donkeys aren't my preferred mode of travel."

"Then Thera it is. You won't regret the decision."

They spent a leisurely afternoon strolling hand in hand along narrow cobbled streets lined with an array of enticing craft shops. At one of the stalls Dom bought her a gold charm bracelet as a souvenir of their visit. She tried to refuse the expensive gift but Dom insisted. He fastened it on her arm and she held it out to admire it, thinking it a sweet, thoughtful reminder of their brief time together. All that walking induced a fierce hunger and they dined at a quaint restaurant overlooking the sea.

They returned to the ship with time to spare for the seven o'clock departure. They stood hand in hand at the railing as the ship steamed out of the bay, watching the cliffs become smaller and smaller. It had been a remarkable day, one Cara would hold forever in her heart.

That night Dom arranged for dinner to be served in his suite. They ate steak and lobster, drank champagne, danced on the veranda to Elton

John and other favorites, and afterward made love on the big bed.

The ship had no scheduled stops the following day as they steamed toward Malta, the next port of call. Dom had some business to attend to so Cara stretched out on a deck chair beneath a shady umbrella, reading a romance she had purchased before leaving Miami. Unfortunately, she accomplished very little reading. Her eyes were heavy. She'd gotten precious little sleep the past two nights and the hot sun and balmy sea breezes combined to lull her to sleep. She must have slept for hours, for when she awakened the sun had lost most of its brilliance.

She'd begun to gather her paraphernalia when Dom came strolling toward her. "I thought you'd be napping in your cabin." He wagged his eyebrows at her. "Neither of us have gotten much sleep lately. And I don't intend to let you off the hook tonight, either."

"I napped here instead. I haven't stirred since lunch."

"Oh, I almost forgot. This wire came for you. I was in the radio room sending out some messages when it arrived, and I offered to deliver it." He pulled a rumpled sheet of paper from his pocket and handed it to her. "It's from Gil."

Cara scanned the message, then read it again more slowly. "He's meeting me in Rome instead of Barcelona. He says he can't wait to see me."

"I know. I read it."

"That's only two days from now."

Dom thought she sounded as disappointed as he felt. He had only two more days in which to fulfill her fantasy. It wasn't nearly enough time.

"You're going back to him, aren't you?"

Cara stuffed the message in her bag. "I haven't decided."

"You'd be a fool to take him back."

She rounded on him. "You have no right to judge me, Dom. You can't possibly know what my life is like. I'm almost thirty years old. I've never been married and my biological clock is ticking."

"You're not exactly over the hill," he scoffed. "Gil isn't the only fish in the sea. Obviously he has doubts about this marriage or he wouldn't have ditched you at the last minute."

"It's true Gil had reservations about marriage, but I think he's worked through them. I owe it to him to listen to what he has to say before making up my mind."

Dom's handsome brow wrinkled in disgust. The very idea of Cara in Gil's bed was distastful. "You don't owe him a damn thing. But I can tell you've already decided to forgive him." His mind worked furiously as an idea began to take shape in his mind. He might be considered ruthless, mad even, but in time he hoped Cara would thank him for it.

"Gil regrets what he did," Cara said. "Forgiving him will depend on . . . many things."

"You don't need to make a decision for two

whole days. There's still Malta and Sorrento. I'm not going to let your ex-lover keep me from showing you the sights. This may be your fantasy, but this is my part of the world. I want to make your visit memorable."

"You've already made it memorable," Cara contended.

Their gazes met and clashed. Dom felt himself harden. The sexual implication was so potent he felt overwhelmed, almost disoriented. He wanted to make love to her. He ached from it, and he could tell she wanted the same thing.

He grasped her hand. "Let's get out of here."

"Where are we going?"

He didn't answer. They took the elevator because it was faster. Moments later they were in his suite. He closed the door and backed her against the panel, pinning her there with his hard body. "The way you looked at me . . ." His voice was taut with desire. "*This* is what you want. *I* know damn well it's what I want."

He stripped her bikini off so fast her head spun. His shorts and polo were discarded in record time. He pressed his body against hers and kissed her hungrily, thoroughly, his hands roaming freely over her ripe curves.

"Now, Dom," Cara moaned against his mouth. "I want you inside me now."

"Ah, Cara mia, I love your honesty," Dom murmured as he grasped her bottom and lifted her against him. Her legs went around his hips and her arms circled his neck. He thrust deeply inside her and she clung to his shoulders, riding the undulating wave of their passion as he stroked them both to gasping completion.

After the first heat of passion cooled, they moved to the bed, kissing and caressing. "I'm sorry about not using protection," Dom said. "It all happened so fast. You have nothing to fear from me. I'm disease free. As long as you're on the pill, I see no problems."

Cara merely stared at him, aware that she wasn't being entirely truthful with Dom. She hadn't taken the pill since boarding the *Odyssey*. She thought she'd brought them but had been unable to find them in her suitcase. She reflected a moment on the possibility that she'd purposely left them behind. This was to be her honeymoon, and she *did* want children.

Dom's mind whirled with confusing thoughts as he held and caressed Cara. He'd never met a woman like her before. When he first saw her he'd visualized a shipboard romance to liven up the boredom of traveling alone. But in a very short time Cara had wormed her way beneath his skin until she seemed almost a part of him. Instead of tiring of her after the first time or two, he wanted her more fiercely each time they came together.

When he'd been told what her fiancé had done to her and learned the depth of her dejection, he made an instant decision to make this trip memorable for her. He hadn't considered the possibility of growing inordinately fond of her. After his first disastrous marriage he'd vowed next time to choose a woman with traditional values, a woman who would willingly bear the children he wanted. Someone he could learn to love in the fullness of time. Unfortunately he'd become so jaded he wasn't sure he could ever love anyone.

He pushed up on his elbow and leaned over Cara. He caressed her face, pushing loose strands of burnished hair away from her smooth brow. "I'm going to ask a question, Cara mia, one I hope you'll answer truthfully."

Cara stilled. "I've already told you all about myself."

"There are still things I don't know. For instance, do you love Gil? Personally, I don't think you do. I wouldn't have been able to seduce you so easily if you truly loved him."

Cara blushed, blaming her fair complexion for allowing it. "You still don't understand, do you? I'm not promiscuous. I don't engage in one-night stands. I've not looked at another man since making a commitment to Gil. You can't begin to imagine how worthless and rejected I felt when Gil dumped me for his ex-wife. Then you looked at me with desire and I felt alive again."

"I'd like to wring that bastard's neck," Dom said vehemently.

"I love my job and am good at what I do," she continued, "but having a career isn't a priority with me. I want to be loved, and to love in return. I want a home and family. Children. At least two. Gil promised me all those things."

"That still doesn't answer my question. Do you love him?"

After a lengthy pause, she said, "I thought I did. Perhaps I still do. That's the best answer I can offer you."

"How do you explain the attraction between us? I felt the magnetism immediately. I know you did, too."

"I was at my lowest when we met. I was devastated by Gil's rejection. Then I saw you staring at me with desire and realized other men could want me. At that moment I *needed* to feel wanted and you gave that to me. I'm in lust with you, Dom. There's no other explanation for it. I'm not stupid. I know when this cruise ends we'll never see one another again."

"Cara, I . . ."

"No, don't say anything. I know there can be nothing permanent between us. We're from different worlds, different cultures. This is my fantasy, not yours. I don't know yet what will happen between me and Gil, but I'll always have this to look back on."

"I was hoping for more time. Wire Gil now, before he leaves Miami" he urged. "Wait until you get back home to confront him. Tell him not to meet you in Rome."

Cara shook her head. "I have to give him a

chance to redeem himself. If he wants to meet me in Rome, I'm not going to discourage him."

"We'll see," Dom said as he leaned forward to kiss her. "This lust thing between us is the best thing that's happened to me in a very long time. Don't leave me tonight. We'll dine in my suite, just the two of us, and pretend Gil doesn't exist."

Cara bit her lip. Talking about Gil had resurrected all those feelings of guilt she'd been trying so hard to repress. She'd never done anything like this in her life. She supposed her vulnerability had led to an affair with the most desirable man in the entire universe, and she couldn't regret it. Being with Dom surpassed her wildest fantasy. She was having her dream honeymoon, forget the wedding. Unfortunately she was honeymooning with the wrong man. That thought led to another. *Was* Dominic Domani the wrong man?

"You order dinner while I shower," Cara said, in effect agreeing to his plans for their evening. She'd be a fool not to make the most of the next two days.

Dom gave her a slow grin. "Your wish is my command."

Dom and Cara watched from their private veranda as the ship docked at Valletta, Malta at seven the next morning. At nine they walked down the gangplank to explore the honey-colored capital jutting out into the Mediterranean between two of the finest natural harbors in the world. First they took in the historic sites left by a legacy of maritime conquerors; then they visited the Grand Master's Palace, Fort St. Elmo, St. John's Cathedral, and a sampling of ancient treasures built by the great knights of the Order of St. John.

Unfortunately they couldn't linger, for the ship was scheduled to sail at twelve-thirty. Nevertheless, they became so engrossed with the sights and with each other that time ran away with them. They returned to the ship with scant minutes to spare.

"That was cutting it close," Cara said as the gangplank was pulled in behind them.

"I wanted to show you as much as possible in the short time we had ashore. We'll have more time on Sorrento."

"Have you been to Malta before?"

Dom's dark eyes seemed to turn inward. "It's where I spent my honeymoon," he said, then quickly changed the subject. "I can't wait to show you Sorrento, the Isle of Capri, the Blue Grotto, and the Amafli Drive. There is nothing in the world like the Amafli Drive. The magnificent vista is worth every hairpin turn."

Cara's eyes glittered with excitement. She couldn't wait to see everything Dom described. She dimly wondered if she would have been as excited had she been with Gil.

The next day the ship eased into its berth at Sorrento. Cara slept late and missed it. Dom told her to take her time because they had all day to see the sights. He disappeared on some mysterious errand while she showered and dressed. After a quick breakfast they debarked and stolled along the beach.

Dom lifted her hand to his mouth and kissed her knuckles. "We'll go to Capri and the Blue Grotto first. You'll love it. There's nothing like it anywhere in the world."

The touch of his lips on her hand made her tingle all over. Everything Dom did to her thrilled her. He was the most romantic man she'd ever met. This was to be their last full day and night together. How could she bear it?

They strolled to where a fleet of hydrofoil boats were taking on passengers. Dom told her that from Capri a smaller launch would take them to the Blue Grotto. Dom bought tickets and they boarded the super-fast boats that traveled on a cushion of air all the way out to Capri in the Bay of Naples.

"This is sooo exciting," Cara trilled, thoroughly enjoying the breathtaking ride.

"Not as exciting as what I have planned for us tonight," Dom mouthed into her ear. "Do you know what I'm going to do to you?"

Cara nearly lost her cool. All she could do was stare at him and shake her head.

"First I'm going to taste every inch of your luscious body." His words were pitched so low, no one but Cara could hear him over the roar of the engines. It was a good thing. "Then I'm going to pleasure you with my fingers until you're shaking and begging me to end it. But I won't. Not until I bring you to heaven with my mouth and tongue. After a brief respite I'm going to . . . He mentioned something so outrageous Cara gasped aloud, earning strange looks from their fellow travelers.

"Dom! Please. We're not alone."

"I know," he growled. "A damn shame, too. I'm hornier than a billy goat."

He looked so disgruntled that Cara couldn't suppress the giggle that seemed to come spontaneously.

"Have you no mercy, woman?" Dom asked with a twinkle in his eye.

"I haven't done a thing, Dom."

"You don't have to. Just looking at you makes me want you. Behave now, we're almost there."

Cara stretched her neck to view the city of Capri perched above the Bay of Naples. The glistening city appeared to hang on the the sheer sides of the cliffs rising from the white sand beach, stacked like layers upon a cake. They left the hydrofoil immediately after it docked and boarded the launch waiting to take passengers to the Blue Grotto. It was a short trip around the island to the grotto, but Cara began to worry when the wind rose and the sea became choppy.

"It's going to be somewhat tricky climbing from the launch into one of the small rowboats. You look a bit perturbed."

"Rowboats? The launch doesn't enter the grotto?"

Dom laughed. Not hardly. Look up. See those rowboats hanging from davits? They'll be lowered into the water for our trip into the grotto. You'll be able to see the opening any minute now. Look over to your right, at the base of the cliff."

Cara gazed at the cliff with growing alarm. She saw nothing that could even begin to describe an opening to an underwater cave. "I don't . . ."

"There," Dom pointed. "See that small aperture near the waterline? That's the entrance."

"You're joking," Cara scoffed. "Not even a rowboat could get through that opening."

Suddenly the launch stopped and Cara saw crewmen scurrying about, lowering rowboats into the water from their overhead perches. Then the captain's voice came over the loudspeaker, asking the passengers to perpare for their descent into the small boats for transportation into the grotto. Dom grasped her hand and pulled her along with the dozen or so other passengers.

Cara watched apprehensively as two passengers to each boat were handed down into the heaving, bucking rowboats. Dom and Cara were the last to leave the launch. Cara hesitated, fearing she'd fall between the two boats and be crushed to death. But Dom's hold on her was firm and steady as he handed her down to the boatman.

Cara clung to the side of the boat as the boatman fought against the waves and the wind to bring them to the small opening in the side of the cliff. Suddenly Cara realized that they would never get through, that the opening was too low to allow them entrance. She opened her mouth to cry out a warning and clamped it shut again when she saw that the boatman seemed unperturbed by their impending doom.

"We have to lie down in the bottom of the boat now," Dom said as the prow approached the dark aperture. He helped Cara scoot from the seat and held her close against him in the bottom. Even the boatman had flattened himself on the seat as they drifted through the opening.

Cara gave a soft sigh as a brilliant, dazzling light surrounded them. She blinked, nearly blinded by luminous flashes of iridescent blue light that bounced off the walls of the grotto and reflected beneath the surface of the shimmering water. It was eerie; so magnificent in its scope that she found no words to describe it. All she could do was gape and file it away in her bag of memories, to be taken out and enjoyed when life's pressures overwhelmed her.

"What do you think?" Dom asked, enchanted by her reaction to something he'd seen a dozen times.

"I think . . . I think it's glorious, splendid, magical—I can't think of appropriate words to describe it. It's something I'll never forget."

"Nor I," he said, bending low to kiss her. The boatman appeared to be dozing instead of enjoying the spectacular scenery, and Dom took advantage of the man's inattention.

He kissed her again, and yet again, wondering how she'd react when she learned what he'd done and hoping she'd forgive him.

Cara drank in the sight of the dancing, twinkling lights in silence, awed by the extraordinary phenomenon she had been privileged to witness. She felt an unexplained sadness when they finally left the Blue Grotto and returned to the launch. In fact, she was quiet all the way back to Sorrento. She couldn't help thinking that this was the last day of her fantasy, her final hours to be with Dom. It was a good thing, she decided. If they were together much longer she'd never be satisfied with her mundane existence. She had to keep reminding herself that this was a once-in-a-lifetime fantasy, one that had no connection to reality.

When they reached the mainland Cara assumed they would be boarding the ship, but Dom rid her of that misconception when he led her to a sleek white Mercedes parked nearby. She assumed he had made arrangements for its delivery with a rental company before they'd left the ship. She didn't suspect anything was amiss until it was too late.

"Where are we going?" she asked as she sank down into the creamy leather upholstery.

"Have you ever heard of the Amafli Drive?"

"Who hasn't?"

"The drive is known the world over for its serpentine curves and spectacular view of the Mediterranean."

"Do we have enough time? Departure is at seven."

Dom avoided her eyes. "Don't worry. I know what I'm doing."

Dom seemed to know exactly where he was headed as he negotiated the narrow streets of Sorrento and turned onto the high road that traversed over towering cliffs overlooking the sea. Some of the hairpin turns they negotiated were so hazardous that Cara held her breath, fully expecting the next curve to be their last. To her vast relief, Dom handled the wheel like a pro, maneuvering the hairpin curves as if he had driven them countless times in the past.

"The view is magnificent," Cara exclaimed. "The endless vista of azure sea against a sparkling blue sky above cliffs jutting upward from the rocky shore is breathtaking. I can't begin to find words to describe it properly. The serpentine road leaves me breathless and more than a little awed. I'll never forget this, Dom. If not for you I would have hibernated in my cabin for the duration of the cruise, feeling depressed, rejected and utterly forlorn. You're my angel of mercy."

Dom gave her a strange look. "I'm definitely no angel, Cara. I hope you still feel that way a few hours from now."

Cara had no idea what he meant and refused to worry about it on such a glorious day. It wasn't until she noticed that the sun had begun to slip low in the sky that she grew alarmed and looked at her watch. "Dom, it's almost five o'clock! The ship sails in two hours. Shouldn't we be getting back?"

She thought she heard him sigh. But he sounded cheerful enough when he said, "I want to show you a place that's special to me. It's a villa that's been in my mother's family for generations. You'll love it."

Her brow furrowed. "There isn't time."

"We'll make time."

"When did we turn off the Amalfli Drive?" she asked, suddenly aware that they were now driving down a narrow two-lane road leading inland toward the mountains.

"A few minutes ago. Don't fret, Cara mia."

"I can't help it."

Cara chafed apprehensively as the car wound upward along the deserted road. She couldn't believe Dom was acting so irresponsibly. What if they missed their ship? "How much farther?"

"We're almost there."

The countryside was thickly wooded and the rutted road looked as if it saw little travel. They passed a small village and continued through without stopping. Then, as they crested a hill, Cara saw the villa sitting majestically at the crown. She stared at it, clearly impressed with the sprawling villa that resembled a small Mediterranean palace.

"We're here," Dom said as he pulled up in front of the villa. He got out of the car and went around to the passenger side to open the door for Cara.

"I really don't think we have time for this, Dom. How long will it take us to get back?"

He guided her up the front steps, opened the door and ushered her inside. "At least a week."

"What?"

"We're not going back, Cara mia. Not yet, anyway."

She gave a nervous titter. "Don't tease me, Dom. Of course we're going back. If we don't, the ship will sail without us."

"That's the idea, Cara mia. The ship is supposed to sail without us."

"Are you mad? What will Gil think when I fail to debark at Rome? You can't just kidnap me like this and get away with it."

"Can't I? Gil wants to take you back to Miami," Dom said. "Your vacation isn't over for another seven days. Give *me* those seven days, Cara. If you marry Gil you'll have to give up all your fantasies. Let me use these seven days to give you enough pleasure to last a lifetime."

"You *are* mad. Just because you have money and position doesn't mean you can kidnap me. Return me to the ship now, Dom, while there's still time. Don't spoil what we've had together."

Dom's square chin firmed. "I can't let you go back to Gil. Despite my playboy reputation, I've never disappointed a woman like Gil did you. In my opinion, he's a bastard. Had he loved you, he wouldn't have needed time to choose between you and his ex-wife. He should have sent her packing. I don't know how you can even consider returning to him."

"I told you, I haven't made up my mind."

He searched her face. "I think you have," he said quietly. "I've thought a long time about this, Cara, and decided you need more time to consider your options."

Cara laughed. "What options? There are only two that I know of. Marry Gil or don't marry Gil."

"Perhaps there are options you're not aware of," he said in a voice filled with promise. At least Cara thought it sounded like promise.

Chapter Four

"Ah, here's Sophia," Dom said as a plump elderly woman welcomed him with a cry of gladness. She rattled off a string of Italian words and threw herself into Dom's open arms. He hugged her tightly, then set her aside. He launched into rapid Italian, apparently issuing orders, for the woman kept nodding and sending sidelong glances in Cara's direction.

"I'm not here because I want to be," Cara said when the woman turned and smiled at her. "Dom kidnapped me. I should be aboard the *Odyssey* right now."

Sofia merely smiled and bobbed her head.

"She can't understand a word you're saying," Dom said complacently. He dismissed Sophia with a few words of instruction about their dinner and the woman trotted happily toward the kitchen.

"Sophia is my housekeeper. She lives nearby in a small cottage with her husband, Vito, the groundskeeper. He doesn't understand English, either. Would you like to go up to your room and freshen up before dinner?" Dom asked in a effort to forestall Cara's anger, which he could see gathering in her turbulent gaze. "Or would you prefer a tour of the villa first?"

"I know what you're doing, Dom, and it's not going to work," Cara returned shortly. "I'm angry, very angry. You planned this before we left the ship this morning, didn't you?"

"Guilty," Dom said, sending her a smile meant to pacify. It didn't.

"Look at the time! The ship has sailed without us," Cara ranted. "Tomorrow you *will* take me to Sorrento." Her voice brooked no argument. "I'll catch a flight to Rome and hopefully arrive about the time the *Odyssey* docks. I may still catch Gil at the terminal."

"I'm not taking you anywhere, Cara," Dom insisted. "At least not for the next week."

"But the ship . . . We can't just disappear without a word to anyone."

"I've already spoken to the captain. Everything was arranged ahead of time. Your suitcases are sitting upstairs in your room as we speak. They arrived while we were sightseeing."

"Well, it appears you've taken care of everything," Cara snapped with asperity. "The only thing you forgot was my permission."

"Do I have it?"

"No. I don't appreciate your underhandedness. Why have you done this?"

He caressed her cheek with the back of his hand, his eyes dark with sensual promise. "You know why."

She slapped his hand away. "There are other things in life besides sex. And that's all we have in common."

"Did you have even that much in common with Gil?" He didn't give her time to answer. "I seriously doubt it."

Dom had hit a raw nerve. No man, not even Gil, had taken her to heights she'd only fantasized about until Dom had proved that occasionally dreams did come true. But that didn't necessarily mean Gil wouldn't be a good husband, or that she couldn't be happy with a man whose lovemaking didn't light up the sky or shake her world.

"I could be happy with Gil," she asserted.

"That's the kind of thinking that convinced me to keep you here until you regained your senses," Dom said, trying to rationalize his decision.

"Why should it matter to you what I do? Whether or not I marry Gil shouldn't be of the slightest interest to you."

Dom frowned. "Are you implying these past few days meant nothing to you?"

"No! That's not what I meant at all," she returned quickly, too quickly. "Our time together has been incredible. You've given me enough memories to last several lifetimes. You've helped me through a rough time, Dom. I couldn't have done it without you. But we both know all good things eventually come to an end."

"It doesn't have to end, Cara."

Cara stared at him in consternation. "Of course it has to end. All shipboard romances die." Her voice was light despite the heaviness of her heart. "Our affair is but a brief interlude in our lives. A little hotter than most, maybe, but one that's bound to cool, and ours is—"

Dom didn't give her time to finish the sentence. He scooped her up into his arms and sprinted up the stairs, his face set with grim purpose. Cara thought he had gone mad as as he kicked open the door, carried her inside and slammed the door shut with his foot.

"Dom, what are you doing?" she asked on a note of panic.

"Proving that our attraction is as hot as it ever was. No amount of rationalizing will change the fact that we still want one another."

"Lust is a powerful emotion," Cara said without conviction.

What she felt for Dom went beyond simple lust, for all the good it did her. She still didn't know what he wanted from her, or why he was doing this. Neither of them intended for their affair to be anything but a brief dalliance. She'd read a great deal about Dom's affairs in the tabloids and and knew she could never be more than another of his conquests.

Dom mulled over Cara's words. He had been in lust before. His first marriage had been the result of that. And after his divorce he'd lusted after other beautiful women. Despite all that, he felt certain his affair with Cara was more than simply physical. The chemistry was right, of course, but there was a depth to it he'd never experienced before. It was that feel of something different that had compelled him to keep Cara away from her fiancé.

"You talk too much, Cara mia," Dom said as he set her down on the edge of the bed. He peeled off his polo. "I'm going to prove to you that our attraction is still alive and as strong as ever. It's not going to cool any time soon."

Cara's breath caught in her throat as she stared at his bare chest. A deep tan stretched across the incredible width of his shoulders and upper torso, interspersed with dark, curling hair. He still had a beautiful physique and she found herself anticipating the moment he would step out of his tennis shorts. Then he was naked and she released her breath in a long, drawn-out sigh as his fully aroused sex burst forth.

He posed before her, hands on hips. "As you can see for yourself, my lust for you hasn't diminished."

She swallowed convulsively, trying to suppress her excitement and failing miserably. She glanced at Dom, aware that he was watching her closely. She could tell by the amused smile curving his lips that he sensed her growing arousal.

He dropped to his knees beside the bed and removed her sneakers and socks.

"Lift your hips."

She wanted to refuse but her mouth had suddenly gone dry. He slid off her shorts and bikini panties and pushed her back onto the bed.

"Raise your arms."

Dear God, he had stolen her mind! She obeyed him like a puppet on a string, waiting breathlessly as he stripped her shirt up and over her head and removed her bra. She moaned as his hands cupped the soft weight of her breasts, brushing the tips with his fingers, gently stroking them into taut crests. Then he took one nipple into his mouth, sucking and laving the throbbing point with the rough tip of his tongue.

Cara gasped, her lungs striving for air. What a liar she'd been to tell Dom her lust for him was cooling. She groped for his hair, tunneling her fingers through the thick, silken locks. She clasped her palms over the nape of his neck, holding him in place as he diligently plied his tongue to her swelling nipples. Her heart was thundering so hard she thought she would expire with the pleasure he was giving her. She groaned a protest when his mouth left her breast. But the groan quickly turned into a sigh when he sought her lips.

His mouth was hot, yet his kisses were gently seductive as his tongue memorized her taste, her scent, her very essence. She responded eagerly, returning kiss for kiss, matching his passion with the intensity of her own.

An eternity passed before Dom's mouth left hers, sliding down her throat to explore tender, vulnerable places before continuing downward with agonizing slowness.

Dom's body was stiffly aroused; Cara felt the hard ridge of his sex pressing against her, demanding, as he took his mouth to that intensely sensitive place between her legs. Suddenly she shoved him away and reared up on her hands and knees. Dom sat back on his haunches, his brow raised inquiringly. He went very still, his eyes nearly crossing as she grasped his sex and took him into her mouth. His hips jerked spasmodically, thrusting into the sweet warmth of her mouth.

Cara heard him cry out and felt his hands on her, shoving her away. Then, with an efficiency of motion, he tossed her onto her back and buried his head between her thighs. She shrieked as he parted her with his tongue and delved deeply. An eternity later she arched sharply upward and climaxed into his mouth. She was still spasming when he rose above her and thrust inside, stroking her to even greater heights as he succumbed to the splendor of his own climax. He stayed inside her until she lay quiescent beneath him, then he carefully withdrew and flung himself down beside her.

"If you call *that* cooling attraction, then I'm Mickey Mouse," he panted. "Every time we come together it gets better and better. If it gets any better than this I'm likely to die from it." He gave her a cheeky grin. "What a way to go!"

"You think you're smart, don't you?"

"I proved a point, didn't I?"

"What point might that be?"

"You don't love Gil. Marrying him would be a mistake."

"Exactly who do you think I should marry?" she asked with a hint of sarcasm. "Do you have another man in mind? It will have to be one who wants children with me. One who is family oriented and has the same values as I do."

"Are you telling me Gil has all those qualities you require in a man?" Dom asked, obviously unconvinced.

Cara's chin raised to a stubborn angle. "One out of three isn't bad. Gil loves children."

"So do I."

She gave an unladylike snort of laughter. "You're a playboy. You've slept with more women than Trump has money."

"You've read too many tabloids. I've slept with my share of women but not as many as you seem to think."

"I didn't ask for numbers and I don't want to

know," Cara said with asperity. "Where is this leading, anyway?"

Dom stared at the ceiling. Where, indeed? he reflected. It was becoming increasingly apparent that he was becoming possessive of Cara Brooks. Not to mention obsessive. He definitely didn't want Gil to have her. Nor any other man, to be perfectly honest. He needed more time to figure out exactly where Cara fit into his life.

"I'm not sure," he said slowly. "But I suspect it will all make sense soon."

"Sorry, I can't wait around. Gil is waiting for me in Rome and your next conquest is probably waiting as well."

He didn't want to hear this. He turned her toward him and pulled her into his arms, placing a tender kiss on her lips. "You've become very necessary to me in a very short time, Miss Cara Brooks. What do you say to that?"

"I'd say that you're letting lust blind you to the truth."

"What exactly is the truth?"

"I wish I knew," she said on a sigh. "When I'm with you my mind doesn't seem to work."

"Then don't think. Don't try to figure this out. Just enjoy it like I am. Can you stop talking long enough for me to make love to you again?"

She did.

Much later Dom left her to shower and change, giving Cara time to take a good look at the exquisite bedroom. It was a large room, lavishly furnished with antiques and elegantly appointed. The papered walls were a soft blue with tiny yellow flowers and the double set of tall windows were draped in midnight blue velvet. Cara gazed out the window, mesmerized by the fantastic view of majestic mountains towering above a dark forest carpeted in green.

Flowered Oriental rugs pulled together all the colors in the room, and the fireplace lent it an old-world charm that soothed Cara's raw nerves. She wondered if the rest of the villa was as elegant and supposed she'd have a week to find out, since Dom was determined to keep her here that long.

Dimly she wondered what Gil would do when he discovered she wasn't on the *Odyssey*. Gil was the kind of man who demanded answers and she supposed he'd not rest until he found out what had happened to her. There was a remote possibility he'd trace her here. That thought made her uncomfortable and she cast it from her mind.

She sighed and shoved herself out of bed. She still had to shower and find something decent to wear tonight. All she had was what she'd packed in two suitcases and nothing was really that fancy or expensive.

Cara's gaze found Dom immediately when she entered the parlor an hour later. He was standing before the hearth with a drink in his hand and appeared completely at ease. Cara thought he looked stunningly handsome in casual gray trousers and open-necked shirt. He looked up just as she entered the room and gave her a slow, sensual smile that made her want to melt.

"You look wonderful," he said. "I'm glad you dressed casually." She had chosen something long, sheer and flowing. "I rarely dress formally in the country. This is the one place in the world I can be myself. No paparazzi. No one hounding me about business. There are no phones here except for my cell phone, and I can turn that off. I come here when I want to disappear from public view for awhile."

"I can understand why; it's magnificent. And so peaceful. Is Sophia responsible for the upkeep of the villa?"

"I'm the only one who comes here anymore. Whenever I'm in residence Sophia sends to the village for a cook and maids. Then there are various cleaning people who come on a weekly basis. It seems to work well. I told Sophia to keep it simple this time, the fewer servants around the better. I wanted this time alone with you."

Just then Sophia appeared in the doorway to announce dinner.

"Shall we go?" He tucked her arm under his and guided her into the formal dining room. Cara paused a moment to savor the ambiance of the room. Above them, the crystal chandelier sparkled like a hundred diamonds, bathing the table and dinnerware in brilliant light, clearly dazzling Cara.

They ate in companionable silence. The food was delicious. The soup was fragrant with oregano and the chicken cacciatore rich with red wine and spicy tomatoes. The salad, served at the end of the meal, cleansed the palate for the desert. Cannoli and espresso, a combination to die for. Champagne and red wine flowed freely throughout the evening.

"Your cook is excellent," Cara complimented.

"Lucia is Sophia's daughter. She lives in the village with her husband and children and comes when we need her. I count myself fortunate to have her."

Dom glanced at Cara but could read nothing in her expression. Was she still angry at him for whisking her off the *Odyssey* and bringing her here? he wondered. It wasn't well done of him but he couldn't allow her to walk out of his life and return to Gil without offering her options. On the heels of that thought came another. Exactly what options was he giving her? Offering marriage after so short a relationship didn't seem the responsible thing to do. God, he couldn't afford to make another mistake. His first wife had taken him to the cleaners, so to speak, coming out of the divorce with a considerable fortune.

His parents had been livid, accusing him of making poor choices. Next time he considered marriage he had to think long and hard about his decision before taking the plunge. He owed his parents a daughter-in-law they could be proud of.

Dom must have realized that his prolonged silence was unnerving Cara for she had begun to fidget. "Would you like to go for a stroll?" he asked. "The evening is warm and the view incredible by moonlight."

She rose so quickly she nearly knocked over the chair. "I'd like that very much."

"Cara, we're not strangers, there's no need to feel uncomfortable around me. We've been lovers for a week."

"It was different on the ship," Cara maintained. "There was no feeling of permanency about it. And we had such a good time exploring Santorini, Malta and Capri. But it's different here somehow. This is your home. I don't belong in your world. I'm out of my league."

"Why do you say that?"

"We're nothing alike. Gil is more suited to me than you are. You're a hedonist, Dom, a man who seeks pleasure for pleasure's sake, a man devoted entirely to self-indulgence."

"Then let me indulge you for the time we have left together. What's the harm?"

She studied his face, admiring the way his taut bronze skin emphasized the stark beauty of his bone structure, and suddenly realized that leaving this man was going to be difficult. She had been vulnerable and aching from Gil's rejection when she'd met Dom. Her heart had been damaged and

Dom had shown her that another man found her attractive.

Dom was special, but far too sophisticated for her. He belonged to society, to the rich and famous and the beautiful people. The world was his playground. He needed a flashy woman he could flaunt before his peers with pride. Still and all, he was a kindhearted man despite his worldliness and she loved him for attempting to soothe her aching heart. He'd sensed her dejection and had stepped in to fulfill a fantasy. It was exactly what she'd needed to lift her spirits. Unfortunately, he'd succeeded too well in his endeavor. In a few short days she'd grown close to Dom, closer than she'd been to Gil. She hated to put a label to her feelings, but if she wanted to be perfectly honest, she'd call it love.

Fortunately, knowledge that Dom wasn't for her kept her from making a total ass of herself and telling him how she felt.

"Cara, what are you thinking? You're so quiet."

She smiled brightly, too brightly. "I was just thinking about the moonlight and the stars. Let's go outside, Dom. A moonlight stroll will provide a perfect ending to my last day here."

He offered her his arm. "Dream on, sweet. I'm not ready to let you go yet."

Cara readied an angry retort but lost it in a soft sigh of resignation. To be perfectly honest, she wasn't ready to leave.

Chapter Five

Chapter Five

Flushed from the lovemaking that Dom had initiated after their stroll, Cara rested in Dom's arms. She knew she should try to sleep but there was so much to think about that her mind refused to shut down. Dom had told her that tomorrow they were going to drive down to Naples and take the family's private jet to Monte Carlo. He was indulging her fantasies at such a furious pace she barely had time to dream up new ones.

Monte Carlo was one of the Odyssey's ports of call, and Cara had been eagerly looking forward to visiting the famous resort. When Dom learned she'd never been to Monte Carlo, he made plans to take her there himself. Never mind that she was supposed to be seeing Monte Carlo with Gil; she couldn't imagine being there with anyone but Dom.

Sleep came before she'd solved the all-important question of what she was going to do when she finally came face-to-face with Gil.

Monte Carlo was fabulous. Cara was enjoying every minute of her visit. She had brushed elbows with the rich and famous and pretended she was one of them. In one of the casinos she'd caught a glimpse of Sean Penn and his wife. In a restaurant she'd seen Sharon Stone, and the star had even spoken to Dom. What a thrill that had been!

The excitement of gambling in the casinos and meeting celebrities overwhelmed her, not to mention the spectacular scenery and cosmopolitan atmosphere. Dom had provided her with chips and she'd gambled cautiously, suffering Dom's laughter when she'd refused to place large bets. Extravagance just wasn't her style. That night they saw a show featuring some of Hollywood's biggest names and then stayed overnight at the Monte Carlo Hotel.

The following day they flew back to Naples and drove up the mountain to the villa, the fairy-tale trip carefully tucked away in Cara's bag of memories. Most vivid of those memories was what had taken place in their bed the night before in the hotel. Their passion had literally exploded. What followed had been pure, erotic bliss.

Cara was relieved that today was to be a day of

rest and relaxation. Between jetting to beautiful places during the day and making love at night, she was exhausted. After lunch that day, she and Dom decided to relax in lounge chairs on the veranda overlooking the terraced garden. There had been no more stiffness between them since Cara had reconciled herself to the fact that Dom wasn't going to allow her to leave until she had given him the week he'd asked for. With only three days left, she'd begun to dread the inevitable leave-taking.

How could she bear saying good-bye? The thought of never seeing Dom again was exceedingly painful, extinguishing every spark of happiness their brief affair had brought her. Dom had added a special ingredient to her life that few women were privileged to experience. She was grateful for having the opportunity to know him. Though life would never be the same, she realized she must go on without him.

Yes, Cara reflected, that's exactly what she would do. Be grateful for the experience and make a future without Dom, no matter how painful. Cara firmly believed their time together didn't mean as much to Dom as it did to her. He was accustomed to courting women and indulging their fantasies while she lived in a tightly structured world where partings hurt. Partings to Dom were viewed as inevitable, she knew. Something that always followed an affair. She supposed she would live through it, though she didn't know how.

"Someone's coming up the road," Dom said, shading his eyes with his hand. He frowned. "Wonder who it could be? No one knows we're here."

Cara watched the small Fiat wend its way up the narrow mountain road. Suddenly she shivered, seized by an inexplicable feeling of apprehension.

"Go inside," Dom said, rising abruptly. "I'll walk around to the front and see who's calling. I'll get rid of whoever it is as fast as I can. I don't want anything or anyone to interrupt the short time we have left together."

Cara didn't argue. She walked through the French doors and continued on to the front of the house, where she could watch through the windows without being seen. She didn't have a good feeling about this.

The car braked at the end of the gravel driveway. A man opened the door and stepped out. Dom didn't recognize him. Sunlight reflected off his longish blond hair and pale complexion, leading Dom to believe the man was a stranger to sunshine. Dom had seen his type before. Men like him usually spent their days in galleries and museums.

Comprehension dawned. *Gil!* It had to be. Dom waited on the front steps, mentally preparing himself for Gil's anger by summoning his own. *This* was the bastard who had jilted Cara on the eve of their wedding and made her feel worthless. *This* was the man who had asked for her forgiveness and intended to give her a life in which she wouldn't be happy.

Gil Tallman was somewhat shorter than Dom. His eyes were light blue, his lashes nearly colorless. He had an air about him that reeked of authority. Without knowing him Dom thought him pompous and overbearing.

"Are you Dominic Domani?" Gil asked pugnaciously as he boldly confronted him.

Dom liked nothing about Gil. Not his tone of voice, his looks, nor his attitude.

"I am. Who are you and what do you want?"

"I'm Gil Tallman." He waited for Dom's reaction. When he received none, he said, "I'm Cara's fiancé. I've come to take her home."

"Ah, you're the bastard who left her standing at the altar," Dom intoned dryly.

Dom's insulting words seemed to irritate Gil. "If anyone is a bastard, you are. You took unfair advantage of the woman I'm going to marry."

"*I* didn't jilt Cara," Dom sneered. "*I* didn't make her feel worthless and unwanted."

"*I* didn't sleep with another man's intended," Gil charged. "*I* didn't take advantage of her vulnerability."

"Cara wouldn't have been vulnerable if you hadn't jilted her," Dom contended.

"Maybe not, but you made her your whore."

Rage seethed through Dom. He was overwrought to the point of violence. Never had he come so close to committing murder. He acted without a thought to the consequences and felt better for it. Doubling his fists, he decked Gil. Gil let out a strangled yelp and hit the ground hard. He lay there unmoving as Dom dusted his hands off with supreme satisfaction.

Suddenly Cara came flying out of the house. She had watched Gil and Dom through the windows and could tell they were arguing, but she hadn't expected violence.

"What have you done?" Cara cried, bending down to inspect Gil's bruised face. "He's not moving. You've killed him!"

"I couldn't be that lucky," Dom said, sneering down at the unconscious man. "He'll come around in a minute or two. The bastard deserved it. How in the hell could you believe yourself in love with a man like that?"

"You don't know him," Cara cried. Truth to tell, she'd been asking herself the same thing. But there was no time for introspection now. Gil was starting to come around. He groaned and opened his eyes.

"Cara! Thank God I've found you." He rose shakily to his feet, glaring balefully at Dom. "The bastard struck me! Get your things. You're coming home with me."

"How did you find me?" Cara asked.

"Not from the captain of the *Odyssey*," Gil said, clearly disgruntled. "He told me nothing beyond the fact that you had left the ship at Sorrento. But if nothing else I'm tenacious. I rented a car and drove down to Sorrento to learn the truth for my-self. I found a boatman who recalled taking you and your . . . er, Domani, to Capri, so I knew you were with a man. I kept digging until I located the man who brought your luggage up here to Do-mani's villa. Cost me a small fortune in bribes." He paused.

"Did Domani seduce you?"

"It wasn't like that, Gil. It just happened. I'm not going to make excuses for something I could have stopped any time I chose."

"This man is a sophisticated con, a master of the art of seduction, whereas you're an innocent in his world." He searched her face. "He did seduce you, didn't he?"

Dom decided it was time to step in. "Stop bad-gering her, Tallman. Cara doesn't need to explain herself to you. You lost that right when you jilted her."

"Who in the hell do you think paid for that cruise?"he all but shouted.

"Who forced her to take the cruise alone?" Dom shot back.

Gil had the grace to flush. "I don't have to stand here and take this. Cara doesn't belong here with you. That's why I'm taking her back home. Whether or not Cara and I end up marrying doesn't matter. Cara isn't sophisticated enough for you. One day she's going to end up regretting the choices she's made."

"Why not let Cara decide," Dom said, turning to

Cara. "Do you want to return home with Tallman, Cara mia?"

No! No! No! Her heart rejected utterly what her mind knew to be the right decision. She was living in a fantasy world that had but one ending. She knew it as well as she knew that marrying Gil would be a terrible mistake. She wasn't now, nor had she ever been, head over heels in love with Gil. Wanting to marry and have children didn't necessarily guarantee a loving marriage. The ease with which she had become Dom's lover proved she didn't belong with Gil.

Cara believed that Gil's words made sense, however. She had to return to the real world sometime and the longer she delayed, the deeper her love for Dom would grow. Even now the pain of loss was so crushing she could barely breathe.

"Cara, tell me what you're thinking," Dom prodded.

She stared up at him, her eyes blurry with unshed tears. "I'm leaving with Gil," she said on a sob. "It's time for me to leave, Dom. We both knew this day was coming. I'm going upstairs to pack."

Dom felt as if his world had just collapsed around him. "You're going back to him? After what he did to you?"

"I didn't say that. What I said was that I'm returning home."

She turned abruptly and disappeared inside the house. Dom followed. When he sensed Gil behind him he whirled around, his face set in determined lines. "Wait out here, Tallman. I don't want you inside my house."

"Don't try to work your wiles on her, Domani. I know your kind. The whole world knows your kind. Cara is nothing to you but a warm body."

Dom sent Gil a look so filled with rancor that Gil stopped in his tracks.

"Very well," Gil said, rubbing his sore jaw. "I'll wait out here. Tell Cara not to dally."

The door to Cara's room was standing ajar. Dom walked inside and quietly closed the door behind him. He saw Cara staring at something in her hands but paid it little heed.

"Are you sure this is what you want, Cara?"

Apparently unaware of his presence, Cara started violently, dropping whatever it was she'd been holding. "I didn't hear you come in. What was your question?"

He repeated his question.

"What I want doesn't matter."

He thought he heard a catch in her voice but couldn't be sure. "It matters to me. I intended to fly you home in my jet when the time came."

She stared at him. "When would that be, Dom? When you tired of me? When I became so hopelessly in love with you I couldn't survive without you?"

Dom shrugged. "Our parting would be a mutual decision. Perhaps . . ." He was going out on a limb here. "Perhaps I'd never tire of you. What would you say to that?"

She gave him a sad smile. "I'd say you were lying. Or having pipe dreams. Our affair has run its course. I'll never forget you, or the way you came to my rescue. No woman has ever lived a fantasy as beautiful as the one you created for me. You promised me pleasure and delivered beyond my wildest dreams."

"Cara, listen to me." He tipped her chin up. "There's something I want to say. Something to which I've given a lot of thought. I think I'm falling in love with you."

He heard her breath catch. "You may feel that way now but it won't last, no matter how sincere you think you are," Cara said. "It's that lust thing again. We had some wonderful times together. The sex was fantastic. Unfortunately, I'm not sure either of us knows the meaning of love."

"If that's how you feel, don't marry Gil. He's not right for you."

"I rather doubt Gil wants me after finding me here with you." She gave him a mirthless smile. "I doubt he ever really loved me."

"Why is he here, then?" Dom didn't like the way she was belittling herself. She sounded so damned forlorn he wanted to shake some sense into her. Then he wanted to take her in his arms and comfort her.

"I suppose Gil's pride is showing. The shoe is on the other foot now. I chose an affair with you over marriage to him."

Dom grasped her shoulders and gave her a little

shake. "Dammit, Cara, don't talk like that. You sound guilt-ridden and guilt doesn't become you. People have affairs every day."

"I don't."

"I was too experienced for you. I swept you away. I seduced you when you were at your most vulnerable. If anyone is to blame, it's me."

She gave him a wobbly smile. "I'm not blaming anyone. What we had together was wildly exciting and I don't regret a moment of it. Don't think of me as a helpless female, because I'm not. I'm a successful editor of a popular magazine. One day a man will come along with all the qualifications I require. And if no one fits the bill, why, I'll adopt that child I want so very much. Meanwhile, I have my work, my friends and my family. So you see?" she said brightly, "there are always options."

"I said I was falling in love with you, you silly fool!"

"Men like you are inclined to love unwisely."

"I have every reason to believe you love me," he persisted.

"I do love you," she said wistfully. "You'll always have a part of me."

"I want all of you."

"No, you don't. You might think that now, but you'll come to your senses once I'm gone."

He pulled her against him, his face so close she could see how deeply he was troubled. Then all thought ceased as Dom's hard mouth came down on hers. His kisses were frantic, almost punishing in their intensity. It was apparent to Cara that he was trying to force her to acknowledge her feelings for him with sexual persuasion. Incredible sex was the one absolute they had in common, and as he carried her with him onto the bed, she realized that would never change.

In one deft motion he stripped off her shorts and panties. His fingers delved through a forest of silken curls, parted the tender folds of her sex, and glided through gathering moisture to reach her heat. She heard him groan and arched up against his hand, bringing his fingers deeper inside her as he teased the petals of her sex.

"Dom, you have to stop," she gasped. "Gil is waiting for me."

"To hell with Gil. I'm coming inside you, sweet."

He pulled off his shirt and skimmed his shorts and underwear down his hips. Cara's eyes widened. He was gloriously nude and spectacularly aroused. With a will of their own her legs opened wide to welcome him as he thrust into her silken heat. Her last coherent thought was that she fit him as if she'd been made for him.

Cara trembled and moaned as Dom rocked against her, and she met his thrusts forcefully, seized with nearly mindless pleasure. Her face was transfixed, her mouth drawn taut, her eyes tightly closed. Suddenly all those sensations Dom had stoked inside her erupted in a white-hot burst of rapture. She screamed his name and went limp beneath him. Dom continued thrusting, wringing one last cry from her before spending himself deep inside her.

When the storm passed, he rose slowly, pulled on his clothing, and sat at the edge of the bed, his head resting in his hands.

"I'm sorry, Cara, I don't know what got into me. That was uncalled for. Forgive me."

Cara lifted her hand to smooth back his rumpled locks, thought better of it, and quickly lowered it. She couldn't give in to weakness now. Not after she'd already made up her mind about leaving. Not with Gil waiting outside for her.

"You're forgiven," she said, avoiding his gaze when he finally looked up at her. "Holding grudges at this point in our relationship is pointless." She scooted off the bed and went into the bathroom.

Dom grew thoughtful as he listened to the sound of running water. This was a first for him. He'd never cared for another woman like he cared for Cara. Why couldn't she believe he was falling in love with her? What did she have against giving their relationship time to mature and ripen? He needed time to discover whether the emotions he felt for Cara were simple lust or once-in-a-lifetime love.

Admittedly his reputation was somewhat tarnished, but men could change, couldn't they? Especially when a man found his soulmate. He regretted every one of those tabloid stories that had paired him with dozens of women he cared nothing about. He knew his reputation was to blame for sending Cara back into the arms of her fiancé and didn't know how to repair the damage. He supposed the best thing he could do for her was allow her time to search her heart.

Cara came out of the bathroom and pulled on a pair of jeans she found folded on top of her open suitcase. Her eyes were swollen and red and Dom wondered if she'd been crying. Hurting her was the last thing he wanted to do.

"Is there anything I can do for you?" he asked, gaining control of his emotions.

"I'm almost packed. You can carry my suitcases down."

"Is there nothing I can say or do to stop you from leaving with Gil?"

"You've done and said quite enough, thank you." Her expression softened. "I'll never forget you, Dom. I'll always remember that you loved me for a little while. I don't think I'll tell anyone about you, though. The memories are too precious to share. You know"—she gave a sad little smile—"I don't think I'll ever indulge in fantasies again. The ending hurts too much and I'm far too practical to believe in forever after."

She sounded so desolate that Dom ached to comfort her, but he didn't dare touch her again. As for forever after, perhaps Cara was right. Forever existed only in fantasies. He thought about his playboy image, aware that he had cultivated his reputation by romancing some of the loveliest women in the world. It had become a way of life. He probably couldn't change now if he wanted to. He'd marry, of course, but his wife would have to be content to remain at home, raising his children while he continued his wicked ways.

Dom grimaced. The scenario he'd just painted sounded unpalatable, even to a man as jaded as he. He didn't want that at all. These past days with Cara had given him a glimpse of a life far different from what he'd been accustomed to. He'd always wanted children, and the prospect of having children with Cara was suddenly something he craved above all things. And a home. He was bored out of his skull with jet-setters. Thank God he'd never done drugs, but he had plenty of friends who did.

Unfortunately, Cara still saw him in the same way the tabloids portrayed him. A womanizer without scruples. A man with jaded appetites and a roving eye.

"I'll carry your suitcases down," Dom said. It was difficult, but he had finally resigned himself to her leaving.

"They're all ready," Cara said, slamming down the lid on the last suitcase.

They stood in the center of the room, staring at one another in tense silence. The air surrounding them was as thick as mist rolling off the Atlantic.

"Don't look so grim, Dom," Cara said, trying to keep her tone light and teasing. "I told you I don't regret one thing about us. We each have our own place in this world and mine isn't with you. Love is fleeting. I'll bet you'll forget me before the Fiat is out of sight."

"That's one bet you'd lose," he said in a voice she'd never heard before. "Come on, if you don't show up soon, Gil will bust in here and carry you out by force." He picked up her suitcases and headed out the door.

They found Gil pacing back and forth before the front door.

"What in the hell took you so long?" he shouted, sending Dom a virulent look. "I suppose the bastard was trying to talk you into staying. I'm glad to see you were smart enough not to listen to him. He's no good for you, Cara. His life is an open book. He uses women and tosses them aside like unwanted baggage."

"Are you jealous, Tallman?" Dom sneered. "Do you hate it because Cara found something with me she didn't have with you?"

"I don't have to stand here and listen to this crap," Gil blasted. "Get in the car, Cara."

Gil opened the door and Cara settled inside while he placed her suitcases in the trunk. Then he slid into the driver's seat, slammed the door and started the engine.

Cara's frantic gaze sought Dom's. His face looked as desperate as hers did, though he did attempt a smile. She looked away, fearing she'd change her mind if she looked at him a moment longer. She wanted to end their affair with dignity, before it died of natural causes.

Dom's smile vanished the moment the Fiat sped away. He watched until the car rounded a curve and was no longer visible. Then he turned away and entered the house. Moments later he was on the cell phone, making arrangements to fly to Paris. He was a playboy, wasn't he? Cara had called him a hedonist and she had pegged him right. Even if his heart wasn't in it, he was going to do what playboys and hedonists did best.

Chapter Six

"How could you do such a thing?" Gil ranted as he negotiated the curving road. "It isn't like you to go off with a man you hardly know. You know damn well he wanted only one thing from you."

"Perhaps I wanted the same thing from him," Cara retorted angrily. She didn't care what Gil thought.

He sent her a sidelong glance. "We were great together in the sack. What does *he* have that I don't?"

"It's difficult to explain. I thought you had ditched me for good. I was despondent and feeling rejected. Dom came along when I needed him most."

"Why didn't you end the affair when I indicated

I wanted you back?" Gil asked. He sounded puzzled and hurt, yet Cara couldn't muster pity for him. "It didn't work out with Lisa, and I felt guilty about leaving you stranded on the ship."

"I don't want your guilt, Gil. I wanted your love. Apparently you're still in love with your ex-wife."

"I was confused, is all. A lot of men get cold feet at the last minute."

"The man who truly loves me won't get cold feet," Cara assured him.

"I assume our marriage is off."

She gaped at him. "You still want to marry me?"

He focused his attention on the narrow road, apparently mulling over his answer.

"It's all right, Gil," Cara said. "I couldn't go through with our marriage now, anyway. I wouldn't expect you to want me after finding me with another man. Just as I wouldn't want to marry a man who can't choose between me and his ex-wife. You may not want my advice but I'm giving it. Go back to Lisa. I think you two belong together."

Gil stepped on the brakes and pulled the car over to the side of the road. "I wasn't going to tell you, but I think it's best in view of your affair. Lisa and I . . . we've been seeing each other for some time. I know we're no good together, but I just can't seem to let her go. We can't stand living together but neither can we bear being apart.

"Why did you propose to me if you felt that way?"

"I hoped you'd help me get over my obsession with Lisa."

"You've been sleeping with Lisa and still you . . . we . . . oh, God, what a fool I've been! No wonder you decided we shouldn't move in together until after we were wed. How long did Lisa wait to climb into your bed after I left it?"

"I truly do care for you, Cara. I wanted our marriage to work. I was even willing to have children with you to make you happy. What Lisa and I have together isn't healthy, it's obsessive. I wanted a clean break with her but I don't have the strength to cut ties on my own. I was hoping marriage to you would . . ."

"It would solve nothing," Cara said with firm conviction. I'm glad you got cold feet and left me stranded aboard the *Odyssey*. It didn't do much for my ego but it saved me from coming to grief later. I'm surprised you bothered to follow me here, feeling as you do."

He paused, then said, "I wasn't going to. When I learned you had left the ship I was going to leave you to your own devices. Then I learned who you had taken up with and knew you were out of your league. Dominic Domani would have used you and spit you out. I felt duty bound to rescue you from a damaging relationship."

She gave an unladylike snort. "Thanks for nothing. I would have left in another day or two without your interference. But Dom isn't what you think. He's kind and generous and—"

"My God! You sound like you've fallen in love with him. Thank God I arrived when I did. His kind eats women like you alive."

Gil started the engine and turned the car back onto the road.

Cara fell silent. It hurt to think that their engagement had been a farce. Gil had never loved her. She was just a means to an end. While she was planning a future with Gil, he was having sex with his ex-wife on the side. She suspected strongly that he would have gone right on seeing Lisa after their marriage. She should have felt the crushing weight of rejection and was surprised she didn't. She supposed she had Dom to thank for that.

The way she looked at it, nothing but good had come from her brief affair with Dom. The hard part was returning to the real world and its humdrum trials and tribulations. She'd never forget Dom, but she hoped that in time the pain of losing him would fade into a dull ache.

"I'm sorry it turned out this way, Cara," Gil said.

"I'm not. How long would you have gone on two-timing me with Lisa? Why in the world did you wire me aboard the ship and come all this way if you didn't want to marry me?"

"But I *did* want to marry you!" he claimed. "I told you, Lisa and I are no good together. We fight all the time. Marriage to you would have been peaceful and less emotionally draining."

"And you'd go on seeing Lisa behind my back," Cara charged.

"You don't know that. I don't even know that. The point is moot now. You had your fling and I told you about my affair with Lisa. It's all out in the open. Of course marriage for us is out of the question now. We'd never trust one another again."

Cara thought that was the understatement of the century. "Where are we going?"

"To Rome. We have reservations on a flight to Miami. We fly out tomorrow. You'll get home in time to rest up a day or two before returning to work."

Cara leaned back and closed her eyes, filing away her fantasies in a small corner of her mind, where she could retrieve them at will and recall the pleasure.

Six Weeks Later

Cara clutched the latest issues of *Star Magazine* in one hand and *National Enquirer* in the other as she walked into her office at *Fashion Wise*. She set down her purse and spread out both tabloids on her desk. With aching heart she studied Dom's beloved features. In one tabloid he was photographed in Paris with a beautiful starlet on his arm. In the other he was at the Cannes Film Festival, flaunting a dark-haired, statuesque Italian model. In each picture he was looking at the woman with an expression Cara remembered well.

He was smiling, of course, his lean face and handsome features literally reeking with sensuality. And yet . . . The photographs revealed something else. She recognized a look of sadness about his eyes. As if no matter how hard he tried to live up to his reputation, there was something definitely lacking.

"You're a fool, Cara," she said aloud. How could she possibly see all that in a photograph? She turned her attention to the articles. The *Star* said Dominic Domani was contemplating marriage to the fiery-eyed Italian model. The *Enquirer* said a leggy Hollywood starlet had captured Dom's heart and was leading him on a merry chase.

Both tabloids reported that Domani had disappeared from the scene a few weeks before and was reemerging again. There was speculation about which of the women pictured with him had been his companion in seclusion. Cara closed her eyes and pictured herself in Dom's arms, making love with him. She recalled his words the day she'd left him. He'd said he was falling in love with her. She gave a mirthless laugh. So much for love.

"Would you like a cup of coffee?"

Cara's secretary stood in the doorway, a smile on her expressive dark features. "Thanks, Keesha, you always know how to lift my spirits in the morning. I didn't have time for coffee at home."

Keesha studied Cara's gaunt features as she

handed her the foam cup filled with strong black coffee, just the way Cara liked it. "Are you all right, Cara? You haven't been yourself since you returned from your vacation."

By now everyone in the office knew that Cara and Gil were no longer a couple and had carefully avoided the subject around her.

Cara sipped the coffee, felt her stomach rebel and clapped a hand over her mouth.

Keesha's brow furrowed in concern. "Are you ill? You look pale this morning. Shall I cancel your appointments? Perhaps you should see a doctor."

"I'm fine, Keesha, thank you for being concerned. It will pass. It usually does." She took another cautious sip of coffee and smiled when it seemed to settle.

"Did you eat breakfast?"

"I . . . no."

"Sally brought in some jelly doughnuts this morning. Shall I fetch you one?"

Cara gagged and looked away. "No doughnut. Are there any crackers in the office? Perhaps that would help settle my stomach."

Keesha stared at her, her dark eyes suddenly filled with understanding. "I'll go see."

Cara settled down into her chair, pouring over articles about Dom and his current lovers. She hadn't expected it to hurt so much. She knew Dom was doing what Dom did best, romancing beautiful women.

She squeezed her eyes shut and remembered

the birth control pills she thought she had forgotten to bring along with her on the cruise. She had wanted to get pregnant during her honeymoon and assumed she'd left them at home on purpose. She didn't realize she'd packed them until she'd found them in her suitcase at the villa. By then it was already too late.

Except for the first two times she and Dom had made love, she'd had unprotected sex. She hadn't actually told him she wasn't on the pill but neither had she lied to him. She hadn't meant to deceive him. She'd been on the pill a long time and assumed it would take a while for her to get pregnant. The last time she'd taken the pill had been the day before she left Miami for her wedding and honeymoon aboard the *Odyssey*.

It was too late to worry about it now, she thought, lightly touching her flat stomach. She was pregnant with Dom's child. Just to make sure, she had taken a pregnancy test after she missed her period. The results were positive. And if she still had doubts, morning sickness arrived soon after with a vengeance.

Keesha returned with a box of soda crackers. "Tori had a whole box in her desk drawer. She's several weeks pregnant and swears they're the only thing that gets her through the mornings." She searched Cara's face. "Are you pregnant, Cara?"

Cara ate two crackers before she felt strong enough to reply. No sense keeping it a secret, she decided. Everyone would know soon enough. "The test came out positive."

"Are you happy about that?"

Keesha's query startled her. Was she happy about becoming an unwed mother? She hadn't allowed herself to really *think* about it yet. She wanted time to savor the joy of having a child growing inside her. These days there was little or no stigma attached to having a child out of wedlock, so she expected no problem there. With sudden insight she realized she wasn't just happy, she was ecstatic. She gave Keesha a smile that lit up her face. "Actually, Keesha, I'm very happy. It's just that I'd always assumed I'd be married when I had children."

"Does Gil know? I know something happened on the cruise that caused a breakup, and I don't want to pry, but I think the father of your child should know he's about to become a daddy."

Cara glanced down at the tabloids still spread across her desk and saw Dom's image waver before her eyes. In the pictures he appeared to be intensely interested in his companion. Or should she say lover? He was indulging another woman's fantasy now, she thought, dashing away a tear from the corner of her eye. She sighed and pulled her emotions back into place before answering Keesha.

"Gil isn't the father."

Keesha's dark eyes widened. "He isn't? I thought . . . That is . . . Sorry, Cara, I didn't mean to butt into your personal life. Is there anything I can get you?"

"No, thank you. I'll call you in for dictation later." Her gaze returned to the tabloids, drawn to Dom's image by something so powerful it was like a physical grip.

"I didn't know you read the tabloids," Keesha said, moving to look over her shoulder. "That's Dominic Domani. What a hunk! He's almost as handsome as Denzel Washington. He was even linked once with Princess Diana."

"I wouldn't put too much store in rumors, Keesha. You know how the tabloids exaggerate. Perhaps Mr. Domani is nothing like the image he presents to the world."

Keesha snickered. "Yeah, and maybe I'm not black. Oh, well, it's time I got back to work." She paused in the doorway. "Cara, if you want to talk, you know where to find me. I know having this baby is a big decision for you. There are options, you know."

"Not for me. But thanks, anyway. Go on, get out of here," Cara said with a smile, "We both have work to do."

After Keesha left, Cara made a few phone calls but couldn't settle down to business. All she could think about was the baby, Dom's baby. There was no possibility that it could be Gil's child because they'd been too busy during the weeks before their cruise to think about sex, much less have any. Besides, she'd been on the pill.

She touched her stomach. She was still flat and probably wouldn't show for another couple of months. Time enough to break the news to her parents. They weren't going to take it well, she knew, but being the kind of people they were, they would support her decision to keep her child.

She allowed herself to imagine Dom's reaction were she to tell him she was expecting his baby. He'd said he loved children. He'd probably support his child lavishly, and she believed he would love it, too. The fantasy ended there, however, for she'd never see Dom to tell him about his impending fatherhood. And even if she were to see him, she doubted she'd tell him. His extravagant lifestyle did not lend itself to home, hearth and family, and she'd never accept a philanderer for a husband. In *her* fantasy her husband would be faithful.

Cara didn't regret having known and loved Dom all those passion-filled nights and days they'd spent together. Nor could she regret this baby she carried beneath her heart. She'd be both father and mother, she vowed, already thinking of the tiny mite inside her as a person. She sighed and put the tabloids away. Looking at them only made her remember.

Cara's morning sickness ran its course another two weeks before she began to enjoy food again. After a few hearty meals the gauntness left her cheeks and she gained the weight she had lost during the first weeks of her pregnancy. She made plans to visit Atlanta the following weekend, to tell her parents about the baby. She was naturally nervous and hoped they wouldn't be too disappointed in her.

One day the door to her office burst open and Keesha flew inside. She fluttered her arms about, apparently too excited to speak.

"Keesha, what is it? You look like you've seen a ghost?"

"He's here!" Keesha gasped, her dark eyes aglow with excitement. "Right here in our offices. I didn't even know he was in Miami."

"Keesha, quit babbling,. Settle down and tell me what you're talking about. Who is here?"

"I think she's trying to tell you that I'm here," Dom said from the doorway. "May I come in?"

Cara leapt to her feet, startled beyond comprehension as she cried out his name.

"Dom! What are you doing here?"

She stared at him. He appeared tan and fit and more gorgeous than she remembered.

"You know him?" Keesha asked, clearly awed. "You know Dominic Domani?"

"Quite well," Dom said, sending Keesha one of those devastating smiles for which he was famous. "I've missed you, Cara mia." His voice held a wealth of feeling.

A glance at Keesha informed Cara that her secretary was as overwhelmed by Dom's sudden appearance as she. And curious. Keesha was a savvy woman. It wouldn't take long for her to put two and two together.

Dom couldn't take his eyes off Cara. She appeared to be flourishing. She had a glow about her that surpassed his vivid memory of her. And there was damn little he hadn't remembered about her. "Can we talk privately, Cara?"

"Oh," Keesha said, as if realizing suddenly that she was intruding upon a very private moment. "I should get back to work. I'll see that you're not disturbed."

Neither Dom nor Cara heard her. That old magnetism that had drawn them together from the beginning was still sound, still vibrantly alive. The air around them fairly crackled with tension. Absence had stretched the bond between them, but it hadn't been severed. What they once had together was still intact and as compelling as ever.

"You're looking well," Dom said, searching her face.

"So are you." God, why was she so tongue-tied? "What are you doing here?"

One dark brow slanted sharply upward. "I hoped you'd be glad to see me." He sounded almost disappointed.

"I am. I'm just surprised, is all. Did that Italian model accompany you?"

"You've been reading the tabloids."

Cara flushed. "Guilty as charged."

"Adriana isn't with me. You didn't marry Gil."

"No, it was a mutual decision."

"I'm glad. You're better off without him."

She shrugged. "I suppose I am."

"Are you seeing anyone else?"

She shook her head. "I've been too busy. But I see you haven't let any grass grow under your feet."

"Guilty as charged," he said, using her own phrase. He walked around the desk until he was close enough for her to see the longing in his eyes. "You're a difficult woman to forget, Cara Brooks. Lord knows I tried hard enough."

He was standing so close Cara was overcome by the familiar heat of his body and the unique, slightly musky scent that was his alone. She must have been mad to think she could walk away from Dominic Domani and expect life to go on. She hadn't seen him for weeks, yet two minutes in his company brought back all those feelings she'd tried so desperately to forget.

"Will you have dinner with me tonight?" Dom asked.

"I don't think we should be seen together publicly. It would be devastating to see my name splashed across the tabloids as your next conquest."

"I *need* to see you, to be with you."

No more than I need to be with you, Cara's heart cried in silent supplication. But she had to remain firmly planted on the ground. No more fantasies, no more dreaming of things beyond her reach.

"Come to my apartment for dinner tonight,"

Cara heard herself saying. Her words shocked her but it was too late to call them back. "Eight o'clock. Don't expect anything fancy. And try not to bring the paparazzi with you." She wrote her address on a note pad, tore off the sheet and handed it to him.

She started to turn away but Dom's arm came around her, pulling her against him. He grasped her chin between his thumb and forefinger and tilted it upward, forcing her to look into his eyes.

"I've missed you so much," he whispered. The glow in his eyes was like looking into the belly of a volcano about to erupt.

She stared at his mouth and desperately wanted to feel those soft, full lips against hers. She wanted to open her mouth and taste his essence, to melt against him, to absorb him into her pores. She wanted to take him inside her, to bring him to that place where their baby rested. She wanted the fantasy he'd begun to last forever.

Impossible dreams? Definitely. Dom wasn't a forever kind of man.

Dom saw Cara's lips part and groaned, seized by the uncontrollable need to hold her against his heart and never let her go. This was the woman he'd traveled across the ocean to reclaim. This was the woman he wanted forever and ever. He wanted to be in her, around her, over her.

Impossible dreams? Dom didn't think so. He knew he could be the forever kind of man Cara wanted. All he had to do was convince her.

Cara opened her mouth to speak and he sealed her words with a kiss; a poignantly tender touching of lips. Abruptly he tore his mouth away from hers, cradling her face between his palms, reluctant to lose the contact he'd craved for so long.

"Until tonight, Cara mia."

Then he was gone.

Chapter Seven

The peal of the doorbell echoed through the silent rooms. Excitement spiraled through Cara as she paused before the hall mirror and gazed at her image. She smoothed an errant tendril of burnished hair away from her forehead, checked her lipstick and eyed her dress critically. The sleeveless chiffon creation still fit her perfectly . . . well, maybe not so perfectly. It did pull slightly across the breasts, and the neckline seemed to show a little more of her, but that couldn't be helped.

She'd worn the chiffon dress once before and was sure Dom would recognize it, but she didn't care; he'd liked it well enough the first time she'd worn it. The doorbell pealed again, more urgent this time. Cara moved toward the door on shaking legs. She had no idea what this night would bring, or whether she would tell Dom about the baby, but of one thing she was certain. She didn't need Dom in order to have this baby, to love it and to support it financially.

Settling a smile on her face, she opened the door, her heart constricting when Dom greeted her with that sensual smile she adored.

"For a minute I thought you weren't going to answer." He held a bottle of champagne in one hand and a huge bouquet of roses in the other. "Are you going to ask me in?"

She flushed and stepped aside, letting her eyes roam hungrily over him. He had dressed casually in perfectly tailored tan trousers, open-necked white shirt and brown sports jacket. A gold chain in the vee of his open shirt caught her eye and she stared at his chest, recalling the heat and hardness of his body. The memories were painfully distracting; she blinked and raised her gaze to his dark, glittering gaze.

"You have a nice apartment," Dom complimented.

Cara wondered how he'd come to that conclusion when he'd looked at nothing but her since he'd entered the room. "It's nothing grand, but it suits me. It's a condo, actually. I bought it two years ago."

Shifting his eyes away from hers, his gaze made a slow perusal of the room and its furnishings, finally coming back to rest on Cara. "It *does* suit you. Did you decorate it yourself? I like the mix of antiques with modern. You've put a lot of thought into it."

Cara nodded, held immobile by the dark intensity of his gaze. She literally had to shake herself to sever the invisible strings binding her to him.

He held out the flowers and champagne. "These are for you. I know how much you love champagne and roses."

She accepted the gifts with a murmured thank-you and headed to the kitchen for a vase. She turned to tell Dom she'd be right back and found him a step behind her.

"I thought I'd open the champagne for us," he explained as he followed her into the kitchen. He sniffed appreciatively. "Mmm, smells good in here. I didn't know you could cook."

"I cook very well. I hope you like Cornish hens and dressing. I was lucky enough to find fresh artichokes in the open-air market on the way home. I remembered that you liked them."

He gave her a seductive smile that made Cara lose her train of thought. "I hope you remember more than that about me because I've forgotten nothing about you. Shall I pour the champagne?"

Cara hadn't consumed any alcohol since she'd learned she was pregnant and wondered how she was going to explain her reluctance to drink with Dom. She watched Dom pop the cork and tried to come up with an answer. Nothing came to mind.

"Where are your champagne flutes?" Dom asked.

Cara found two flutes in the cupboard and set them down on the ceramic tile counter. Dom poured and handed one to her.

"A toast," Dom said, holding his flute aloft. "To us. To pleasure. To forever."

Cara's glass froze in midair. "That's a strange toast, Dom. Nothing is forever. Especially not us."

He gave her an enigmatic smile. "Not as strange as you think, Cara. Will you drink with me?"

He clinked his glass against hers and raised it to his lips. He didn't drink, though, until Cara took a tiny sip of her own champagne. She set the glass down almost immediately and reached for a vase. She felt Dom's gaze on her as she arranged the roses and glanced at him from the corner of her eye. He was staring at her oddly, a puzzled expression on his face.

"Isn't the champagne to your liking?" he asked.

"I've . . . lost my taste for champagne."

"Would you prefer wine? I'll be happy to go get something more to your taste."

"No, please, I like champagne, it's just that . . . well, lately alcohol seems to upset my stomach. It's nothing, really," she quickly added when his brow creased into a worried frown. "Don't let me stop you from enjoying your own champagne. Take it into the living room while I finish up in here. Dinner is almost ready."

* * *

Relaxing in a cream-colored leather easy chair, Dom lifted his expensive alligator skin–shod feet onto the ottoman and sipped his champagne. Cara was even more beautiful than he remembered. During the past few weeks he'd tried his damnedest to forget her. He'd romped on the Riviera with the loveliest women on the continent and took in all the delights Paris and Rome had to offer, and he still felt empty. He must have been mad to let Cara leave him without a fight. These past weeks he'd discovered something about himself he hadn't known before. He'd learned that he was as old-fashioned in his views as his parents were when it came to marriage. He readily acknowledged his first marriage had been a mistake and vowed that his next would be his last. And it would be for love.

"Dinner is ready," Cara said, interrupting his reverie.

Dom leapt from the chair and offered her his arm. She hesitated but a moment before slipping her arm beneath his. He raised her hand to his lips and kissed her fingers as he escorted her to the dining room. Dom took a moment to admire the room before seating Cara, thinking it but another reflection of Cara's excellent taste. The antique cherrywood table and hutch were polished to a high sheen, complementing the cream brocade-upholstered chairs. The modern prints on the walls and antique furnishings maintained the mix of old and new throughout the condo, creating a pleasant and relaxing atmosphere.

Dom couldn't recall when he'd enjoyed a meal more, and he owed it all to Cara's enchanting company. Though she seemed somewhat distracted, the conversation flowed easily as long as it was conducted on an impersonal level. Dom complied with her unspoken wishes, keeping things light and trivial.

After the meal, Dom offered to help with the dishes. It was a first for him but the offer was genuine. Cara declined, however.

"Tomorrow is Saturday. I'll just pile everything in the sink and do them tomorrow." She scraped her chair back. Dom hastened up to help.

After the dishes were neatly piled in the sink they returned to the living room. Dom sat on the comfy leather sofa and patted the seat beside him. "Come sit beside me." If he didn't kiss those sweet, pouting lips soon he was going to expire, he thought as he watched her sit somewhat stiffly beside him.

"Why are you nervous, Cara?" he asked, when he noticed that her fists were curled tightly in her lap.

"I'm not nervous."

"No?" He picked up her hand and unclenched her fingers. "You could have fooled me."

"Why are you here, Dom?"

"Cara, Why is it so difficult to understand that I

349

might want to see you again? Have you forgotten already those days and nights we spent together? Perhaps they meant nothing to you but—"

"No, please," Cara pleaded. "Don't say things you'll regret later. I'll always be grateful to you, Dom. You were there when I needed you. You brought me from the depths of despair with your caring and attention. You made all my fantasies come true and gave me the confidence to believe in myself again. No man has ever given me more."

Placing his hands gently on her shoulders, he turned her into his arms. "Don't you see, Cara mia? I *want* to give you more." Tightening his arms around her, he rested his forehead against hers. "I've learned a great deal in the past few weeks. One of the things I discovered is that I enjoy having you around. I like you as a person"— he gave her a wicked grin—"and I absolutely adore you as a lover."

A dull red advanced across Cara's cheeks. "How long will the attraction between us last? How long before another woman strikes your fancy? I'm not a model, or a starlet, or royalty. I'm just plain me. I want a home, a family, a loving husband committed to marriage. We're poles apart in our wants and needs."

"What makes you think I don't want those same things?"

He cradled her face in his hands and kissed her—just a small peck, but it was enough to make him want more.

"You want me, don't you, Cara?"

His question must have hit a nerve for he felt a shudder ripple through her. "Need you ask?"

"Very good." He kissed her again, more deeply this time, visibly pleased with her answer. "Now we're getting somewhere."

"What do you . . ."

Her words ended in a surprised squawk as his kiss forced her silence. Her arms crept around his neck and she melted against him.

"It's still there," Dom whispered against his lips. "Those same old feelings that made us so good together. Can you feel it? My heart is pounding and blood is surging through my veins. I missed this. I missed *you*."

He whispered her name into her ear, over and over, his voice raw with passion. "You do need me, Cara. Admit it."

She was so dizzy from his intoxicating kisses, she would have admitted to anything. "I need you, Dom. God help me, I *do* need you." It was true. Excitement had left her life the day she and Dom parted.

"Thank God," he said urgently as he gathered her into his arms and rose in one fluid motion. "Which way to the bedroom?"

"Down the hall," Cara said, pointing with her foot. It never occurred to her to resist. She had no will where Dom was concerned. "First door on the right."

The door was standing ajar. Dom pushed

through, flipped on the light switch and gently eased her down his body to her feet. Cara was unable to prevent the shiver that slid down her spine as he turned her around and she felt his hands fumbling with the zipper at the back of her dress. He gave a tug and the dress slithered down her body, pooling around her feet. Then he unfastened her bra and tossed it aside. His hands covered her breasts and he pulled her against him, her back resting against the solid wall of his chest.

She sensed confusion in his voice as he said, "You're larger than I remembered."

Before she could reply, he slid his fingers beneath the waistband of her panties and slid them down her hips. She stepped out of them and he flung them away to join her bra.

His hands returned to her breasts and she moaned as he brushed his thumbs against her sensitive nipples.

"I missed you, Cara," Dom whispered into her ear. "I want to make love to you."

"You've been traveling in rather stellar company," Cara charged as he turned her to face him. "How did you find time to miss me?"

"It wasn't difficult when you were the first and last person I thought about each day. I remembered how good we were together, how wonderful it felt to be inside you. I want to be there again."

He shrugged out of his coat and pulled his shirt from his trousers. His seductive smile made her tingle all over as he dropped to his knees and buried his head against her stomach. Then he slid his hands between her legs, parting them as his head dipped down to taste her, trailing tantalizing kisses along the insides of her thighs and back up to the sweet apex of her sex. His tongue darted into her moist crevice and licked her.

"Dom!"

He made a low sound that was rather like a growl and licked her again. Pleasure pooled and then burst inside her, extracting a sharp cry from the back of her throat. When Cara's knees begin to buckle, his arms came around her to hold her steady for his plundering mouth and tongue, until she slumped over, drained and replete. Then he gathered her into his arms and carried her to bed. He caressed her with his dark gaze, making her burn and ache for him, as he tore off his clothes.

He made love to her again, lavishing tender attention on every part of her body as she arched beneath him and cried out, begging him to come inside her.

"Not yet," he said in that sexy, accented drawl she loved so much.

He stroked her into a savage frenzy; his mouth and hands were everywhere, touching her, caressing her breasts and licking and suckling her nipples, until she thought she'd die of pleasure.

When he thrust inside her, Cara wrapped her legs around his slim waist and clasped him tightly. Digging her fingers into his shoulders, she arched her back and lifted her hips to take him deeper.

He seemed to grow even larger inside her and her muscles contracted around him. She felt him shudder, heard him cry out.

"Cara! Oh, God, oh, God, oh, God! Come with me."

His words flung her over the edge, releasing the pressure building within her. Gyrating in wild abandonment, she spiraled downward into an abyss of pure pleasure.

For a long time nothing stirred but the sound of their uneven breathing.

"I'm too heavy for you," Dom said when he finally found the strength to speak.

"Don't leave me yet," Cara whispered, holding him in the cradle of her thighs. She couldn't bear for him to leave her body yet. Having him inside her again after their lengthy separation was sheer heaven.

"I don't want to crush you." But he didn't move, not until he had softened and slipped out of her. Then he shifted to his side and pulled her against him.

"Are you still on birth control pills, Cara? I didn't use any protection."

She hesitated, then said, "No, I haven't been on them since . . . well, for a long time."

"What if I got you pregnant?"

Cara shrugged. She couldn't be any more pregnant than she already was. "Perhaps it isn't the right time."

His penetrating gaze unnerved her. His words

even more so. "I found something that belongs to you at the villa."

He got up and padded over to his discarded jacket. He picked it up from the floor, fished in the pocket and flung it back down after he found what he was looking for. Then he returned to the bed and handed her a small container. Cara knew what it held without looking inside. Her birth control pills. She'd discovered them in her suitcase before she left the villa and remembered holding them in her hand when Dom had burst into the bedroom and made love to her. Then she'd forgotten about them.

"Where did you find this?"

"On the floor beside the bed. The packet is full. You hadn't taken any."

"I thought I'd forgotten them at home," Cara said, flushing. "I was surprised when I found them in my suitcase at the villa."

"You told me you were on the pill."

"I *had* been on the pill. I took them until the day before I boarded the *Odyssey*. When I thought I had left them at home, it didn't really matter because I wasn't expecting to have sex after Gil jilted me. You used protection the first two times we were intimate so I didn't really worry about getting pregnant. But then you *didn't* use protection and it was too late to say anything, so I just let the matter drop."

He deliberately stared at her breasts. "You've filled out since I last saw you."

"You're imagining things."

"You wouldn't lie to me, would you?"

"Is that why you're here? To find out if I'm pregnant? Why bother? If I *were* having a child," she said, "it doesn't have to interfere with your lifestyle."

"*Are* we having a child, Cara?"

"Dammit, Dom, it's none of your business! You'll probably be gone tomorrow anyway so what does it matter? The next time I see you in the tabloids, you'll be courting another great beauty."

"What will it take to convince you that we belong together? I'm not leaving Miami, Cara."

"What?

"Domani cruise lines just added two new cruise ships to our fleet. They're to be based in Miami. I've been placed in charge of our operations down here. But forget all that. I want to know if you're carrying my child. No lies, just the truth."

Cara suddenly felt as if she'd been stripped bare and her innermost secrets revealed. On a swiftly indrawn breath, she said, "It wasn't my intention to trap you."

"I know that. Am I to assume, then, that you *are* pregnant?"

She nodded slowly. "But it changes nothing."

His gaze caressed her face. "We'll be married immediately. A short civil ceremony by a notary, I think. We can have a big wedding in Athens. I'll fly your entire family and any friends you'd like aboard my private jet for the ceremony."

"You can't dictate my life for me," Cara charged. "What if your parents don't like me? What about my job? Where will we live? What about love?"

"My parents will adore you. You're exactly the kind of woman they want for me." He kissed the tip of her nose. "I've been looking for you all of my life, Cara Brooks. I own homes in several countries, but Miami will remain my home base for as long as our cruise lines flourish in Florida.

"As for love," he said, rising up on an elbow and leaning over her, "I've never loved a woman until you came along. I've searched the world over for someone like you. Our meeting was fated; it had to be. I tried to forget you, Cara, to continue living life as I always have, but I wasn't happy. Something was missing. It was you, Cara."

Cara shook her head, certain she was dreaming. Fantasies didn't come true. Fantasies were dreams one tucked away and retrieved when life became dull and unbearable. One didn't actually live one's fantasies. Men like Dom weren't for real. One read about them, occasionally met them, but never, ever, was loved by them.

"Dom, this whole idea of you and me is ridiculous. We don't—"

"Do you love me, Cara?"

"—belong together. We're from different worlds. It won't—"

"Do you love me, Cara?"

"—work. We're two different—"

"Do you love me, Cara?"

"—people." She paused to catch her breath, then blurted out, "I *do* love you! But I won't have you if you want me because of the baby."

"I intended to claim you long before I found the birth control pills or entertained the notion that you might be pregnant. Did you think I'd marry you for the baby's sake alone? It's not necessary today. Single women have babies every day and no one condemns them for it. I want you because I love you."

"Did you suspect I was pregnant when you saw me today?"

"Perhaps subconsciously. You were radiant. Not that you aren't always beautiful, but there was a special glow about you that was different. Then, when I saw your breasts and noticed that they were larger and more sensitive than I recalled, I began to suspect. Refusing to drink the champagne was the clincher. Do you have any idea how pleased I am? I'm going to want more than one child, though."

"You're happy about the baby?"

"Ecstatic. I'm really an old-fashioned guy despite my image. I've always known what I wanted, I just never found it until you came along. You will marry me, won't you, Cara? I've already got my eye on a home on Biscayne Bay. As for your job, you can continue working, if that's what you want."

"You wouldn't care?"

"Actually, the corporation is considering

branching out into new territory. One of them is publishing. Your magazine could be our first acquisition. How would you like to become a publisher?"

"You're going too fast for me, Dom. I'm still working on the marriage part."

"Say it, love, say you'll marry me."

"Only if you promise me something first."

"Anything, love, anything within my power to grant."

"Promise you'll always love me."

"Until hell freezes over."

"And promise me pleasure."

Pulling her on top of him, he spread her legs and thrust hard, filling her with himself. "All the pleasure you can handle."

SIERRA

Connie Mason

Bestselling Author Of *Wind Rider*

Fresh from finishing school, Sierra Alden is the toast of the Barbary Coast. And everybody knows a proper lady doesn't go traipsing through untamed lands with a perfect stranger, especially one as devilishly handsome as Ramsey Hunter. But Sierra believes the rumors that say that her long-lost brother and sister are living in Denver, and she will imperil her reputation and her heart to find them.

Ram isn't the type of man to let a woman boss him around. Yet from the instant he spies Sierra on the muddy streets of San Francisco, she turns his life upside down. Before long, he is her unwilling guide across the wilderness and her more-than-willing tutor in the ways of love. But sweet words and gentle kisses aren't enough to claim the love of the delicious temptation called Sierra.

_3815-3 $5.99 US/$6.99 CAN

SHADOW WALKER
CONNIE MASON

Bestselling Author of *Flame*!

"Why did you do that?"

"Kiss you?" Cole shrugged. "Because you wanted me to, I suppose. Why else would a man kiss a woman?"

But Dawn knows lots of other reasons, especially if the woman is nothing but half-breed whose father has sold her to the first interested male. Defenseless and exquisitely lovely, Dawn is overjoyed when Cole Webster kills the ruthless outlaw who is her husband in name only. But now she has a very different sort of man to contend with. A man of unquestionable virility, a man who prizes justice and honors the Native American traditions that have been lost to her. Most intriguing of all, he is obviously a man who knows exactly how to bring a woman to soaring heights of pleasure. And yes, she does want his kiss...and maybe a whole lot more.

_4260-6 $5.99 US/$6.99 CAN

Dorchester Publishing Co., Inc.
P.O. Box 6640
Wayne, PA 19087-8640

DEBRA DIER
LORD SAVAGE
Author of *Scoundrel*

Lady Elizabeth Barrington is sent to Colorado to find the Marquess of Angelstone, the grandson of an English duke who disappeared during an attack by renegade Indians. But the only thing she discovers is Ash MacGregor, a bounty-hunting rogue who takes great pleasure residing in the back of a bawdy house. Convinced that his rugged good looks resemble those of the noble family, Elizabeth vows she will prove to him that aristocratic blood does pulse through his veins. And in six month's time, she will make him into a proper man. But the more she tries to show him which fork to use or how to help a lady into her carriage, the more she yearns to be caressed by this virile stranger, touched by this beautiful barbarian, embraced by Lord Savage.

_4119-7 $4.99 US/$5.99 CAN

Dorchester Publishing Co., Inc.
P.O. Box 6640
Wayne, PA 19087-8640

Please add $1.75 for shipping and handling for the first book and $.50 for each book thereafter. NY, NYC, and PA residents, please add appropriate sales tax. No cash, stamps, or C.O.D.s. All orders shipped within 6 weeks via postal service book rate. Canadian orders require $2.00 extra postage and must be paid in U.S. dollars through a U.S. banking facility.

Name_____
Address_____
City_____ State_____ Zip_____
I have enclosed $_____ in payment for the checked book(s).
Payment <u>must</u> accompany all orders. ❑ Please send a free catalog.

FLAME
CONNIE MASON

"Each new Connie Mason book is a prize!"
—Heather Graham

When her brother is accused of murder, Ashley Webster heads west to clear his name. Although the proud Yankee is prepared to face any hardship on her journey to Fort Bridger, she is horrified to learn that single women aren't welcome on any wagon train. Desperate to cross the plains, Ashley decides to pay the first bachelor willing to pose as her husband. Then the fiery redhead comes across a former Johnny Reb in the St. Joe's jail, and she can't think of any man she'd rather marry in name only. But out on the rugged trail Tanner MacTavish quickly proves too intense, too virile, too dangerous for her peace of mind. And after Tanner steals a passionate kiss, Ashley knows that, even though the Civil War is over, a new battle is brewing—a battle for the heart that she may be only too happy to lose.

_4150-2 $5.99 US/$6.99 CAN

Pure Temptation

Connie Mason

"Each new Connie Mason book is a prize!"
—Heather Graham

Spirits can be so bloody unpredictable, and the specter of Lady Amelia is the worst of all. Just when one of her ne'er-do-well descendents thought he could go astray in peace, the phantom lady always appears to change his wicked ways.

A rogue without peer, Jackson Graystoke wants to make gaming and carousing in London society his life's work. And the penniless baronet would gladly curse himself with wine and women—if Lady Amelia would give him a ghost of a chance.

Fresh off the boat from Ireland, Moira O'Toole isn't fool enough to believe in legends or naive enough to trust a rake. Yet after an accident lands her in Graystoke Manor, she finds herself haunted, harried, and hopelessly charmed by Black Jack Graystoke and his exquisite promise of pure temptation.

_4041-7 $5.99 US/$6.99 CAN

Three Heartwarming Tales of Romance and Holiday Cheer

Bah Humbug! by Leigh Greenwood. Nate wants to go somewhere hot, but when his neighbor offers holiday cheer, their passion makes the tropics look like the arctic.

Christmas Present by Elaine Fox. When Susannah returns home, a late-night savior teaches her the secret to happiness. But is this fate, or something more wonderful?

Blue Christmas by Linda Winstead. Jess doesn't date musicians, especially handsome, up-and-coming ones. But she has a ghost of a chance to realize that Jimmy Blue is a heavenly gift.

___4320-3 $5.50 US/$6.50 CAN

Dorchester Publishing Co., Inc.
P.O. Box 6640
Wayne, PA 19087-8640

Please add $1.75 for shipping and handling for the first book and $.50 for each book thereafter. NY, NYC, and PA residents, please add appropriate sales tax. No cash, stamps, or C.O.D.s. All orders shipped within 6 weeks via postal service book rate. Canadian orders require $2.00 extra postage and must be paid in U.S. dollars through a U.S. banking facility.

Name_____
Address_____
City_____State_____Zip_____
I have enclosed $_____ in payment for the checked book(s).
Payment <u>must</u> accompany all orders. ☐ Please send a free catalog.

Surrender to the fantasy...

Indulge yourself in these sensual love stories written by four of today's hottest romance authors!

CONNIE BENNETT, "Masquerade": When shy, unassuming Charlotte Nolan wins a masquerade cruise, she has no idea that looks can be so deceiving—or that her wildest romantic fantasies are about to come true.

THEA DEVINE, "Admit Desire": Nick's brother is getting married—to the woman who left him at the altar two years before. And when Nick sees them together, he realizes he wants Francesca more than ever. But little does he know that she, too, will do anything to have him in her life again.

EVELYN ROGERS, "The Gold Digger": Susan Ballinger is determined to marry for money. She doesn't believe in love at first sight—until she meets Sonny, a golden boy who takes her to soaring heights of pleasure—and gives her so much more in the bargain.

OLIVIA RUPPRECHT, "A Quiver of Sighs": Valerie Smith is a lonely writer with an active imagination. But she's missing one thing: experience. Then she meets Jake Larson, a handsome editor who takes her writing—and her body—to places beyond her wildest dreams.

___4289-4 $5.50 US/$6.50 CAN

Dorchester Publishing Co., Inc.
P.O. Box 6640
Wayne, PA 19087-8640

Please add $1.75 for shipping and handling for the first book and $.50 for each book thereafter. NY, NYC, and PA residents, please add appropriate sales tax. No cash, stamps, or C.O.D.s. All orders shipped within 6 weeks via postal service book rate. Canadian orders require $2.00 extra postage and must be paid in U.S. dollars through a U.S. banking facility.

Name_____
Address_____
City_____State_____Zip_____
I have enclosed $_____ in payment for the checked book(s).
Payment **must** accompany all orders. ❏ Please send a free catalog.